MISFOLDINGS

J H Tache

*To M for having and holding
me for better, for worse, in
sickness and in health.*

It is never too late to get back on your feet. Though we won't live forever, make sure you accomplish what you were put here for.

ABIGAIL ADAMS

CONTENTS

1. JULIA AND DEREK (1987)

On hearing that Julia Ellison was leaving education, the headmaster had asked her to stop by his office and had tried to convince her that she was bright. He had noticed the change from a happy thirteen-year-old into an introverted sixteen-year-old and suspected bullying may have had something to do with it. He worried that by failing to spot it the school had let her down. Julia would not say so directly but the head realised school had been something of an ordeal for her, and he knew that the family business offered an alluring alternative. Teachers had fed back that Julia spent much of break time in the Arts and Crafts classroom turning out quite impressive sketches, watercolours and pieces of tapestry or embroidery. So as not to sever the connection with education altogether and leave open the possibility of a change of heart, the headmaster suggested Julia at least take Art A-level. She obliged him, excelled, got a top grade in one year, then left school.

Julia enjoyed working with her parents in the family business in Ely and was not dismissive of the idea that she might take it over when the time came for them to retire. *Ellison Interiors* was not a mainstream fabric and wall-paper shop. Milton and Sylvia Ellison had identified a niche in the Cambridgeshire market for a bespoke interior design service that specialised in designer fabrics. The high end, though by no means the top end, of the market had been cornered by Laura Ashley for years; but their stripes, checks and flowers in repetitious muted palette did not excite any more.

There was money in Newmarket of course, but Cambridge was becoming wealthier too. Milton and Sylvia signed up to the textile trade fairs in Milan and Munich, from which they introduced a range of new wools, silks and bamboo fabrics with exciting, sometimes dramatic, contemporary designs. Shifting colour and pattern from wall to curtains required furniture to take a back seat, as it were. IKEA's affordable and cleverly designed ash and beech veneered furniture and the new designer wall paints in fifty shades of grey or cream provided the perfect neutral backdrop for *Ellisons'* contemporary textile art, and demand soared.

After seven years in the business, Julia had become knowledgeable and skilled. She knew the thread counts, picks per inch, and warp and weft cover factors for the various fabrics, but she talked to clients in terms of the hand of a fabric. Just as a sommelier might describe the nose and palate of a wine, Julia would encourage clients to touch the fabrics on display and would draw from her stock of sensuous similes to liven up the usual descriptors of cool, slick, smooth, heavy, stiff and so on. She could cut and sew expertly too, but her strengths, like her mother's, were good taste and an eye for what would work in a particular room.

This interior design service took Julia into large and very large houses in and around Cambridge, and adjoining Suffolk. She learnt from clients, many of whom had impeccable taste as well as the money to indulge it. These encounters began to affect her in unexpected ways. She became aware of her Fenland accent; so, she listened acutely in order to modulate, inflect and articulate her own speech accordingly. Also, she saw evidence of a wider engagement with culture than she knew and wanted a part of it. For a while, she had been regretting the fact that she had left school with only one A level and had come to feel that her horizons were too narrow.

Then, a week before Julia's twenty-fifth birthday, the Ellisons' harmony and happiness were hit into the outfield. Sylvia discovered that Milton had been having an affair with a family friend over several years. She was devastated and unforgiving. In the following months, both couples started divorce proceedings and Ellison Interiors was put up for sale.

Sylvia kept the family home, but Julia realised she could not cope for long with the atmosphere of bitter resentment that settled there. It was time to move out. So, she refused the offer to stay on under the new owners.

The advertisement for a Trainee Sales Negotiator at Tuckers, a Cambridge Estate Agent, caught Julia's eye. It didn't state a requirement for particular educational qualifications. In fact, in-house training and support to acquire relevant qualifications were offered as an inducement, which interested Julia especially. She thought too she would enjoy helping people buy or sell their property, particularly those looking to set up a new home. Tuckers was on Hills Road and only a couple of blocks from Cambridge Station, making for an easy commute from Ely until she found a place of her own in Cambridge.

When Julia was shown into his office for interview, Mr Tucker rose to his feet. Not from courtesy but because her beauty demanded it. In order to militate against this sort of thing happening, Julia usually wore no makeup and pulled her hair back severely into a tight knot at the back of her head. It helped too to wear somewhat loosely fitting sweaters and blouses; the latter with never more than the top button undone, in order to conceal curves of the sort that induce most men to tune in to *Strictly Come Dancing* on Saturday nights. On this day, however, Julia was wearing a subtly flattering blue business dress suit that she had made herself. When he first lifted his eyes to acknowledge the applicant, Tucker saw sparkling aquamarine eyes beneath beautifully shaped eyebrows set in an oval face with perfect bone structure, all framed and crowned by cascading waves of glossy gold-streaked auburn hair. Julia had learnt the usefulness of a smile to release the smitten from this spell.

Once Tucker had found his tongue, welcomed her and got some way into the interview, he realised two things about Julia. Considering the impact she had made on him, he was surprised to find her shy, which was peculiar. Tucker couldn't imagine how someone with these looks, not to mention that

3

crowning glory, might not be supremely confident and extrovert. In fact, Julia was not comfortable with her beauty. It had attracted too much attention from the boys at school, which alienated the girls, some of whom, driven by envy, had bullied her. Since too much attention from boys morphed into the wrong kind of attention from men, Julia contrived ways to disguise herself as plain.

Once attention was away from her appearance and Tucker started on the subject of property, Julia relaxed and surprised him by her proposal for residential property sales. She thought in terms of homes not properties; whether for singles, newlyweds, families or elderly couples, she was concerned that a property should fit, or that it could be made to fit, the client's style of living so as to become a home. She had excellent ideas on how to present an empty property in a way that made it feel lived-in still.

Tucker didn't think that Julia would become his top-selling agent, but he felt she would bring another dimension to his team that could repay dividend. Also, I would like to look upon this woman, he thought. He offered Julia the job. The learning curve at Tuckers was steep: the geography of the city's streets, the amenities and character of various neighbourhoods, the sort of people buying here or there, and how to value properties, photograph and market them. When Julia was permitted to take on clients, she did very well. Clients would comment very favourably in the 'after sale' questionnaire, noting in particular how helpful she had been in emphasising the potential in a property and how it could easily be made attractive.

Derek Black walked into Tuckers one Saturday lunchtime. He had spent the morning walking from estate agent to estate agent down Regent Street. The two-up-two-down Victorian house in York Terrace, in which he had been living for six of the nine years that he had been employed at Astons on the Newmarket Road, was getting on his nerves and he wanted rid of it. Most solicitors over-worked in order to make partner. Derek was no exception; work intruded heavily into his evenings and weekends. So, he had not stripped the wall paper, had not put in a new bathroom, had not replaced the pine kitchen and had not sorted out the small back garden. The state of the house depressed him, which is why he had decided to sell York Terrace and buy a new-build, fully-fitted apartment. Better still, he would try to find one that had also been curtained and carpeted as a show property.

Julia looked up as Derek entered the office and began to peruse the summary posters of properties for sale. She watched him rise on his toes to look at the topmost row. We should lower the display, she thought. He's not that short after all; five seven, perhaps. She went up to Derek to find out how she might help. He turned, looked at her, saw that her smile undermined the effort at plainness, and felt heat and colour come to his cheeks. If there was one thing that helped Julia to feel confident, it was apparent shyness or embarrassment in another. She smiled again, which enabled Derek to sit down and tell her what he was after.

Julia was better informed than the agents he had encountered that morning. She knew that the Peugeot garage and showroom on the corner of Hills Road and Cherry Hinton Road, and the Fire Station just the other side of the railway bridge, were to be demolished to make way for large condominium-type developments aimed at the increasing number of commuters to London. The two developments were to have a gym, swimming pool and plenty of underground parking that would be easily accessible through internal lifts. Tuckers would be marketing both apartment blocks.

Ah, this is more like it, thought Derek; it's pretty much what I had in mind. So, he told Julia he would consider the floor plans and specifications of the two developments over the coming week and come to a decision. Also, he asked Julia to handle the marketing and sale of his present property, which is why, at eleven o'clock the following Saturday, Julia turned into York Terrace carrying her Filofax and camera, and two bunches of flowers.

The facades in York Terrace were among the smallest in Cambridge, but several houses, had been extended at the rear and into lofts to create quite decent living space for families. Number thirty-two was not one of these. White plastered brickwork and a glossy red door made it stand out in a terrace of yellowish grey Cambridge brick. To the right of the door were two small sash windows, one above the other. A hanging basket of flowers by the door would make a better picture, thought Julia, but the bright sunshine and the absence of parked cars prompted her to photograph the exterior anyway. When Derek let her in, she stepped directly into the open-plan lounge and kitchen-cum-breakfast areas. In answer to his offer of coffee, Julia suggested she walk round the house to take measurements and note features first; they could talk things through over the coffee afterwards.

Julia was relieved that Derek had engaged a cleaner to tidy up earlier that morning. The front bedroom was a decent size and the back bedroom had been turned into a bathroom, which needed to be replaced. Julia tied curtains back, arranged the flowers into two vases, moving them from room to room as she went, and photographed the rooms from all angles. It did not take her long to take dimensions and sketch a floorplan. Derek suggested he receive Julia's verdict at the small picnic table in the garden. He surprised her by serving warm *pastéis de nata* with the fresh coffee.

'They're from a fabulous Portuguese bakery that has just opened in Norfolk Street,' he said. Julia had not tasted these custard tarts before.

'I could find a place in my heart for these,' she said, 'they're delicious. Thank you.' Derek was not at ease. He was shy in the company of attractive women. His mother had discouraged him from dating as a teenager. There'll be time for girls at university, she would say; better that you concentrate on your studies. This left him ill equipped for such encounters when he got to university. Even now, in his late twenties, he would approach only plain-looking girls whom he judged unlikely to refuse an invitation.

Derek was hugely attracted to the young woman seated at his garden table and so he felt quite acutely embarrassed. I know she knows, he thought, sending blood rushing to his cheeks. Julia thought it might help if she could get Derek to talk about himself. So, she explained that she liked to consider clients 'holistically' when relocating them. Perhaps Derek could tell her how he moved around the neighbourhood: where he worked and the route he would take to get there, where he did his shopping, where he socialised and so on. She didn't intend to be nosey and didn't come across that way. Julia's conclusion was totally unexpected.

'Mr Black, I believe you'd be making a big mistake if you were to sell this place.'

'Really? Why, that's an astonishing thing to say. What do you mean?' asked Derek, cooling rapidly.

'I've been thinking about your routine,' began Julia. 'You have an easy walk to work along Sturton Street and East Road, and the distance to the train station is even shorter. You get yummy cakes from a Portuguese bakery round the corner in Norfolk Street. At the weekend, you breakfast at Hot Numbers on Gwydir Street. There's a choice of Italian, Indian, Turkish and Moroccan restaurants along Mill Road. The Cambridge Blue and Kingston Arms are on your doorstep and you've told me that you like both pubs. And a five-minute bike ride gives you the choice of the Grafton, Beehive and Newmarket Road shopping centres.' Julia spread out her hands to imply that this was a *no brainer.* 'From the point of view of amenities, this is pretty hard to beat.'

'Miss Ellison, are you talking yourself out of a double commission?'

'Quote honestly, Mr Black, I believe you wouldn't thank me if I were to sell you an apartment in the new developments on the Hills Road. You'd have to cycle to work in rush-hour traffic. You'd have quite a high annual condominium charge. And when we were talking earlier, you didn't mention a passion for tenpin bowling, which is the only facility you get around there that you don't have here ten times over.'

'Of course, you're right about all that, but the problem is the house.'

'Oh yes, I can see that, Mr Black, and I have a suggestion.'

Derek held up a hand and said: 'That's the fourth time you've called me Mr Black and it's making me feel ancient. Do you think we could be less formal? Please, call me Derek.' Now, colour came into Julia's cheeks, which Derek noticed, and he added quickly: 'not if it makes you uncomfortable, of course.'

'I'm okay with that... Derek. Then, I'm Julia.'

'Well, Julia, what would *you* do about the house?' Julia's enthusiasm overcame the embarrassment of the earlier moment.

'I would extend the house backwards and upwards into the loft. Its value would soar, and that's separate from the increase we're likely to see in the value of property generally in the Mill Road area.' Julia opened her Filofax and sketched out floor plans to illustrate how one might extend the ground floor backwards to enlarge the kitchen and to accommodate a washroom and a conservatory, how a second double bedroom could be located over the extended ground floor, and how the staircase could be revised for access into a new loft conversion, which would make a large study.

'Well, that would certainly transform the place, Julia, but I don't think I could cope with such a project. Don't forget there's the matter of upgrading the bathroom, and redoing the plumbing and wiring'

'If you don't want building going on around you, and frankly who would, Tuckers could easily find you an apartment to rent for six to eight months. Also, you might consider engaging someone to manage the project.' Derek took another look at Julia's sketch and they bounced ideas about. Julia could easily imagine the new spaces and, having noted how the property was oriented, she described how light would flood into the house through full-width patio doors, large windows and skylights.

'You've certainly given me something to think about, Julia. I would rather invest in the property than pay hefty stamp duty to the Chancellor. I'll consult a couple of builders and see what estimates they come up with.' Just then Derek had an idea. 'You know,' he said, 'it occurs to me that I don't even have time to check on builders once work gets under way. If I do go down this route, I could do with help in keeping an eye on things. I don't suppose you would consider acting as my agent, would you?'

Julia surprised herself by finding she was inclined to say *yes.* She wasn't entirely clear why, but she would hardly be entering into a binding contract by saying *yes,* would she?

'I might be,' she said, 'I could quite easily call by the house before and after work at Tuckers to check on the builder. Actually, it wouldn't be difficult to pop round during the day too. So, yes, I would be interested.'

'Then you really have given me a realistic alternative, Julia. I'll call you in a couple of weeks, if I may.' On this note, they parted, leaving Derek to muse on the conventional wisdom that men think about sex every seven seconds. Given the evidence of the last hour I'd say that's an underestimate, he said to himself.

Julia turned over the morning's events in her mind as she made her way to Tuckers. The fact that one does not wear a wedding ring does not mean one is unmarried, but everything about number 32 screamed *bachelor.* She smiled at the thought that the flowers she had taken to the house seemed uncomfortably out of place. I think he's interested in me, she thought without feeling awkward by it, perhaps because *he* seemed so embarrassed by it. So many others strut about, cocking their heads and parading their plumage as if to say: surely, I'm irresistible. Turning to her own impression of Derek, she thought: He's quite good-looking. Not a Robert Redford or a Richard Gere, but neither of those chaps had walked into Tuckers.

Julia didn't mind that he wasn't tall, though she would have to avoid high heels. His hair was dark brown and curly but looked soft. A pair of spectacles had been lying on the desk, which suggested he had been wearing contact lenses. He was trim from walking everywhere but could do with some gym work. On the other hand, Julia would have been put off by anyone with an unhealthy focus on body shape. The bookshelves indicated a range of interests. Also, she had liked the mantelpiece photograph of the happy-looking couple in their early sixties; his parents, she assumed. Derek had mentioned that he worked at *Aston's,* whom Julia knew to be a law firm, and the conversation had left little doubt that Derek was hardworking. He ticks several boxes, she thought.

Derek telephoned Julia in the middle of the following week to say he was interested in her proposal and to ask if she would like further discussion to happen over dinner one evening. They agreed on early Friday evening at *Prana,* a recently opened Indian restaurant on Mill Road that sought to present Indian cooking as a fine dining experience. The décor was modern. There were no pictures of the Taj Mahal on the wall and no Indian music. Julia had slipped out to a hairdresser at lunchtime and asked for a grown-up style. The hairdresser suggested a French chignon. She arrived exactly on time and was pleased to see that Derek had got there earlier. He rose as Julia was brought to the table.

'How nice to see you again, Derek. This is lovely,' said Julia as she turned to let Derek help her out of her coat. She was sure that, behind her, Derek inhaled deeply.

'You look stunning, Julia,' he said as he pulled the chair back for her to sit. They dealt with business quite quickly. Derek confirmed his interest if Julia were willing to liaise with the builders every weekday. He preferred to lease an apartment for six months with an option to extend for another three months. Julia had made inquiries of a local builder, who indicated that he could take on the work in four months or so if they could get planning permission in time.

She recommended a visit to a kitchens and bathrooms store down the Mill Road because of their continental kitchen catalogue, high-end German appliances and reliable after-sales service. It would also be quite easy for her to pop into their showroom should issues arise. She lowered her voice conspiratorially: 'and I know a wonderful interior decorator firm in Ely.'

Julia was more than happy with the terms offered. So Derek said he'd draft a contract and send it to her at Tuckers. That settled, they started the soft tread into one another's past and present. Julia learnt that Derek had read Law at Jesus College. The best in his year had been taken up by the big London Firms while in their second year. Derek had not got into an efficient work routine until his third year and missed out at the annual milk round. Surprised and impressed by Derek's academic performance in the final year, Derek's tutor telephoned a colleague at Astons to recommend him. Derek was a Yorkshireman, though Cambridge had wiped away his accent pretty well. His father had worked for Rowntree and Derek had benefited from a Rowntree scholarship to one of the few remaining grammar schools in York. Excellent A-levels and a historical connection between Jesus and the schools in his part of Yorkshire helped Derek in.

Exploring gently around these biographical facts, Julia uncovered a young man who hadn't fitted in at Cambridge. Derek had too much self-doubt for that. The confidence and bravura of Cambridge contemporaries coming from a public-school background intimidated him; more so those with a much better mind than his, and the combination of big brains, good looks and female gender overwhelmed him. In the early years after graduation, Derek had kept in touch with others from his year, but the City's corporate world seemed a different universe to his non-specialist solicitor's practice. Until he met Julia, Derek had been content to connect socially with a couple of other Aston lawyers over a few pints down the road in *The Burleigh Arms* most Friday evenings.

11

Derek may have felt *Yorkshire* but, with Julia, he acted *Cambridge,* though careful not to overdo it. He realised she was very bright but that she didn't know it. His Cambridge Scholar's persona impressed her, as did his professional status. This hand could win me this high-stakes game, he thought. I'll play it carefully. Before regular meetings to discuss progress with the building work, Derek sought out what was on in Cambridge in the following week or two, and invited Julia to join him; casually, as if he were going anyway. Julia most enjoyed the live music at The Corn Exchange with groups like Dire Straits and Kaiser Chiefs, but she became interested in theatre when Derek introduced her to the University's Amateur Dramatic Club's theatre and The Playroom at Corpus Christi College. She thought the students precociously talented.

The building project went very well. Some six months later, with Derek comfortably settled in an apartment, the builders moved in. Julia's charm and persuasion kept momentum going. So, over the subsequent eight months, number thirty-two morphed into a modern, energy-efficient, well-lit home that was twice the original size. Derek reserved a dinner table for two at *Prana* for the day after he moved back into York Terrace. He hoped to take advantage of this celebration. He had something in particular in mind and at the end of their meal Derek made his move.

'Julia, I know you're looking for a place in Cambridge. Well, you've given me a beautiful new home. Would you like to share it with me? Nothing would please me more.' Oh, that is just so clumsy, he thought. That's just typical of me: sit on the fence. Propose, yet don't propose! Aren't I the confident one!' He went red rather fiercely. While Julia knew that Derek was strongly attracted to her, this invitation took her by surprise because a clarion call couldn't have declared Derek's emotions and intentions more clearly than his crimson countenance. She reached for his hand.

'Oh Derek, is this a proposal?' she asked gently, holding his gaze.

'I-I would have put it so much better if I were s-sure you would accept,' he said, his speech sticking slightly, 'but I don't want to scare you off.' Julia squeezed his hand affectionately.

'Thank you, Derek. You're very sweet, but you've taken me by surprise. Yes, I must move away from the rancour at home. I should have done it sooner. In fact, I've agreed to move in with Amy Smith. She's the blonde girl at Tuckers. She's just bought a two-bedroomed apartment in *Highsett* on Hills Road and needs to rent out a room. The two of us get on very well.' Derek looked deflated. Julia shook his hand gently. 'Hey, don't misunderstand me, I am fond of you and I am excited at the thought that we may become close.' His spirits lifted.

'What a find, Julia! *Highsett* is perfect for Tuckers and for the train to Ely.' Mention of trains prompted him to check the time. 'Speaking of which, Julia, we should get to the station or you'll miss your train.' Derek's muddled proposal had kindled in Julia a feeling of affection towards him and as they walked down Tenison Road she took his arm, drawing in closely, which was a new intimacy. Julia was not sure when the thought of sex entered her mind; she became aware of wetness between her legs. When they got to the station, she turned to face him, moistened her parted lips and kissed his mouth softly. Derek drew her onto his erection. When they came apart, she said:

'I see I'm giving you a hard time.'

'I can't help it. You look even more beautiful tonight, if that could be possible. You're simply intoxicating.'

'Do you know,' she said, pressing into him again, 'I'm not getting on a train tonight.'

2. SYSTEM FAILURE (1982)

As my eyes roll back in my skull,
The life leaves my body.
System failure! System failure!
Where were you when I needed you?

If I Were You

'**D**ad! Dad!' Paul cried out as he rushed to kneel beside his father. Anguish and dread almost over-whelmed him. Oh God! Please, don't let him be dead. Seemingly in response to this supplication, Charles began to breathe noisily, climaxing into loud snoring, then spluttering snorts, before waning into quiet shallow breaths; but he did not wake. Paul shook Charles and, whether because of this or despite it, the deep breathing resumed. He picked the telephone off the floor, tapped the cradle to regain the line and called the emergency services.

'We need an ambulance. It's urgent... My dad has fallen down stairs... No, I can't rouse him...Yes, he's breathing but not regularly... Has he got a pulse? Hang on, I'll try to feel for it... No, I can't feel it at all, but he must have one, obviously!' Don't lose your temper, now. She's probably going down a checklist. '... It's 16 Lemur Drive, Cherry Hinton... You will?... No, I won't move him. Thank you. I'll switch on the porch light so they'll see where to come.'

The ambulance was quick to arrive. Not much longer than it had taken Paul to fetch blankets and wrap them over Charles. The paramedics inserted a plastic airway into

Charles' mouth, applied a stabilising collar to his neck, determined that there was no sign of an arm or leg fracture, set up a saline drip and then lifted Charles onto a stretcher. Paul took some reassurance from one paramedic's observation that, as Charles withdrew his arms and legs reflexively when pinched, a severe stroke seemed unlikely.

'Your dad is stable,' he said to Paul. 'He feels warm to the touch and, while it's difficult to gauge the amount of blood he's lost, there is a steady pulse at the wrist, even if it's a bit thready.' Quite what the fellow meant by this Paul didn't know but he took heart from the paramedic's reassuring tone. As he followed the ambulance through the late Friday rush-hour traffic, Paul cursed. Damn his father for insisting he stay on in his own home after the death of their mother two years ago. Damn the Alzheimer disease with which Charles had been diagnosed five months earlier. Damn the staircase down which Charles had fallen. Damn the telephone table that had cut open Charles scalp and may even have cracked his skull. Damn, damn, damn! Paul was so distracted, it was just as well he was following in the wake of the wailing ambulance; traffic lights, other motorists, cyclists and pedestrians went unnoticed as his mind went over the scene at his Dad's. The house had been warm, he recalled. Hypothermia would have made the situation worse. A small mercy for which I'm thankful.

Charles was wheeled into the medical assessment area where a dark-blue uniformed nurse took charge. Paul was ushered to reception to provide Charles' personal information and medical history. He was assured that Charles was being assessed and told to wait. The Emergency Room reception was filling up with people, of whom most were in obvious discomfort and more in need of the unoccupied chairs than himself. He walked towards the entrance, then stepped back again when the automatic sliding door opened to admit a blast of cold air. Fortunately, his mobile phone picked up signal at that spot and he called his sister's mobile number.

'Hi Paul, I'm just getting the girls ready for their bath.

15

Could you give me another hour?'

'Katy, I realise you have your hands full at this time of the evening, but you'll want to know that dad has had an accident.' Katy gasped. Something clattered to the floor with a metallic sound.

'Oh no! What is it, Paul?' she asked, the rising stress audible in her voice, 'Is Dad okay?'

'He's had a fall but he's stable. I've got him to the hospital and the doctors are with him right now. I couldn't check on Dad this morning because his phone was engaged. When his phone didn't disengage, I drove over after work and found him at the foot of the stairs. It seems Dad hit his head against the telephone table. He was still in pyjamas and could have been on the floor some hours before I turned up.' Paul heard the girls clamour for their mother's attention.

'Katy, you look after the girls. Don't worry just now.'

'Just tell me what the doctor has said.'

'No-one has come back to me yet. My guess is that dad is concussed. Of course, I'm concerned about the angioma. I've made a note of it in the admission form..... Hang on, Katy, someone has called my name. I must go. Look, I'll report back after the kids' bedtime. Bye.' He ended the call. An overweight woman, dressed in ill-fitting grey tunic and trousers, who had come through the doors from the patient area, called out for Mr Marshall again. Paul raised his hand and walked over.

'The doctor wants you, Mr Marshall. He wants to ask some questions.' Paul was led to Charles' bedside where a man in green scrubs was bent over Charles, listening to his chest. At Paul's arrival, he straightened up, took the stethoscope out of his ears, swung it round the back of his neck, and extended his hand.

'I'm Dr Raj,' he said with a smile. 'Your father's condition is stable, Mr Marshall. I can hear some crackles in his chest. That's very likely early infection but we'll get the physio to see him and start antibiotics... Look, could you expand on the Admission Questionnaire that you filled in, please?'

'What would you like to know, Doctor?'

'You've listed Alzheimer's disease under *Other medical conditions*...'

'Yes, Dad was diagnosed five or six months ago. Katy, that's my sister, and I thought it was depression following Mother's death with cancer a couple of years earlier. Of course, it's very likely dad *was* depressed; but forgetfulness became the problem as his grief eased. Nothing major, mind. Just finding it difficult to recall names and where he has put things. He had been repeating himself recently. I also put down that he has a small brain angioma. It runs in the family.'

'Oh yes, that should show up on the scan. Now, you've indicated here that your dad lives alone. How has he been managing?'

'Katy and I provide some support, but not a lot. Dad manages the routine of shaving, bathing and dressing well enough. His socks might not match, and frequently one or both are inside out'. Both men smiled at this. 'The house is all electric; no gas cooker or fire. My sister delivers cooked meals on alternate days, which Dad microwaves. Also, he's good at keeping reminder notes. He sticks to the corner shop for essentials and I order the rest online and arrange a weekly delivery to his home to coincide with my visit.'

'It's important to know that he was pretty much independent before his fall, Mr Marshall. Then here's the position. Your father has a head injury and requires specialist care. I'll refer him to the neurosurgery team, and I expect him to be admitted to the Neuro Critical Care Unit where he'll be assessed and treated.'

'Explain *head injury* please, Doctor.' Dr Raj pointed to two chairs and they sat down.

'Well, we've cleaned up the scalp wound, and my col-

17

league is suturing it as we speak. X-rays show no skull fracture, which is good news of course. As is the fact that there are no signs to suggest extradural or subdural hematoma – that's bleeding from the covering membrane of the brain. A large volume of blood over the brain would be dangerous. To be on the safe side, we'll get a CT scan on your dad tonight. If a haematoma shows up on the scan, the neurosurgeons may have to take him to theatre to remove it. Setting that aside for the moment, one is left with the question of damage to the brain itself. You see, Mr Marshall, at the moment of impact the soft brain inside the skull is squashed and twisted when the head comes to a sudden stop. This movement may tear some of the bundles of nerve fibres that make up the brain. The NCCU team will keep your father stable, prevent the brain from swelling and assess the extent of this component of the injury.' Paul was taken aback.

'Do I understand you correctly, Doctor? Are you telling me the outcome is bleak?'

'Just that it's uncertain. Things ought to be clear after the scan. I suggest you call hospital reception tomorrow morning to confirm that your dad is on NCCU. Visiting hours are quite flexible on the Unit.' They rose, shook hands and Paul expressed thanks. He was shown to his father's side. Paul took his father's hand and kissed it. How he loved this gentle man.

Seeing the light on in the front room despite the late hour, Paul parked the car and walked up to the window. A gentle tap on the glass with his car keys brought Katy to the door. She hugged her brother in shared concern.

'Oh Paul, you're here at last. How is he?' Katy looked as if she had been crying.

'Hey Sis, I'm sorry to have dropped the news on you like that and then cut you off as I did. Things are stable. I didn't want to wake the girls. So, rather than telephone, I thought it better to stop by to fill you in.'

'Come in. I'll get us a drink. I've been in need of one but thought better not, in case I have to drive out to the hospital.' Paul joined Henry, his brother-in-law, in the front room and Katy followed quickly with two glasses of red wine, one large one small. Katy kept the large one. She listened intently to his report. It didn't sound as reassuring as Paul seemed to think. The name 'Neuro Critical Care Unit' implied that her father was critically ill. She decided she would get to the hospital as soon as possible the next day. Things were a little fraught in the morning, but Henry and Katy had the girls dressed and breakfasted, the washing machine and dishwasher loaded, and the beds arranged when Paul came by. Henry planned a trip to Wimpole Home Farm, which both girls would enjoy.

'Charles Marshall, did you say?' asked the receptionist, looking up from the computer screen, 'and his date of birth, please?' With that information and Charles' home address, she located Charles on Ward G7.

'Not on NCCU, then?' asked Paul, surprised.

'G7 is DME: *Medicine for the Elderly*. Walk through the Concourse to the lifts. G7 is on the seventh floor.'

Three staff members sat at the nurses' station. One was showing the others how to enter data onto the IT system. Paul and Katy were ignored for a short while. Then, having sorted out some issue on the screen, one of the nurses looked up, took the inquiry and pointed down the ward.

'Room 19,' he said, 'and I've got a note here to inform the doctor that you're here. I'll bleep her, but go on down.' Charles occupied a single room at the far end of the ward. His head was bandaged, and he was lying on his side; kept in position by several pillows placed behind his back. Another pillow was placed between his bent knees. He was receiving fluid by intravenous drip. Urine was draining into a bag that hung from the bedrail and a feeding tube went into his nose. Katy's attempts to rouse Charles provoked only incomprehensible muttering and purposeless movements of his limbs.

'I think dad is a little better than last night,' said Paul

19

quickly, seeing the alarm in Katy's face. Half an hour later, both of them were in tears. Margaret Tilley had come in at half past seven. Her shift started at eight o'clock. Hand-over was rushed as her colleague had had a busy night and wanted to get away on time.

'I'm so sorry this is going to be a bit of a rush,' she said, after shutting the door behind her and introducing herself, 'I have to get back to Casualty soon.' They sat on orange, moulded plastic chairs at the end of the bed. Clearly, Doctor Tilley had no expectation that Charles might be able to understand what would be said.

'The news isn't good, I'm afraid. It appears that Mr Marshall has suffered quite severe brain damage in the fall.' There's no easy way to break bad news, she thought, as she saw Paul and Katy's shock.

'But last night your colleague seemed hopeful and talked about surgery. Have there been complications?' asked Paul.

'No new complications, but the CT scan shows brain swelling. Surgery would have been appropriate if a haematoma had been found overlying the brain. In Mr Marshall's case, there is no blood clot that requires evacuation. That's not to say there isn't bleeding. You see, that's the problem. The scan shows bleeding into the substance of the brain stem.' Katy became very agitated. Paul put an arm around her shoulders to steady her and forced himself to concentrate. He realised he would need to catch the essence of what they were being told in order to have some chance of searching profitably for more information on the internet later.

'It's not easy for us to follow, Doctor; but do go on. You said you had patients waiting and we mustn't hold you up more than necessary.' Maggie Tilley disliked being in this position: having to give bad news to someone whom one hadn't met before, having to press on with an explanation of the facts when what was needed was sympathy, not knowing the full details of the case. She inherited this patient, and several others, from yesterday's team and she would be handing most of the cases on to another team the next day; hardly continuity of care. Ah well, things are as they are, she said to herself, I can only try my best.

'Thank you, Mr Marshall; do interrupt me if I'm not clear. Now then, the lobes of the brain connect with this brain stem, which is located in the back of the head and tapers into the spinal cord in the neck. What makes the brain stem a vital structure is the fact that the nerve control centres for breathing, for the circulation of the blood, and for consciousness are located in it.'

'That sounds like a dangerous place in which to have bleeding.'

'Exactly, Mr Marshall. It explains why your father remains unconscious. At the moment of impact, movement of the soft brain damaged the nerve fibres in the brain, which has caused the brain to swell. The swollen brain cannot expand upwards and outwards because of the rigid bones of the skull vault; but there is some room around the brain stem. So, it comes to be squeezed downwards, around the brain stem, distorting it and rupturing the delicate blood vessels within it.' This came at Paul too quickly for him to decipher.

'Is there nothing that can be done?' he said, taking Katy's hand in his own.

'There's no useful operation, which is why the neurosurgeons didn't admit your father to their unit. Of course, there are several issues to discuss regarding his care. Charge Nurse will catch you before you leave.' Maggie Tilley stood up to leave. 'I'm so sorry about your dad,' she said, extending a hand. Maggie stopped by the Charge Nurse's office before leaving the ward.

'Hi, Sam. I've talked to Mr Marshall's son and daughter and told them about the poor prognosis. The daughter was about to break down, poor thing. Look, I haven't talked to them about the Integrated Care Pathway. Dr Gillespie may wish to do so himself.'

'Off you go Maggie. I'll see the relatives. Do come and see us when casualty quietens down. There's always a cup of tea and a biscuit for you here.'

Paul and Katy stayed at their father's bedside for an hour or so. A nurse came to turn Charles onto his other side. Otherwise they were left alone. They grieved. Both of them hurt a great deal but they had been close always, and the fact that they could share their sorrow helped. When they felt composed, Katy and Paul returned to the nurses' station. Sam Marley looked up.

'You must be Mr Marshall's relatives,' he said. 'I've been hoping to catch you. I'm Sam Marley, the Charge Nurse.'

'Katy Price and Paul Marshall,' replied Katy, 'Charles is our father.'

'May I ask if you're next of kin?'

'We are. Mum died two years ago.' Marley ushered them into his office and offered tea, which was refused. After reassuring himself that Katy and Paul were up to it, he brought up the question of care.

'Mr Marshall, Mrs Price, I believe Dr Tilley has told you about the CT result and the implications. Dr Gillespie, the consultant under whom your father has been admitted, will be round this afternoon. He's been informed of the details of your father's medical condition, but Dr Gillespie wants to assess your father himself. After that, we'd like to arrange a meeting with you; that's to say, Dr Gillespie, the Senior Physiotherapist on duty this weekend and me. Could you come back to the ward later this afternoon? I believe the others expect to be free at half past three.'

Katy and Paul agreed to return at that time and left for a late sandwich lunch in the concourse. They checked in with Henry who insisted Katy needn't worry about him and the girls and added that he would cook up a spaghetti Bolognese for supper. There were quite a few people getting something to eat around them. Paul and Katy found a table to one side and, over their M&S sandwiches and Café Costa flat whites, they remembered their father and reminisced together about the family life they had shared.

Charles had become headmaster in the school in which he had taught History for many years. His appointment to the headship had almost been by acclaim as he was both respected and popular among staff and students. Whether teaching, managing or leading, Charles' approach had been collaborative, supportive and encouraging, and he had been like this as a father. He let Mother keep discipline in the home with the result that he had been the more demonstrative parent. The headmaster stayed out of the home. In the home, Paul and Katy had known only a dad: one full of the stories of the world, one who excited their imagination and one who nudged them gently toward curiosity and learning.

Paul and Katy stood a head taller than their dad, but in many other respects they had his features: speckled brown irises in eyes on a slight downward slant away from a somewhat womanly nose, which is to say a nose most women unhappy with their own would ask for from their plastic surgeon, and blonde curly hair, which turned white on Charles' head but refused to fall from it. Paul would look at his father and see his future; Katy would look at Paul see her daddy. Through laughter and tears, their shared reminiscences helped them. They found themselves able to talk about the issues that Dr Gillespie was likely to raise. They were clear in their minds that their father's life should not be prolonged if there were no chance for a good recovery.

Following the usual courtesies and expression of commiseration, Dr Gillespie soon raised this very issue when they were shown into his office. He described the basic care of an unconscious patient, emphasising hydration by intravenous drip, two-hourly turns and skin care, and use of the catheter to drain the bladder. Of course, if there were any sign of discomfort, Charles would be given painkillers. To do more was a matter for discussion. Without chest percussion by the physiotherapist at least four hourly a chest infection was likely to develop. Protecting Charles' lungs in this way, keeping him fully nourished and preventing blood clots developing in the leg veins would be essential in the event that recovery of brain function was expected. In the absence of such an expectation, however, these additional measures would simply prolong life in a coma.

Dr Gillespie emphasised the irreversible and severe nature of the brain damage. On top of that, there was the Alzheimer's disease, wasn't there? Dr Gillespie didn't hurry them. He let Katy and Paul ask questions and showed no impatience in answering but, frankly, it boiled down to whether Katy and Paul would agree that Charles' life should not be prolonged unnecessarily. Thank Goodness we've had a chance to talk this through together, they thought. Both said they did not want their father to suffer.

On Monday morning, G7 seemed a different place to Katy. Two very elderly women were lying on trolleys in the ward corridor. One was wrapped in a blanket of silver foil. Many more nurses and other health care staff were around. All seemed to have their hands full; some were helping elderly patients to and from the day room; two nurses pushed a medicine trolley from bed to bed and dispensed pills of various colours in little plastic cups; two ward assistants had started to serve lunch to the occupants of the four-bedded room just inside the entrance; and Sam Marley was on the telephone at the nurses' station. It looks chaotic, she thought.

'It's yesterday's cold snap,' Marley said to Katy in response to the somewhat startled look he saw on her face. 'I'm just trying to arrange the early discharge of some patients to make room for new admissions. The poor dears are piling up in Casualty. You go down to your dad now. I'll come and find you.'

The door to Charles' room was shut. This wouldn't have been remarkable except that none of the other doors were shut. Katy found Charles positioned uncomfortably. He had rolled forward; his face was pressed against the side rails and his arm dangled down between the rails. Charles was groaning. Distressed at the thought that he might be in pain, Katy hurried to push Charles' shoulder back so that his head was brought onto the pillows. The movement upset Charles, though Katy couldn't immediately identify the problem. Charles was bringing his hand up toward his face. His eyelids weren't fully shut, and his eyes rolled upwards, showing the whites. Katy stroked his unwashed tangled hair, spoke softly into his ear intending to soothe him, and held his hand down so that he wouldn't scratch his face. Then, she noticed that his lips were cracked. Katy touched his tongue and found it bone dry. The feeding tube was no longer in Charles' nostril.

Someone had placed a plastic jug full of water, which was covered with an orange lid, and a glass on top of the bedside cupboard. Katy poured a little water into the glass and manoeuvred Charles sufficiently to bring him more onto his back than his side. She placed a tiny amount of water into his mouth. The sigh that Charles gave in response seemed one of relief. His tongue sought the moisture. He's thirsty! Could he have been trying to reach the water jug? thought Katy aghast, and if he has, surely Dad can't be brain-dead. The bile rising in her throat, she walked back to Marley's office, saw through the open door that he was off the telephone and then knocked, forcing herself to do so lightly. Seeing the concern on her face, Marley asked:

'Is anything wrong, Mrs Price?'

'Yes, actually. Dad doesn't seem to be unconscious. He's thirsty and that's hardly surprising given his mouth is dry. Aren't you giving him fluids? I suspect he's been trying to get to the jug of water.' Katy was getting mad; she knew it but couldn't control herself. 'For Heavens sake, what's the point of placing a jug of water out of reach! With a lid on it! Why hasn't he been helped to a drink? Maybe Dad isn't as brain damaged as all of you say.'

'Mrs Price, the doctors are quite certain about the diagnosis,' said Marley, getting to his feet so as to ward off the verbal onslaught. 'Your father has got a devastating bleed into the brainstem. There's no way back, I'm afraid.' He went on: 'Still, it's possible that Mr Marshall is sensing pain and discomfort. Look, I'll check on him just as soon as I've sorted today's bed problem. A painkiller has been prescribed and we can dispense it as required.'

Katy's anxiety was not allayed. She telephoned Paul and suggested he try to see Charles earlier than planned, before the night staff came on at seven o'clock. Paul got to the hospital ward as the senior nurses of the day and night shifts were in conference. He went down to see his father and found him unresponsive. Paul called out *Dad* quite loudly and shook Charles' shoulder, but there was neither a groan nor any movement to indicate that Charles registered the stimulus at any level. He found a junior nurse from the outgoing team and asked about his father's state. She told him that Charles had appeared distressed, as if in pain, and had been given diamorphine to ensure any pain was relieved.

'Is that medicine sedating? You see, my sister thought our father was improving. Now, he seems worse.'

'Diamorphine does have a sedative effect, but it's the strongest painkiller. Charge Nurse thought your dad was in considerable distress,' replied the nurse. Paul decided to waylay Marley who emerged some fifteen minutes later, dressed in his overcoat, and clearly keen to leave the ward. He seemed a little irritated to find Paul outside the office.

'Mr Marshall, it's nice to see you. I hope you've found your dad settled. He was agitated earlier and obviously in pain.'

'But why would he be in pain?'

'The head wound, I'm sure. Look, Mr Marshall, I'm in a rush. I've got to get home. My wife works nights, you see. I'm here again tomorrow afternoon and we could talk again if you could come in a little earlier.' Paul had to let Marley go. Then he found the Night Sister and asked her not to give any sedative to Charles overnight, adding that he and Katy would return together next morning. When they made their way into the ward the next morning, Maggie Tilley intercepted them.

'Hello Mrs Price, Mr Marshall. Could I have a word, please?' Maggie ushered them into an unoccupied treatment room for privacy. 'I'm sorry to tell you that your father's condition has deteriorated. He has a chest infection. This is usually the way with seriously head-injured patients. It comes as a merciful release.' Doctor Tilley didn't expect the anger that she saw in Katy's eyes. Katy blew up. She let Dr Tilley have it: the doctors and nurses had got it wrong, had starved Charles, sedated him unnecessarily, hadn't prevented the chest infection with physiotherapy, and would be guilty of killing him.

Paul, never having seen his father in the seemingly more responsive state, didn't know how to react. He touched Katy on the shoulder, but his hand was angrily pushed away. Katy was out of control and, thinking that she might attack Dr Tilley, Paul grabbed her in a bear hug. Katy wrestled in Paul's clutches for some moments; then she burst into tears and her knees gave way. It was difficult for everyone. Unhelpful things were said on both sides. None of it helped Charles. He died that night.

3. MUSIC AND FRIENDS

I've done a lot of living and I've found
No matter where you go the whole world 'round
They always go together hand in hand
Where there's one there'll be the other, music and
friends.

Simani

D on and Pat Black were small and round but nimble enough on their feet to walk up and down the Yorkshire Dales in their retirement, albeit with a bit of a waddle. This time outdoors had given them a ruddy complexion. Don had wispy white hair that had thinned only slightly over the crown. Pat's grey hair was permed into rather tight curls. They chuckled easily at one another's jokes, liked their Rowntree neighbours, owned their small terraced home and attended church on Sundays. The extra bedroom and bathroom at York Terrace encouraged them to visit their son in Cambridge for a long weekend every four to six weeks.

After nine years of asking Derek whether he had a steady girlfriend, Pat quickly realised Derek needed no encouragement this time. Every visit, she saw that the body language between Julia and her son was more intimate, which provoked contrasting emotions in this doting mother. Her lovely talented son may have left their home a decade ago, but she felt he still held his mother in his heart. What chance did she have against this creature endowed with the beauty of youth and more? Pat realised such thoughts were unbecoming and unfair to Julia and did her best to push them away. She concentrated on never saying the wrong thing.

On the other hand, Don just loved being around Julia. He would ask about the houses she had been into and the people she had met through work. Julia would have a marketing brochure of a particularly grand Cambridge home every time Don was expected. The two of them would pour over the photographs and floorplans. A keen and competent DIY man, Don suggested ways he would improve the house, and Julia would talk Don through different arrangements of the furniture and furnishings in the various rooms. Julia would always select a property with a granny flat, or the potential for one, and say: and there would be room for the parents here, wouldn't there? It seemed to Derek that Don helped fill the void left in Julia's life by Milton's departure, following his betrayal of the family, and he offered this explanation to his mother who seemed perplexed by the relationship. The more Julia got to know Don and Pat, the more she could see just how much Cambridge had changed Derek.

Since Derek worked late most weekday evenings, Julia used this time to make connections of her own, both with and beyond her colleagues at Tuckers. She thought the local church might be a good way to ease into the community around upper Mill Road. She was comfortable in church. The family had attended Sunday morning Choral Eucharist at Ely Cathedral regularly. The majestic lanterned cathedral, which sat atop the city and dominated the surrounding fenland, was well attended. Milton used to say it was important for business that they participate, and he would network over coffee after the service. Sylvia did as much voluntary work as their thriving business allowed; usually contributing and arranging fresh flowers on a Saturday evening around six thirty, when evensong ended.

For Julia, the wave upon wave of transporting polyphony that filled the exuberantly decorative high octagonal tower was acutely pleasurable. Add sunlight streaming through the stained glass to illuminate the gorgeous painted ceiling of the nave and Julia thought the experience utterly heavenly. Faith was another matter and better not questioned, she thought. She loved the poetry of the eloquent age-old prayer book but doubted that she could pray spontaneously and sincerely.

So, some six months into life in Cambridge, Julia went to Sunday Eucharist at St. Barnabas on Mill Road and introduced herself to the vicar afterwards. The Reverend David Richmond was tall, stooped, and a had a benevolent bespectacled face beneath barely combed, thick white hair. He was as adept with the guitar as the keyboard in raising hearts up to the Lord. He loved his flock and embraced its newest member. Julia liked him instantly.

David invited Julia to tea and used the occasion to explore her interests and to discover how he could help her integrate into the parish community. She found it easy to talk about her background, about the trauma of her father's infidelity, about her expectation that she might be married within the year, and especially about her wish to make new connections and find new interests.

'As you enjoyed the Cathedral's choral music so much, would you be interested in joining our choir? We need voices, you know.'

'I think I've got a decent voice,' said Julia, "my Mum says so, but I don't know how to read music properly. I just follow the notes up the lines or down.' David Richmond got up and went over to an upright piano.

'Sing this hymn, Julia, would you? Just let yourself go and don't mind how loudly it comes out.' Julia took up the hymnal and, after David's opening chords, sang out. David was astonished.

'Julia, you have a beautiful mezzo voice. How on earth don't you know it? I can tell you that our director of music would willingly teach you how to read music to get you into the choir'

'Would he?' asked Julia, very pleased at the idea. 'Well

then, I would be a willing student and what a great way to make new friends! Thank you for being so encouraging.'

'There are about twenty voices in the choir. They are lovely people and pretty committed. The choir rehearses on Thursday evenings at seven thirty. Could you make it?'

'Do you know, Thursday evening suits me very well. I'll come along this Thursday.' As David showed Julia out, he said:

'Do bring your Derek along, won't you? If you're planning to marry at St. Barnabas, we should arrange three or four meetings to prepare spiritually for your life together in Jesus Christ. A wedding is rather more than choosing readings and hymns.' Julia smiled in acknowledgement.

'He does well to remind me,' she thought, 'it's easily forgotten.' Julia's newfound enthusiasm for singing, augmented by an easily acquired ability to read her musical line, gave her pleasure, brought friends, and made her feel she belonged. St. Barnabas couldn't match Ely Cathedral for architectural wonder and beauty, but it offered a more intimate relationship with other congregants, many of whom were similar in age to Julia and Derek. Cambridge being the sort of town it is, almost everyone Julia met was interesting in one way or another. She became acquainted with teachers, doctors, nurses, artists, musicians, research scientists and University lecturers. Yes, and more lawyers.

Fiona Jefferies was the other mezzo in the choir. Her speaking voice was low in register and very masculine, which rather went with Fiona's short crop and side parting. In song, however, Fiona's voice had a bold, rich quality, and projected powerfully. Initially discomfited by the new member who stood next to her every Thursday evening, Fiona soon saw it was a reawakening of desires she had played with in her time at New Hall. The alternative had been pleasurable, but she had settled on a preference for men. She was happily married to Matthew and had two children, both of whom were now in school. What was the harm in acknowledging that one felt attracted to beauty?

Having been reserved for the first month or so, Fiona resolved to be warm and welcoming to Julia, who was pleased at the thaw in Fiona's frostiness and enjoyed the opportunities for a chat that came after choir practice. It didn't take her long to discover Fiona was practical, efficient, high-achieving and nothing short of miraculous. She was slightly older than Derek, Julia reckoned, and apart from having two children, being committed to the choir and being an active member of the parents and teachers' association, she was a consultant at Bolingbroke's Hospital where she specialised in cancer medicine.

One might have thought there was little in Julia to engage Fiona intellectually given their widely different backgrounds, but Fiona noticed that Julia was hungry and quick to learn, especially about contemporary fiction, music and art. She felt an obligation to encourage Julia in this and was rewarded by increasingly interesting conversations when the two of them met, especially since the subject of the NHS and everything connected to it would be pushed aside. So, from time to time, Julia would accompany Fiona to her home in St. Barnabas Street after choir to pick out books from the Jefferies' shelves and, in turn, she added the catalogues from exhibitions she would have visited in London.

By way of appreciation and gratitude, Julia offered to babysit the girls occasionally so that Fiona and her husband could have time together. Matthew lectured in Social Sciences at the University, usually in late mornings and early afternoons, which meant he could sort out the girls in the morning, cycle them to school and collect them at half past three. Fiona would take over after their tea, bathing them and then reading bedtime stories to them. On two evenings each week in term, Matthew would cycle to his College for supervisions, usually staying on to dine in Hall on one or both nights. Fiona's choir commitments meant the two of them could think of *us*-time only on Wednesday nights.

'I can't tell you what a novelty it is to be going down to the pub with my wife,' said Matthew when Julia first came to babysit the girls. She arrived at five o'clock and joined the girls for their tea. Naturally, Ottilie and Charlotte, known to everyone as Ottie and Lottie, were shy at first, but Julia had bought a 'Cheeky Monkey' game to break the ice. Trying to collect most bananas on the tree, while watching out for other cheeky monkeys trying to steal them, should do the trick, Julia had thought; and it worked a treat. Julia joined in with the water play at bath time and read one of the bedtime stories before leaving Fiona to settle the girls for the night.

As to her wider circle of friends, Julia and Amy Smith became pals and, with other acquaintances, enjoyed occasional girls' nights out, but Julia did not discuss Derek with Amy; nor did she suggest going out as a foursome when Amy started a relationship with a car salesman. On the other hand, the relationship with Fiona deepened. Julia came to love the girls, to appreciate Matthew's humour and equanimity, and to trust Fiona. When the Jefferies returned, never late, from their Wednesday evening reconnects, Matthew would open a bottle of wine and the three of them would chat for an hour or so before Matthew put Julia in a taxi. Of course, Derek came up in conversation several times.

As Julia prepared to go home on one such evening, some five months into their friendship, Fiona asked:

'Would you like us to meet him, Julia?' She's reading my mind, thought Julia, appreciatively.

'I'd like that. Derek would too, I know. Shall we go to a restaurant together or get bar food at the Cambridge Blue?'

'Neither,' said Fiona, 'bring him to dinner here, one Wednesday evening.'

'Absolutely! Derek sounds an interesting fellow. I'll prepare an aubergine parmigiana,' interjected Matthew, 'and if Derek wants to bring a bottle, nudge him toward red.'

Julia and Derek went around to the Jefferies a fortnight later. The four of them had a lovely evening. Fiona had cleared away toys, reading books and discarded children's clothing, so that evidence of children was confined to the several framed photos on the mantelpiece and sideboard. Fiona called them to the table quite quickly, reckoning that Derek would feel at ease sooner if they gathered over food rather than face one another across the sitting room.

Matthew's aubergine parmigiana was only the starter. He had also prepared a main course of Swedish meatballs piled up in the manner of the Ambassador's Ferrero Rocher, over which he poured thick tomato salsa, and a side of mashed potatoes into which steamed broccoli and carrots were inserted absurdly. If this was designed to trigger mirth and ribbing, it worked. Conversation never tired and they found each other's company pleasant and stimulating. Following choir practice the next day, Julia and Fiona walked arm in arm up St. Barnabas Street.

'Thank you for yesterday evening, Fiona. Derek enjoyed meeting you very much. Did *you* like him?'

'Of course, we liked Derek. It was a pleasure to meet him,' said Fiona as they came to her front door; 'come in for a glass of wine, Julia.'

'Oh Matthew, there you are. Would you mind finishing off that marking in the study?' said Fiona, which Matthew correctly understood to mean *we want some privacy*.

'You didn't say very much yesterday, Julia. I'm sorry not to have steered the conversation away from the University and the state of the NHS,' said Fiona as they settled into the sofa, each with a large glass of yesterday's Merlot.

'Oh, don't worry about that. I enjoyed seeing Derek so animated. Any subject is better than the Law; he has enough of that.' Julia kicked off her shoes, brought her legs up beneath her, and turned to face Fiona expectantly. 'So, what do you think of him?'

'That's an easy question. I think Derek is good-looking, intelligent, well-read, charming *and* he has a sense of humour. If you mean do I like him? Yes, both Matthew and I enjoyed his company very much.' Fiona took Julia's hand in hers and, suppressing a momentary feeling of jealousy, she added: 'and he *is* head-over-heels in love with you, Julia.' Who wouldn't be? she thought and, resisting an urge to stroke its soft skin sensuously, let go the hand.

'Is it so obvious?'

'From the way he looks at you, the way he attends to you, the way he reaches out to touch you, I've no doubt at all; but you'll know this.' Then, Fiona asked matter-of-factly: 'Does the relationship work in bed?' which caused Julia's cheeks to colour.

Over the dozen or so times that Derek and Julia had had sexual intercourse, they had come to know how to gratify each other. Julia enjoyed Derek's prolonged foreplay. Hers was not the explosive climax that turned most men into putty post-coitally, but it was more than she had experienced with other sexual partners. She discovered that Derek loved her hair. He would reach for it, draw it through his fingers and smell it deeply; and, within a few seconds, his kissing would grow hungrier. She rather envied the fact that Derek's climaxes were the sexual equivalent of the New Year's Eve fireworks off Sydney Harbour Bridge. Still, she loved to linger in his arms afterwards and receive his grateful overtures.

'There's no need to say anything, Julia. Your face says it all. Obviously, the sex *is* good,' said Fiona with a friendly laugh. Then, she turned serious and asked: 'So, one comes to the difficult question, my darling. Do you *love* him?'

'Oh, Fi! I think I do. I want to be with him, to share our days and dreams. He's not hysterically funny but I like his wit and he has a nice laugh. It's lovely when we laugh together at some movie or play. He makes me feel very special despite the fact that I haven't had much of an education. In fact, he values my opinion and encourages me. You know, I would like to make a home out of his house, and to have his children. Is this love, Fiona?' Fiona leaned over and hugged Julia.

'Love builds as two people make their lives one, navigating happy times and sad times together, celebrating successes and supporting one another through setbacks. One can't have all that from the off, Julia, but I'd say you're making a pretty good start.' Julia felt elated at Fiona's reassurance.

'Thank you so much for listening, Fiona. I'll stop analysing the relationship and just experience it; feel, not think, when I'm with Derek.' Fiona walked Julia to the door. 'Now, I expect to be the first to know when Derek proposes,' she said, touching Julia's lips with her own, briefly.

4. EXPERT WITNESS

S tanley Posner took the stairs two at a time, pushed through swing doors into the Histopathology Laboratory and strode down the corridor to the dissection room. He was nearly forty but athletically slim, six foot three, and handsome from eyes as blue as the Mediterranean. He parted his straight blond hair on the left and slicked it down with a spare amount of gel. He disliked keeping anybody waiting but simply had too much to do. The fact is his research was coming to a critical point. Several others were exploring the same research question and he wanted to get to the answer first. Research demanded more and more of his time. Fortunately for his patients and students, once engaged in a task Stanley would give his full attention to it. So, no diagnostic problem went unsolved and no student left his side other than enlightened.

Javed Iyer waited patiently for his chief. He had joined Stanley a couple of years earlier to train as a neuropathologist and he felt privileged to have the opportunity. Cambridge was the first place to which he had travelled outside India and it was the last place he thought would accept him. Javed read medicine at Cochin and then switched to an internship in Pathology at Trivandrum. Kerala was no longer a medical backwater. Specialisation had come to medical services and the new Institute of Neurology and Neurosurgery wanted their own specialist pathologist. Javed showed interest and the Institute's Director lost no time in contacting a former colleague in Cambridge about training opportunities for his man. Kerala State Government provided him with some financial support.

Only three years younger than Stanley, Javed was his antithesis, being a little man with black beady eyes in a dark brown bald head, over which long strands of black hair connected one ear with the other. Had Stanley been one to judge a man by appearance, Javed might not have stood a chance. Stanley found his manner too diffident at the start, but came to realise he was gentle rather than diffident. Still, a handicap not a virtue as far as Stanley was concerned. One had to be tough to get on. Nevertheless, Javed was committed to the specialty and was quick to learn. He grew in confidence and began to present his views on medical cases with professional decisiveness, when appropriate. So, Stanley came to the view that Javed would make a skilled pathologist; he would train him and the *quid pro quo* would be that he could push more of the routine work onto his shoulders.

'Good morning, Javed. Is this going to take long? How many cases have we got?' Javed stood up.

'Good morning, Dr Posner. There's only one brain for examination today. It's a Coroner's case. The autopsy took place three weeks ago.'

'Right, tell me the story,' said Stanley as he put on a green plastic apron and pulled on a pair of surgical gloves. He picked up the brain in both hands and examined it, while Javed read the referral note from Her Majesty's Coroner.

'The brain is from a seventy-year-old man, called Charles Marshall. The coroner writes that Marshall, known to have Alzheimer's disease, fell down the stairs in his home and suffered irreversible brain trauma. There was no scope for surgical intervention.'

'Have we got the case notes?'

'No, the autopsy was done by John Walker. He has the hospital case notes. Doctor Walker hasn't written a report yet.'

'He'll be waiting for our own report on the brain before he completes the *Cause of Death* statement for the Coroner. Frankly, he ought to have passed the entire case to us. As it is, neither one of us gets to see the whole picture.' Stanley put the brain down on the dissection board, stepped aside, and said: 'Well, take over. What's your assessment so far?'

'The brain weight is pretty good for a seventy-year-old, and there isn't much shrinkage of the gyri on the surface of the brain. This doesn't suggest severe Alzheimer change.'

'Correct! Now, what about trauma to the brain?' Turning the brain upside down, Javed pointed to small areas on the undersurface of the frontal lobes.

'The surface is damaged where the brain scraped over the rough floor of the skull at the moment of impact. There's tissue loss focally, but it isn't much.'

'Agreed! Do you see evidence that the brain was dangerously swollen after the head injury?'

'The brain wasn't swollen at the time of death, but I do think it was swollen for a while after the injury. This groove along the inner part of the temporal lobe is evidence. I'd like to examine the area more closely after we've sliced the brain,' replied Javed. Stanley nodded approvingly.

'Before slicing the brain, you must separate the brain stem from the cerebral hemispheres.' Javed inserted the scalpel blade at just the right angle, swung the blade across, and pulled the brain stem away from the brain hemispheres. To their considerable surprise, the cut surface showed four discrete foci of haemorrhage in the brain stem. 'Hey now! This indicates a much worse problem than the surface observations suggested,' remarked Stanley, 'how do you interpret this?'

'On the face of it, the haemorrhages are consistent with severe trauma to the brain. The blood vessels have been torn apart, either by twisting forces applied to the brain stem directly at the moment of impact or the brain swelled so much after impact that it crushed the brain stem.'

'Right! Whichever mechanism has operated, the presence of these haemorrhages in the brain stem could argue for severe and irreversible brain trauma.' However, Stanley's expert eye had picked out peculiar features. 'Now, look closely, will you? Use the magnifying lens.' Javed peered at the brain stem surface.

'Well, an odd feature is that the bleeds appear so sharply discrete. There's no damage to tissue around them. Another oddity is the fact that there's no bruise-like colour change at the edges to suggest blood breakdown products.'

'Exactly! I don't think these are haemorrhages at all,' said Stanley, 'we could be looking at a malformation: a cluster of thinly walled, but unruptured, blood vessels, which have been in the brain stem for many years, if not most of the man's life – an angioma. As far as this case is concerned, a red herring!'

'Is it heritable?' asked Javed

'Cerebral angiomas may be familial and inherited from one generation to the next,' Stanley answered. 'Now let's move on to the question of the Alzheimer's disease. Slice the brain hemispheres and display the slices in the trays. I'll be back in ten minutes.' Stanley walked round to John Walker's office in order to have a look at the case notes, but Walker was out. So, he grabbed a coffee in the tearoom next door, then returned to the dissection room. Javed smelled the coffee and thought: I could have done with a cup, too. He stood aside to let Stanley examine the surface of slice after slice of brain, arranged from front to back.

'Your assessment?'

'Firstly, there are no other haemorrhages or angiomas. Secondly, the hippocampus on either side seems reasonably well preserved. Usually, the hippocampus is shrunken in severe Alzheimer's disease.'

'You're right. Of course, the naked eye appearances can be misleading, but this doesn't quite fit with a fellow suffering from severe dementia,' confirmed Stanley. He added, with a note of frustration: 'but we don't know the severity of his dementia, as we don't have the clinical notes.' We can get a pretty good idea from checking the tissue under the microscope, thought Javed.

'Dr Posner, I'll take samples and get the lab to prepare them for microscopical examination in three weeks; two, if the inquest is coming up soon.'

'Three weeks will do, Javed. Bring the slides to me after you've had a look at them yourself and drafted a report.'

'I'll do that,' said Javed, pleased to have the opportunity to demonstrate his increasing knowledge and expertise. Stanley returned to his office and settled down to examine and report surgical biopsies. Much as he would have liked to get on with research, the biopsies were from living patients in the postoperative neurosurgical wards, now awaiting the pathologist's verdict: Was it a brain tumor? Was it malignant? Did the molecular genetic test suggest the tumor could respond to treatment? How long has the patient got? A pile of thirteen cases had been brought to Stanley's in-tray while he had been examining the brain with Javed. Stanley put thoughts of research and of the puzzling Coroner's autopsy case aside and concentrated on the job in hand.

Three weeks later, Javed and Stanley were seated at Stanley's double-headed, teaching microscope with the set of tissue sections from Charles Marshall's brain. Stanley sat at the controls while Javed, seated at right angles, looked through the second pair of eyepieces. Stanley liked to examine all the sections before hearing what Javed had to say.

'Have you been able to get a look at the notes,' he asked while completing his examination.

'Actually, I haven't' replied Javed, feeling this failing personally. 'Apparently, the Coroner's Officer has retrieved them. The Coroner wanted the notes urgently. The inquest is likely to be held as soon as he gets the two pathology reports.'

'Hmm, I wonder what's going on,' said Stanley. 'Anyway,

let's get on with it. What do you think?'

'You were right about the blood in the brain stem. It *is* an angioma. The blood is confined within thin-walled blood vessels. They're intact. No bleeding occurred. The angioma has got nothing to do with the cause of death.'

'Agreed! And what of the Alzheimer's disease?' challenged Stanley.

'Again, it's much as we suspected at brain dissection. The Alzheimer-type change is restricted to the hippocampus, which is pretty much what many seventy-year-olds have and still function perfectly adequately.'

'That's right. I hope Doctor Walker has found a cause of death elsewhere in the body, because there's nothing in the brain to explain it.'

Stanley liked David Hillman, Her Majesty's Coroner for Cambridgeshire and Huntingdonshire. So, he usually arrived half an hour before the scheduled start of an inquest to pay his respects. The lawyer was a grandfatherly figure – Father Christmassy even, were he not clean shaven – with a plethoric face acquired through fine vintages. He kept discipline in Court, but always allowed relatives as much time as was reasonable to put their questions, and he ensured that no expert witness obfuscated.

Stanley was surprised to see camera crews outside the Coroner's Court. A single reporter from the local newspaper was the norm. He drove round to the back of the courthouse, parked his car in the space reserved for him, and used the back entrance. David Hillman's door was open, and he called out to Stanley.

'I'm glad I've caught you, Doctor Posner. My officer is at the front entrance looking out for you. Come in, please. Do sit down while I call to let him know you're here,' he said, indicating a chair.

'How are you, Mister Hillman?' asked Stanley when David Hillman finished the brief call, 'I'm surprised to see the press out in force. Is it the case in which I'm to give evidence?'

'It is, Doctor. The son and daughter of the deceased have talked to the Cambridge News and BBC East. They're very unhappy about the care their father received in hospital, I can tell you,' said Hillman with feeling. 'Quite a few of your clinical colleagues and representatives of the Hospital Management Team will be in court. However, that's not for you to worry about. I've been looking out for you because I want to discuss your report before we go into Court.'

'Of course, what is unclear about it?'

'Oh, there's nothing unclear. Your reports are always clear and to the point. You make complicated stuff comprehensible, and I'm grateful for that. In fact, your report couldn't be clearer: you haven't found evidence of severe brain injury and the Alzheimer's disease is mild, but the clinical diagnosis is exactly that – irreversible brain injury and severe Alzheimer's disease.' David Hillman threw open his arms in exasperation. 'The question is: how did your very competent, indeed eminent, colleagues get things so wrong?'

'I have to be honest. Though my registrar tried two or three times, he wasn't able to get hold of the clinical notes. I haven't read them. So, I don't know the thinking of the admitting doctors or of those who looked after the deceased subsequently. If the clinical notes are here, I could look through them to see if anything catches my eye, but the inquest is scheduled to start in fifteen minutes.' When the inquest started was up to Hillman.

'Don't worry about that, doctor,' said the Coroner, waving aside Stanley's concern., 'I'll send word that there will be a thirty-minute delay. Will that be sufficient?'

'I'll have a go,' said Stanley. He took up the thick folder of notes, to which the Coroner pointed, and carried them to a room down the corridor reserved for the pathologists. John Walker's coat and brief case indicated he was already in his

43

place in the courtroom. Stanley was relieved not to run into him. He sat at the table, opened the clinical notes at the date of admission and started reading. So, the cerebral angioma *was* familial, said Stanley to himself when he saw the form that Paul Marshall had completed the night he had brought his father to the Emergency Room. Stanley turned to the Radiology section and found the radiologist's report on the head scan. Aghast at what he read, he went through the report again. Stanley knocked on the Coroner's door and went straight in when Hillman called out: Come!

'I think I've found the error,' said Stanley, showing some anxiety, 'but, my theory is based on a very brief perusal of the notes. You'll have to confirm or refute it through witness interrogation.'

'Just take me through it with your usual clarity, doctor.'

'Right, so the clinical diagnosis of severe brain injury was made on the radiologist's report that there was extensive bleeding into the brain stem. Now, if there really had been fresh bleeding into the brain stem following the fall, the conclusion would have been correct; but in this case there was no bleeding at all.' Stanley pointed to a line in his own report to the Coroner and went on: 'You see here in my report that I found a benign angioma in the brain stem. It's incidental. I mean it has no relevance except that the angioma has been wrongly diagnosed as fresh bleeding. The angioma is an inherited malformation. The son knew it ran in the family. He knew his father was affected. In fact, he mentioned it to the admitting doctor in the Emergency Room.'

'Wasn't the radiologist told about it?' asked Hillman.

'I checked the entry for *Clinical Details* on the scan request form. There's no reference to the familial history of cerebral angioma. Whoever filled in the request form wrote only: *severe head injury*.

The coroner held up his hands. 'Stop there, doctor. I've heard enough. Let's leave the rest to the courtroom. I'm very grateful for your help, as always. Now, you had better join Doctor

Walker in court. I'll come through in five minutes.' The coroner got to his feet and Stanley shook the hand that Hillman
extended. Then, he made his way to the courtroom.

'You've cut it fine,' said John Walker, as Stanley took
a seat beside him. Stanley understood this to mean *what
have you been up to?* The next moment, the Coroner's Officer
entered the courtroom and called out: All rise, please. The
coroner followed him in and sat at the bench. Actually, it
wasn't more than a raised table. Nor was there a witness box.
Evidence was given while seated in a chair beside the bench.
David Hillman's court was spacious, and large windows fitted
with frosted glass made for a comfortable well-lit room. Instead of a pocket square, a ruffled red silk handkerchief over-
flowed from Hillman's jacket breast pocket. Wireframe half-
moon spectacles blunted the amiability of his features, but
marginally. He also tried to frown at first but couldn't sustain
it. Hillman started by welcoming everybody, starting with
the relatives.

Paul and Katy sat to the right of the bench. They were
accompanied by two lawyers, the much younger one presumably an associate. In front of the bench, sat four lawyers,
all looking pretty senior. David Hillman introduced them to
Paul and Katy as the legal representatives of Bolingbroke's
Hospital NHS Trust. In the next row back, sat consultant
physicians and surgeons, some of whom Stanley knew personally, and with whom he interacted professionally at least
weekly. Charlie Mitchinson, known as Mitch, was director of
the Head Trauma Unit in the Department of Neurosurgery
and a much-respected brain surgeon. Stanley liked Mitch but
had much more to do with the brain tumour surgeons, as they
were the ones who regularly sent tissue biopsies from the op-
erating theatre and waited for Stanley's pronouncement of
the tissue diagnosis.

Stanley did not know Gillespie personally but recognised him as one of the consultant geriatricians. A Charge
Nurse and Nursing Sister sat next to Gillespie. They wore
anxious expressions. This is probably their first time at an in-

quest, thought Stanley. The two benches at the back of the room were filled with journalists, who started to scribble in notebooks from the off. Then Hillman got proceedings moving.

'Ladies and gentlemen, the purpose of this inquest is to establish the date, time and cause of death of Mister Charles Marshall. There is no doubt about the first two points as Mister Marshall died in Bolingbroke's Hospital, while under the care of the medical and nursing staff there. So, for the purpose, I shall record the date and time at which death was certified in the clinical notes. Now, by *cause of death*, I mean that this inquest will seek to answer the *how* question, which is to say: what is the sequence of events that led to death? The doctors in charge of Mister Marshall's care have confidently attributed death to severe irreversible brain damage from a head trauma. The police investigation indicates that violence is not suspected at all. The scenario that Mister Marshall fell down the staircase of his home accidentally is not being questioned. The issue that this court must establish is whether the fall did, in fact, result in a degree of brain injury from which recovery was impossible, and which left Mister Marshall vulnerable to terminal pneumonia. So, to be clear, this inquest is neither a civil court nor a criminal court. Only matters of fact concern us. Anything else is for another place and another time. I trust you have explained this to your clients?' Hillman looked from one set of lawyers to the other, inviting confirmation for the record.

'We have explained the position, Sir' said the older man for the relatives. The Trust's lawyers indicated the same.

'Then we shall start with the evidence of my pathologists. Doctor Posner, please take the witness's chair.' Stanley did so and the coroner's officer brought over a Bible, which Stanley took in his right hand and declared that he would say the truth, the whole truth and nothing but the truth. Here we go, he murmured to himself.

'Thank you, Doctor. Please tell the court your name, employment and qualifications.'

'I am Doctor Stanley Posner. I am a Reader in Pathology at the University of Cambridge and I hold an honorary appointment as a consultant pathologist at Bolingbroke's Hospital. I specialise in diseases of the nervous system.'

'Doctor, four months ago, you examined the brain of the deceased on my instruction. Please tell the court your findings.' Stanley looked at Mitch and thought *nothing but the truth, so help me God.* He spoke out clearly and monotonously because he wished neither to emphasise one fact over another nor to introduce any emotion.

'I found evidence of recent trauma to the brain. This consisted of contusions, which are just superficial scrapes, on the under surface of the brain at the point where it overlies some ridges of the bony floor of the skull. These scrapes occur when the moving head comes to an abrupt halt; for instance, during a fall, when the head hits a piece of furniture or the floor. Whereas the brain and skull would have been moving with the same speed before impact, at impact the brain continues to move within the stationary skull.'

'Would you say the contusions were severe, doctor?'

'They were not severe. Certainly, not sufficient to result in significant impairment of brain function.'

'Did you find any other effects of brain trauma?'

'No, Sir.' This evidence caused excitement among the relatives. Katy punched the air.

'Stop that!' the Coroner warned, 'or you won't be allowed in court.' Paul and Katy's lawyer was quick to apologise, and assured the Coroner his clients would not interrupt proceedings again. There had not been any reaction from Mitch and Gillespie, but the nurses seemed agitated. 'Did you find any brain pathology unrelated to trauma?' asked Hillman.

'Yes, I did. A cluster of abnormal wide-channelled, thin-walled blood vessels were present in the brain stem. It's called an angioma. On naked eye examination, I mistakenly thought it may be haemorrhage...' there Mitch, I've given you what help I can and I hope you appreciate it, thought Stanley as he continued...'but microscopical examination left no doubt that it was an incidental finding. I mean, that it is likely to have been present for many years, probably changing little and causing no symptoms.' Hillman continued the line of questioning:

'Doctor Posner, what appearance would the angioma have on a brain scan?'

'It could mimic bleeding into the brain stem. Indeed, I've already stated that I thought it was a bleed when I dissected the brain, before using the microscope.' Suddenly, Paul was on his feet:

'But I told them about the angioma,' he shouted. Two policemen moved forward quickly from the back of the courtroom and were about to take hold of him, when Hillman signed to stop them. Then to Paul, he raised his index finger by way of warning.

'Mr Marshall, I am aware of the concerns you have, and of the strength of feeling with which you hold them. I have assured you severally that this inquest will establish the true facts surrounding your father's death. You must allow it to do so without interruption. You will have to remain silent if you wish to be present during the proceedings. Now is this absolutely clear to both of you?' he asked, directing his question at Katy as well as Paul. Both of them nodded. Turning back to Stanley, Hillman asked:

'Did the deceased have Alzheimer's dementia, Doctor?'

'The brain showed changes of Alzheimer type.'

'I think you've nuanced your answer, presumably in the interests of accuracy. Would you explain?'

'I found changes typical of the Alzheimer disease process but restricted to the part of the brain known as the hippocampus, which implies that the deceased was forgetful in life. Dementia implies a more serious handicap in which a patient becomes progressively unable to cope with activities of daily living: feeding himself, bathing and dressing. Dementia occurs when the changes extend beyond the hippocampus to affect the rest of the brain.'

'Has either the Alzheimer change or the angioma caused death, Doctor?'

'No, Sir. Neither separately nor in combination with one another or with the brain contusions. I'm assuming the cause of death was found elsewhere in the body by my colleague, Doctor Walker.'

'Help me here, Doctor. If there was neither significant brain injury nor severe Alzheimer's disease, what explains the patient's unresponsive state on admission to hospital?'

'In my opinion, the patient did have brain injury that resulted in brain swelling, but this was not irreversible. The brain had prominent grooves on its underside, which indicate it had enlarged sufficiently to fill the main compartment within the skull. The grooves are the persisting impression on the brain surface where it has been forced over the firm edge of an opening in the brain's cover or envelope. However, the brain was not swollen at the time of death.'

'You are doing your best to make the science understandable, Doctor, I know; but I am finding it complicated. I'll ask the question in another way: do the brain changes fit the picture of a patient whose mental function is deteriorating progressively?'

'On the brain changes alone, I would say that the patient was concussed on admission because of brain swelling, but I would guess that his mental function would have been improving significantly before death. Some other illness must have intervened to cause death.'

'Thank you, Doctor Posner,' said the Coroner and, turning to the lawyers, he asked: 'does anyone have further questions for this witness?' To Stanley's surprise, they had none, and the Coroner invited him to step down. 'Doctor Walker, please take the oath?' said the coroner. John Walker did so and, when asked, stated his qualifications and experience, as Stanley had done earlier. Then, he proceeded to recount his autopsy findings, though not quite so fluently because of a tendency to break up his speech with an *Ah*, an *Eh*, or an *Um*.

'When I examined the *ah* body externally, I *eh* found evidence of recent weight loss, even allowing for the *ah* generally loose skin of a seventy-year-old. Old puncture wounds in the *eh* bend of the arm related to the *ah* insertion of intravenous lines. On the back of the body, I found sores over bony prominences, which were consistent with bed sores.' Hillman wanted clarification.

'What is a bed sore, doctor?'

'Well you see, a bedridden patient is *um* prone to breakdown of skin at the *ah* points in the body that bear most weight; the buttocks and heels if the patient is left lying supine, for instance. A patient who is *um* unable to turn himself or who is *ah* malnourished is susceptible; there are other risk factors.'

'Can bed sores be prevented?'

'*Um, eh,* Obviously, one must deal with the patient's medical problems in order to mobilise him as soon as possible. However, the *ah* most important manoeuvre is to turn the patient regularly; at least every six hours, but more frequently when the *eh* risk is greater.'

'Thank you, Doctor. Tell the Court of your findings relating to the cause of death, please?'

'The immediate cause of death was *ah* pneumonia, which is the term for a lung that is airless because *um* pus fills the *ah* airspaces. It is caused by infection with pus-forming bacteria and *um* typically occurs in bedridden patients in the *ah* terminal phase of some other illness.'

Hillman cut in: 'So, by *immediate* cause of death, do you mean that the pneumonia was the terminal event, not the reason for the apparently unresponsive state of the patient on admission?'

'*Um*, That's the case. Yes.'

'Then, could we get to the primary cause of the death, Doctor Walker?' began Hillman somewhat impatiently. 'Doctor Posner has given evidence to the effect that the cause is not in the head. Your evidence so far tells us the pneumonia is a common complication that brings about death in seriously ill patients. The central question is: what made the deceased seriously ill?' John Walker straightened up, puffed his chest and smoothed back his hair with his right hand affectedly.

'I *eh* believe, I have an explanation, Sir. At autopsy, I found that the *um* pancreas weighed less than normal for the organ in *ah* a man of the stated age. I took samples of tissue from the pancreas and *ah* prepared sections for microscopical examination. These sections showed fibrosis and *ah* chronic inflammation. I conclude the deceased had *ah* chronic pancreatitis.' This declaration had a triumphal note to it.

Bollocks! said Stanley under his breath. He'll never get that past *this* coroner. Hillman is no fool.

'Thank you Dr Walker, the Court notes your *Cause of Death* as *Pneumonia complicating Chronic Pancreatitis*,' said Hillman turning to the Clerk who seemed to have no difficulty recording it; 'but Doctor, is there anything in the clinical notes to indicate that the deceased had symptoms relating to chronic pancreatitis when he was first admitted to hospital?' Walker hesitated; then blushed. Again, his right hand brushed his hair back along the temple.

'Actually *ah*, no. There is nothing in them to suggest that.' Hillman continued relentlessly.

'Doctor Walker, you began your evidence by telling the Court that the deceased had lost weight recently. Could rapid weight loss, say from starvation, to pick an extreme example, cause changes in the pancreas?' Walker looked very uncomfortable. After more Um-ing and Ah-ing, he admitted he did not know.

'Would you be able to find out over a short recess, Doctor?'

'I could search the *ah* internet for papers on the *ah* subject," replied Walker.

'Then, this inquest is adjourned for thirty minutes.' The Court rose with the Coroner who then left the court. The Coroner's Officer went up to Walker and took him off to some back office. When the inquest resumed with Walker still under oath, he reported that he had found scientific papers that reported similar pancreatic changes in starvation.

'Thank you, Doctor Walker. That will be all.' Hillman looked at the lawyers, who shook their heads, and then said: 'We shall let Doctor Posner and Doctor Walker get back to the hospital. Doctors, feel free to leave the Court.' Stanley and Walker left the room. Stanley was about to say something when Walker interjected:

'Sorry, must rush,' he said and stormed off.

Next morning, Stanley called in at the newsagents in the hospital concourse. Banner headlines screamed out at him: *Hospital starves 70-year-old! Drugged to death for a hospital bed! Daughter's pleas go unheeded as hospital withholds food and drink!* The story had made the broadsheets, as well as the tabloids. He bought a copy of *The Daily Telegraph,* and a coffee from Costa; then, he settled down at a table to read:

> *A recently widowed, retired headmaster, wrongly diagnosed as a terminal case, was starved to death in order to vacate the hospital bed. 70-year-old Charles Marshall was admitted to Bolingbroke's Hospital after falling downstairs. Despite being told that he had a small inconsequential angioma of the brain, the surgeons misinterpreted the angioma as a sign of irreversible, severe brain damage. Mister Marshall's daughter, Katy Price, pleaded with the nursing staff, trying to convince them that her father's conscious*

level was improving, but the doctors and nurses drugged Mister *Marshall with morphine, and withheld nutrition and fluids.*

Under sharp questioning by HM Coroner, Mister David Hillman, the consultant geriatrician in charge of the case admitted to placing Mister Marshall on an 'End-of-Life Care Pathway', modelled on a scheme for palliative care developed in Liverpool. James Gillespie said: 'The surgeons were absolutely clear that the prognosis was awful; that there was no hope of recovery.'

Mister *David Hillman, Coroner for Cambridgeshire and Huntingdonshire was particularly critical of Trust Managers for establishing financial incentives for Wards and Departments to increase the number of patients put onto the End-of-Life protocol. Just how widespread is this horrific policy of indiscriminately sedating old people and starving them to death?*

Paul Marshall and Katy Price, Charles Marshall's son and daughter, wept when they faced the press outside the Coroner's Court in Huntingdon after the inquest. 'We saw it happening. We told them Dad was regaining consciousness. The doctors and nurses are guilty of gross negligence at least.' The coroner delivered a narrative verdict, leaving the police to consider criminal proceedings. The solicitor for the Paul Marshall and Katy Price said that they intended to sue the Trust for considerable damages.

Oh no! thought Stanley, this looks like trouble and some of it may come my way.

5. THE GIFT HORSE

On the fourteenth of February, some two and a half years after their first encounter in Tuckers, three bouquets of red roses from Derek were delivered to Julia's office desk; two more than previous Valentine's Day despatches. They had a table reserved at Midsummer House that evening, which is where Derek proposed marriage. Julia affected surprise. Derek delivered many romantic touches and a diamond larger than she had seen on any finger. She found Derek's nervousness, and obvious relief when she accepted, endearing.

They married in late summer at St. Barnabas and held a reception at Jesus College. Milton took Julia up the aisle but did not attend the reception, as had been agreed. Matthew and Fiona and Derek's parents witnessed the marriage. Amy was bridesmaid while Ottie and Lottie made the most charming flower girls. Considering the hazard of Milton and the new Mrs Ellison, the day was a success.

Julia had resisted Derek's suggestion that she move in with him after their engagement. Now, she enjoyed being swept up into Derek's arms and carried over the threshold into the home that she had helped create. And he held her up triumphantly; she was his, at last; at those smug, strapping sportsmen so successful at seducing the sexiest girls at uni, he wanted to shout out *just see me now, see what I've got*.

A fortnight before the wedding, Derek asked Julia what gift she would like from him. She surprised him by asking for music lessons. He turned to Fiona for help with this one and she gave him the names and telephone numbers of two music teachers in the area, whom she knew through church, assuring him that Julia would get on very well with either of them. So, when Julia came downstairs to the smell of a cooked breakfast, late next morning after a long night of lovemaking, Derek told her that he had engaged a music teacher who specialised in voice and piano for six months, starting on their return from the honeymoon. She was thrilled, but Derek had gone one better; again, with Fiona's help. Returning after a magical week in Paris, Julia entered the house to find a baby grand piano in the living room.

'Oh, wow!' she cried in amazement. 'Derek, what have you done!"

'Darling, you'll need a piano even if you only take singing lessons. I've hired it for six months, with an option to purchase it after that. If the piano doesn't interest you, just tell me if there's another instrument that you'd like to try.' Julia put her arms round Derek's neck and kissed him.

'This is so thoughtful! Thank you, sweetheart, but why not an upright? This piano is beautiful, but doesn't it take up quite a lot of room?'

'Ah, that's me being selfish, Julia. With this piano you'll face the room and I shall be able to drink in your beauty as you play, and whether you play well or not will be irrelevant,' he said, running his fingers through Julia's silky hair. Julia pressed in closer and felt his hardness. She whispered in his ear: 'Ooh, shall I unleash the animal inside?' Then, she did just that and showed her gratitude for his thoughtfulness and love in yet more imaginative ways than when on honeymoon.

Over the next two years, Amy and another Tuckers Girl married and then came news that first one then the other was pregnant, which brought the question of children of her own to the fore for Julia. Of course, the subject had come up from time to time. While Derek was consistent in wanting at least one child, he put no pressure at all on Julia and was happy to let her discover if, and when, she wanted them. In fact, Julia's relationship with the Jefferies' daughters left him in no doubt that she would want motherhood sooner or later. As with other things medical, Julia turned to Fiona for re-assurance that having a first child at thirty did not present problems.

'Let the relationship, not age, decide the issue,' advised Fiona. She added: 'there are no significant risks until the mother is thirty-five. Remember, though, that it can take a while for normal cycles to return after you discontinue the pill.' Naturally, Julia's twenty-ninth birthday and the happy news from Amy were not insignificant deciding factors, but Julia did feel ready and Derek's enthusiastic reaction made her joyful. She discontinued the contraceptive pill and, after an erratic couple of months, her periods returned, but ir-regularly and scantily. Despite reassurance from her GP, Julia became concerned as the months passed. It occurred to her that she and Derek ought to have intercourse more fre-quently to be sure of catching ovulation.

'Do you think we could have sex every other day?' she asked, when in Derek's arms late one evening. Derek laughed, not realising her concern immediately.

'What a treat! But we might be close to that already, on average,' he said.

'Well, I think we'll be sure to catch the right time if we're regular about it,' said Julia. 'You know, with a recovery day for you in between.' Derek became worried about Julia's proposal for a systematic approach.

'Darling, we could lose some of the magic if this be-comes more about procreation than pleasure. Please try not to worry. I read that it often takes several months for things to settle after taking the pill for several years.' Julia stroked his chest lovingly.

'I promise I won't worry, and I promise you magic,' she said, reaching down to him again.

Julia knew very well what most aroused her husband. Every other day, she would have her hair impeccably dressed in one or other ever-inventive up-style with a single holding pin, and she would be fragrant from her bath. Derek knew he would have sex, but not where in the house or when. The starting gun would be the moment Julia would face him, pull the pin from her head to let her hair fall loosely, and shed her clothes to reveal either erotic lacy underwear or her naked body. Thoughts of her up-dressed hair and those curves would excite him as he approached the house. The sight and smell of her when she welcomed him would swell him further, so that when at last he beheld her paradisal state he could give no consideration at all to foreplay. This erotic game meant Derek never failed to perform but it did not bring colour to the control line of Julia's pregnancy test kits. When she saw her GP, he was reluctant to test Julia but not Derek.

'I'm sure Derek won't mind undergoing a sperm test,' Julia said to him, 'but I think I'm the problem. You see, I haven't been able to detect a temperature rise in several months. Isn't there a blood test that could check if I'm ovulating, before I bring Derek along?'

'Yes, there is,' the doctor agreed. 'I'll check your blood levels of oestradiol and follicle stimulating hormone; then, if these are normal, I'll want to check your husband before doing more tests on you. Are you alright with that, Mrs Black?'

'Yes, I understand doctor. Thank you.'

'We should have the results in a week. Please bring your husband with you when you return to discuss the results with me. It would be best if you were to ring the surgery tomorrow to make an appointment, after you've checked your husband's availability.' So, Derek was with Julia when the doctor explained the implication of a very low oestradiol level and a very high level of follicle stimulating hormone.

'Your suspicion seems correct, Mrs Black. The blood tests indicate you may not be ovulating. It's possible that this is a temporary consequence of long-term contraceptive use, but there is the possibility of premature ovarian failure.'

'And that means?' asked Julia.

'That your ovaries may not be producing eggs at all, which would mean you could be infertile.' Derek heard the sob and instinctively reached out to Julia and took her into his arms as she broke down.

'Why me?' asked Julia for the first of many times, while Derek sought to stop her tears. He had helped her into an empty consulting room in the surgery so that the doctor could see other patients until she had settled sufficiently to return. 'What have I done to deserve this?'

'Darling, don't blame yourself,' said Derek gently to the head buried into his shoulder. 'This is just biology not working as it should; just bad luck, not divine retribution.' As he held Julia in his arms, he became sensible to the scent of her hair and the silkiness of it against his skin. Even at this moment, when we've just been given life-changing news, my loin comes alive, he thought not without some shame. Is there something wrong with me? What would she think if she found I'm aroused? Sex on the brain so inappropriately. Then, he saw it wasn't the fact that he was thinking of sex that disturbed him; rather, the realisation that his own emotional response to the news of Julia's sterility was neutral; no dejection, no despondency, mild regret perhaps.

Derek shifted position so as to keep Julia from discovering his erection. Then he lifted her face, kissed her, and said:

'Darling, let's not think the worst; not until we've heard what the doctor has to say. You know that medicine is making remarkable advances. I mean, there may be help for us.' Responding to the hopeful look on her face, he added: 'When you're feeling up to it, the doctor will have us in again. Perhaps there's some treatment available.' That's right thought Julia; she hadn't given the doctor much of a chance to talk about treatment. She felt thankful for Derek's ability to return things to their proper perspective, for his solidity as well as his comforting support; and she pulled herself together.

They weren't called back until the end of the morning clinic. The doctor apologised, saying that it was all about targets. Had he re-inserted them sooner, the other patients would have been seen more than fifteen minutes after the scheduled appointment, which would see the practice penalised financially. Derek assured him that the time they were kept waiting was helpful to both of them, and he thanked him too for fitting them into the same clinic. Julia nodded her agreement and reassured the doctor that she was alright and wanted to hear about the options open to them, but her heart sank when he asked how they felt about adoption. Derek surprised even himself by his reaction.

'No, no! Not that. Not someone else's child. We wouldn't love it, would we? Perhaps it wouldn't love us,' he blurted out. Blimey, so that's how I feel, he thought, either my child or none. 'Look, I'm sorry for that,' he said quickly, 'I don't know where that came from. Of course, we won't rule anything out until we've considered the issues carefully. It's just that I, we, hope you could point to some medical breakthrough that might help us have our own child.'

'Don't worry about how you might put things,' said the doctor, 'I understand how difficult this is for both of you. Is there some way for you to have your own children?' he asked rhetorically. 'Well, the answer is: possibly and partly. He went on to tell Derek and Julia about the Bourn Hall Clinic, just west of Cambridge, where the first test-tube baby had been made. The clinic now led in the field of *in vitro* fertilisation. He couldn't say whether the team at Bourn would be able to stimulate Julia's ovaries into making eggs, but he spoke with some optimism about an egg donor programme that was being set up.

'How would that give us our own child?' asked Julia. She was upset that the doctor didn't seem sanguine that IVF treatment would work for her. He had passed on to egg donation all too quickly.

'Well, Mr Black would have exactly the same genetic tie to a child conceived through egg donation as he would to one

59

conceived naturally. You see, the donated eggs would be fertilised in a test-tube by his own sperm. In your case, Mrs Black, there would be no genetic tie, but.... and this is an important *but*.... you would have a strong biological tie because the fertilised egg would be placed into your womb. It would be *your* pregnancy, which the two of you would share. The baby would grow inside you. It would be you that would give birth to the child and you that would feed it at the breast.'

Julia was sceptical. 'Would I bond with the child?'

'I believe so, Mrs Black,' the doctor said. The smile he gave Julia indicated he felt certain she would. The doctor went on to sound a note of caution. He reminded them that the techniques were experimental. Success could not be guaranteed, and donors were few, usually women undergoing IVF treatment themselves. At this early stage of the programme, the limited number of willing donors meant that a close match between donor and recipient was not possible.

'How do these things work, doctor? Would you be writing to Bourn Hall? Is the waiting list long? Could one withdraw from the programme at any time?' asked Derek, one question after another coming swiftly to mind.

'Peter Brinsden has just taken over as Director. I'll write to him. They will send an appointment; both of you should attend, of course. I expect they have a long waiting list, so don't get anxious if you hear nothing for a month or so.' Realising that the doctor would need to get lunch before the afternoon clinic got under way, Derek signalled Julia that they should go. They expressed their thanks and left to face the biggest decision either of them had ever had to take.

One imagines that such a crisis might strengthen a marriage as the partners investigate, deliberate, consult and decide on the way forward together, based on affection, care and love for one another; or a marriage could fall apart through irrationality, lack of empathy, selfishness and blame. What transpired with Julia and Derek was neither one nor the other, but the tremor did crack the foundations. Derek decided that he would go along with whatever Julia wanted in the matter of egg donation; not an easy decision actually as Derek was unsure how he would feel toward a child that resembled neither himself nor Julia. After all, such an outcome was quite possible; the donor's genes could predominate, couldn't they? Still, there was a chance to see himself in the child who would be half his. And if he felt such ambivalence, how must Julia feel, given the certainty that the child would not resemble her at all?

All Julia could do was ask questions, one question leading to another, but she couldn't answer them. Why do I want a child if it isn't my own? Is it enough that it will be Derek's child? Isn't it enough that I have Derek to love? Do I need to love a child? Is it that I need the love of a child? Will I love the child? Will the child love me? Julia asked these questions of herself continually. She asked them of Derek too, but his assurance that he would support her in whatever she decided did not help to answer them.

In fact, Derek's reading into the legal aspects of egg donation introduced difficulty. It seemed that the legislation that was being drafted to deal with the ethical issues raised by the new egg donor programme would require infertility clinics to keep information about any person born as a result of egg or sperm donation, and that the child would have a legal right to that information at the age of eighteen. But I wouldn't want the child to know I wasn't its mother, exclaimed Julia when Derek reported his searches. When would I tell it: I'm not your mummy? At five? At ten? How would a child of five or ten respond to that? Does the law think It would be easier at eighteen? Should I teach the child to say *Daddy* but not *Mummy?*

I'd rather not tell the child anything, ever! It would be our child entirely. Demonstrating singular lack of empathy, Derek asked: what if the child noticed it looked nothing like you, possibly nothing like either of us? As the child grew up and learnt about test-tube babies, might it not ask questions? And what if someone else told the child? Julia insisted no-one need know specifically about the egg donation. Pat, Don, Sylvia, Amy, whoever, could be told Julia had been trying IVF, that the hormone treatment had been successful in stimulating the production of eggs, and that the resulting baby belonged to both Derek and her *totally* – genetically, biologically, gestationally, naturally, nurturingly, whatever!

Ay, there's the rub. One other will know: Derek. And this niggle gradually became a central concern for Julia. They loved each other. Theirs was a young and happy marriage. But her parents had been happily married too, until they weren't. What if Derek were to blurt out in front of the child the fact that I wasn't the natural mother in a fit of pique or anger? And if it came to divorce, to whom would a court give custody? Nor need the context be so extreme as marital breakdown. Suppose they disagreed about which school to send the child or whether the teenager could stay out late, might Derek, feeling strongly about the point, suggest the decision should be his, his veto, his casting vote, because of his genes? That would hurt too.

Julia reached out to Fiona, the only person other than Derek in whom she confided. She and Derek were due to attend Bourn Hall clinic the day after next. She had tried not to involve anyone other than her husband but his *I'll go along with whatever you decide* position was not what she needed. Rather than support in the form of acquiescence, Julia wanted someone to take an opposite view to her own, to challenge her view directly, to be told she would be a fool not to accept the gift of another woman's eggs. Just maybe, she thought, Fiona will help me see the issues differently, more clearly. Was it the fact that Fiona was a physician sworn to patient confidentiality that gave Julia the confidence to trust her? She thought it was more than that. Though she couldn't put a finger on it, couldn't name it, this feeling was reinforced when Fiona hugged her, held her, and comforted her as she broke down, overcome by her painful narrative. Fiona held Julia until she regained control, and a little longer.

Reaching for Fiona when she had said all she could,

Julia pleaded plaintively for an answer: 'What should I do, Fi? What would *you* do?'

'If it comes to egg donation, my darling, I cannot think of a greater gift one woman could give another,' she replied, visibly moved, 'except for a life-saving kidney.' She thought for a moment; then decided it might be easier to answer Julia's second question. 'I know what *I* would do. I would take the chance to love another person wholeheartedly, selflessly, unconditionally. I would not tell the child about the circumstances unless asked directly; then I would answer honestly. There is risk, but I would take it. I know my heart would be broken if this went wrong and the son or daughter to whom I had given birth, given life, given love, turned away from me. You see, before Ottie, I wanted a child. It was a strong emotion.' After a pause, she added: 'That's the bottom line, I think. Do you want a child badly enough to accept the risk?' Though they said more before Julia left, little was added, but Julia saw the question clearly now.

So it happened that, following Julia's further blood tests and a laparoscopy, when Peter Brinsden saw them again and told them that egg donation was the only potential remedy for Julia's inability to conceive a child of her own, she said she didn't think she could go through with it. Fearful that Derek would regard her anxiety that he might not keep the secret as a hurtful lack of trust, Julia said simply that she did not think she could love another woman's child. How would you feel, do you think, if we needed a donation of sperm instead of eggs, she asked Derek; and, as he had indicated previously, he admitted that he would very likely feel the same way.

In the days following the final visit to Bourn Hall, Derek became concerned about Julia. She slept badly and was tearful. She did no more than pick at food though she prepared dinner for both of them each evening. Where previously he would return from work eager to look upon, smell and touch the beautiful woman that had prepared herself for his sensual pleasure, Julia no longer bothered to change her outfit, freshen her makeup or do more with her hair than carelessly grab it in an untidy knot.

Recognising depression, perhaps even a bereavement reaction, he found a flight to New York and a room at the Waldorf Astoria, and the two of them crossed the Atlantic for the first time. The towering skyscrapers, the music at the Met, the art in MOMA, the Guggenheim and the Frick, the charm of The Village, the buzz of Broadway and the big, big stores infused them with shared awe and excitement. What with the distance from Cambridge and with so much to feast the eye, distract the mind and excite sensation, Julia could not help but be drawn out of her melancholy. The Big Apple worked its magic. They reconnected with one another and with life.

Fiona was very concerned when she found that she was pregnant again, four years after Lottie, but Julia was excited at the news and quite thrilled when Fiona asked her to be godmother to their new daughter.

'I know it's early days, but have you a name in mind, Fi?' Julia asked.

'It'll have to be Dorothy, won't it?' said Fiona with a wicked wink, 'as we already have Ottie and Lottie'. The penny dropped and Julia laughed out loud.

'And now Dottie!' she exclaimed with hilarity, and she loved Dottie from that moment.

6. DISSATISFIED

J ulia took music practice seriously. Before touching the keyboard, she would go through some fifteen minutes of finger stretches and finger strengthening exercises, which soon became something she did habitually whenever her hands were idle. Scales, broken chords and arpeggios bored most of Ian Kristofferson's pupils, but not Julia. She challenged herself to increase speed in these exercises without compromising accuracy or rhythm. Kristofferson was a curious specimen. He was tall and lanky but folded himself up at the piano from a low seat so that he seemed to hang onto the keyboard by his fingertips, as if trying to haul himself up or prevent himself slipping off. He played with pursed lips, inhaled sharply with every musical phrase, and never made eye contact with her.

Julia thought him peculiar but acknowledged that he was a brilliant teacher. His engagement and her commitment made each music lesson a rewarding experience for both. Teacher and student would talk about every piece of music, however basic, before starting work on it. So, from the first tentative touches of the keyboard, Julia would attempt to capture the emotion of the piece, which is why Derek was a willing listener, even to music arranged for beginners. By the third anniversary of their marriage, she could perform two or three new pieces for Derek on the first Friday of every month; their private concert – she played for *him*.

Julia's private music lessons helped her singing. The St. Barnabas Choir had become more ambitious, giving concerts in the church hall three or four times a year in addition to supporting Choral Evensong and the occasional Sung Eucharist. Julia was being given solo parts, but it was the friendship within the choir that most mattered to her. She continued to be especially close to Fiona. While Derek did not follow her into a deep relationship with the Jefferies, probably because he knew Julia confided in them, he socialised well enough and, tactfully, the Jefferies made no reference to anything to do with Derek and Julia if they had learnt of it from Julia in Derek's absence..

If, to her rewarding music lessons, one added the facts that Julia loved Derek, had a beautiful home, felt valued at Tuckers, felt fortunate in Fiona's faithful friendship and joyful in her role as godmother, one would not be surprised to hear that, by the third anniversary of her marriage, Julia thought herself blessed. In Derek's case, job satisfaction was essential to happiness as he invested so much time in work and around this time, some three years into his marriage, Derek had begun to think about Astons in negative terms.

He had signed up for the ten-year reunion of his matriculation year at Jesus College. The year group gathered one afternoon in early July, listened to a talk by one of the Fellows, attended choral evensong in the College Chapel and then gathered in Hall for a feast. Alumni tended to sit in their former subject groups, unless some stronger bond existed, such as the Boat Club.

Derek sat with the lawyers. Most worked in the City. At this ten-year point, quite a few among those who had been hired directly out of University were partners. On making junior partner, their salaries had doubled or trebled. They expected to be earning one to two million pounds within a few years. Not that it was all about money. Their roles had changed with seniority: less hands-on technical legal work and more business development. They were responsible for maintaining existing client relationships and for creating new ones. Their perspective, initially legal, had broadened into a commercial and strategic one. Listening to this, Derek came away with the feeling that he was stuck in a rut at Astons.

Naturally, Julia became concerned when Derek began to complain about work. One evening when she thought Derek seemed relaxed, she broached the subject by asking whether anything had changed at work recently.

'Actually, the problem is that *nothing* has changed. I've been doing the same legal work for years at Astons. I'm an employee of the firm, not a stakeholder. There's no opportunity for more responsibility and better pay.'

'Is more money, important?' asked Julia.

'It's not vital, but I would like to clear the mortgage on our home; and with more money we could grab weekends away, travelling more comfortably so I'm not tired when back at work. There's lots to spend money on, starting with you.' Derek took Julia in his arms, kissed her and said: 'Our anniversary is coming up and I haven't got you anything *really* expensive since the engagement ring.'

'Derek, I don't need anything like that!'

'Why shouldn't you have beautiful things, Julia? The Astons partners' wives are dripping with jewellery. You dress beautifully but I know you catch the seasonal sales. What about a new car? A new house?' Julia couldn't believe her ears.

'Hey, where has this come from?' she asked with concern. She had reached up to hold his face in her hands.

Derek smiled. 'Don't worry, my love. I'm not unravelling. Let me fetch more wine and I'll tell you about it.' Having refilled the two glasses, Derek returned to Julia's side.

'You know that I met up with old mates from Jesus in September. Well, they've done so very much better than I have. Several are partners or within touching distance of being made up to partner. The rest know they'll make it soon as they're on fast-track schemes to a partnership. Two or three have been partners for three years already. Now, this means a much, much larger salary, but the thing that matters most to me is that their employers value them. They've been made stakeholders. Their work is more interesting, more challenging, more rewarding. It's got me wondering whether Astons is interested in me long-term.'

'I'm relieved it's not about money,' said Julia.

'Money is important, Julia. Everyone in the business judges your worth by it. *Does your firm value you?* translates into *how much is your firm willing to pay you to hold onto you?* I know you feel fortunate in what we have, but my contemporaries have a lot more to show for their efforts. Also, there are things I want.'

Julia tried to lighten the conversation. She ran her fingers through Derek's hair and asked: 'What would you *most* like, darling?' That this cue for an end to introspection and a start to lovemaking was missed, indicated Derek's depth of feeling on the question of promotion.

'I would quite like a larger house with a large mature garden. The Aston partners live on the West side; on Bentley Road and Barrow Road, for example; or around Grange Road. These houses come with gardens of a third of an acre and are full of lovely tall trees. Our back extension reduced the already small garden to a pocket handkerchief-sized patio that barely takes four chairs and a table. Also, there's no privacy. Yes, I do dream about a home and garden on a grand scale. While I appear not to be interested in the *What if* games with the property brochures, which entertain Dad so much, I do sneak a look at them afterwards.'

'Could we ever afford one of them?'

'Well I would like us to have the chance of owning one, but we won't have the option on my present income. On a partner's salary, we could manage that kind of move within eight to ten years. In fact, I should feel I've failed you if it hasn't happened by the time I'm forty-five. You know, Julia, I think it's time I had a talk with the senior partner.'

Lionel Aston may have been in his late fifties, but he was

trim, tall, with the back and shoulders of an oarsman and the perfectly manicured hands of a Harley Street physician. He maintained an affluent tan through a series of short vacations that took in Florida at Christmas, skiing in Saint Moritz, some southern hemisphere destination in bleak midwinter, Easter in Mauritius and summer in the Med, thanks to his IBM ThinkPad, AOL e-mail and the new digital Motorola International 3200, which unshackled him from the office, at least for short periods at a time. He loved technology.

As far as offices went, his was impressive enough. It was the largest in the building, on the top floor. From it he looked out over Midsummer Common and the Cam with several College boathouses along its North bank. Lionel had chosen the West corner office so as to face the Common and away from Elizabeth Bridge, the main artery into the City from the North. He preferred to arrive at the office between half past nine and ten o'clock, avoiding the rush-hour traffic, and work until seven thirty or eight, depending on social engagements. His choice of office and working hours had more to do with the fact that the office was bathed in sunshine all afternoon and evening, till sunset. In the lengthening evenings, he liked to stand at the window to watch the students open up the boathouses, get an eight into the water and set of for Baits Bite Lock at pace. What a time that was! he would say to himself, nostalgically.

Lionel was not surprised at Derek's request for a meeting. Marriage changes a man's perspective and ambitions, he reminded himself, not least the fact that Derek and Julia would be thinking of children. Before the meeting, Lionel asked for reports on Derek's work from the other partners. The partners talked about the Firm's associates regularly, but for this meeting Lionel asked for a written, detailed assessment from each of the specialists. The reports were generally positive. None glowing, though Derek's hard work was acknowledged. One partner suggested the Firm might set him some test; let's see if he'll sink or swim. Instead of his usual *Come!* Lionel went to the door and welcomed Derek.

'Do come in, Derek. It's a pleasure to see you,' said Lionel amiably, 'come over to the window.' Lionel had poured sherry and handed a glass to Derek, saying: 'It's almost six; too late for tea.' Looking out over the common at the sun setting over Jesus College and the Cam, Lionel said:

'You were at Jesus. Did you row? I was in the first boat at Queens', you know. I loved going on the river at just this time in the Easter term, with the bumps to look forward to after Tripos. Or was it rugby?'

'I was in a boat. The third boat; just for fun. I haven't rowed since.' It seems that the old man enjoyed his undergrad days, Derek thought to himself. Then, thinking he'd done enough to make Derek feel at ease, Lionel Aston got down to business.

'Would you be more comfortable on the sofas or at the table?' They sat at the meeting table, out of the sun. 'Your letter indicated that you wished an opportunity to discuss your future relationship with the Firm. How would you like it to play out, Derek?'

'Well, Mr Aston, every associate counts the years to being made up to partner. I am thirty-nine next birthday. I've been with Astons for sixteen years. In that time, I've rotated round the partners and acquired technical legal skills across the business. My client book shows that I have brought new clients to the Firm through recommendation. If Astons sees me as partner material, I should like to know it, to agree a route to achieving partnership and to get there before I'm forty-five.'

'Very good! I'm glad you got to the point. I'll do the same. There is no opening for another partner in this office. However, we're presently considering a merger with a large law firm in Maidenhead. The idea is that each of us will keep our brand locally, but we'll create a new firm located in London. One partner from each firm will start up the London office. Initially, other staff will be at senior associate level. However, each of us will be identifying one of our present lawyers for specialist training. The two individuals will be promoted to partner in three years if progress is satisfactory, and they'll be placed in the London office. I hadn't considered you because you're recently married and at the point when you're likely to be starting a family. Commuting puts pressure on a family with small children. Now, I've had second thoughts, because the partners have reported favourably and think you suited to the role. Do you wish to hear more?' So, it's London or look for another Cambridge Law firm, thought Derek. Well, let's hear what they have in mind.

'Commuting does not present a problem, Sir. What's the specialism you had in mind?'

'The Cambridge Science Park is already a success and is going to grow bigger still. There's also talk of a new Business Park. The University anticipates major advances in technology, in engineering on smaller and smaller scales, and in the life sciences. You would focus in this field, which is to say you would engage with academics wishing to found companies and with venture capital funds. Your brief will be to hone your knowledge of intellectual property, corporate and tax law, as they apply to all aspects of venture capital transactions. The full partners will bring along combined expertise in mergers and acquisitions, private equity, and corporate real estate. Over the next three years, you would work with our present leads for the Science Park. Then you would be seconded to the London office as junior partner with responsibility for venture capital. Thereafter, promotion and salary will depend on the number of clients and amount of business you bring to the office. It's likely the office will be in Shoreditch, as close to Old Street tube station as property prices allow. So, the commute would be to Liverpool Street.'

Lionel stood up to refill his glass. 'I'll ask for your reaction in a few minutes,' he said and walked over to the window. In fact, he could observe Derek through his reflection while giving him some space. He returned to the table when he saw that Derek had straightened up in his chair.

Derek was excited by the proposal. It ticked many

boxes: the opportunity to specialise, a three-year period of mentorship, interesting and challenging work, and a route to partnership. The only downside was the move to a London office, but this was mitigated by the fact that commuting would be three years down the line.

'Just your reaction, Derek. Don't feel committed one way or the other.'

'Firstly, Sir, I'm grateful to you and the partners for giving time and thought to the matter. The opportunity to contribute significantly to a new business venture for Astons excites me. Promotion to partner within three years is as much as I hoped for, indeed sooner than I would have been prepared to wait. So, my reaction is a mixture of excitement, interest, pleasure and relief.'

'I'm glad to hear it. You'll want to talk things over with Julia. So, shall we say that you'll let me have a firm answer by Friday?'

'That's plenty of time, Sir. Thank you.' The two men rose and shook hands warmly. Derek asked for his regards to be passed on to Mrs Aston, then left. Julia knew the meeting had gone well from the animated manner in which Derek announced that he was home. She peeped round the kitchen door and held up a bottle of champagne.

'Hey, you look happy. Would a glass of this be appropriate, darling?' she asked with a smile.

Julia was delighted at the change in Derek's mood and outlook. Astons have come up with the goods, she thought with relief. She brought the champagne to the conservatory table, urged Derek to give her the news and sat close to him to feel the charge of excitement he emitted. She was joyful to find Derek enthusiastic and energised by the prospect of promotion. As Derek recounted his conversation with Lionel Aston and explained the implications, she came to realise there was a significant price they would have to pay. From the moment Derek accepted the new job they would have less time together. Although commuting would not come into the equation for three years, Derek would have to work hard to acquire the specialist legal knowledge and expertise necessary for his new Venture Capital portfolio. This would mean long hours from the start. She understood this and knew that it was a necessary sacrifice. She desperately wanted her husband to feel fulfilled and, their relationship apart, this depended on job satisfaction.

Julia was mindful of the support she had received from Derek. He had not put her under any pressure to have his child through egg donation. Nor had he referred to the matter since she declared her decision. He had not stayed away from her. If anything, he was an even more ardent lover. Julia felt she owed him much and so she determined she would support him in turn. She would make his home a place where he could decompress and reconnect, as some American had put it recently. A call before leaving the office would ensure he found dinner ready for him when he got home. She would keep her weekends free to be with him. And she would be mindful of the need to keep their relationship passionate and erotic.

When Derek called on Lionel Aston to accept the proposal, he found a contract had already been drafted that included a significant increase in salary. Within a week, Derek was moved to a larger office close to the partner leading on Science Park-related business. In making this long-term commitment to the Firm, Derek found that Julia and he began to receive personal invitations from partners to dinners and drinks parties. Previous social encounters had been restricted to business social events. While Derek enjoyed this step up the social ladder, he was embarrassed to reciprocate, thinking that it would not do for it to be known that he still lived in an un-leafy little street off the multi-ethnic Mill Road, which explains why conversation in York Terrace touched on large West Cambridge homes more often than hitherto.

It occurred to Julia that moving to a house in West Cambridge was becoming something of an obsession with Derek. She felt no embarrassment about their home and the neighbourhood. Invariably, visitors complimented them on the house, though Derek would say that it was because the house created a much better impression once inside than would have been made on anyone turning into York Terrace for the first time. Much as she loved York Terrace, Julia promised Derek she would look out for a buying opportunity. She remembered that the amount of money one earned in Derek's world was the significant measure of success. He had told her so after that reunion dinner. How much more richly rewarding he would find friendship than fancy houses or fast cars, she thought, but then he has no time to foster friends. Increasingly, Julia saw Fiona, Matt and their girls in the early evenings or on Thursday nights, without Derek and she regretted the fact that his working late prevented him from keeping pace with her own enriching friendship with the Jefferies.

Just when Derek thought they might manage the monthly mortgage payments on a sizeable house, Nigel Lawson began cutting income tax and house prices rose. High-end house prices rose faster and higher than the other categories. Ensuing inflation pushed up interest rates dramatically, and then more, doubling over eighteen months to sixteen percent. Large West Cambridge houses moved out of Derek and Julia's financial reach; forever, it seemed. Then recession hit and house prices fell, and the prices of high-end houses fell faster than the other categories. It was not until late 1992 that the market bottomed out. Tuckers became hopeful that property would start to move again in the new year.

One afternoon in early March, Julia returned from her lunch break to see Amy dealing with a well-to-do elderly lady. Julia guessed she wanted to downsize. When, at the end of their business, Amy had escorted the client to the door, she turned back to Julia with a grin from ear to ear.

'Here it is! Julia, the house you and Derek have been hoping would come up. The client is desperate to sell. The house and garden are too big for her.' She pulled Julia over to her desk. 'Just look at these photos. I mean wow! It's lovely.'

The poor dear lost her husband just as prices crashed three years ago. She's having a difficult time of it and wants to move into an apartment in Pinehurst on Grange Road. This is the chance of a lifetime – I mean getting one of *these* houses at *this* asking price...' and she pointed to the sum written in her notebook. Julia hadn't been able to get a word in edgeways. Now that she had looked at the photographs and noted the asking price, she found she was lost for words.

'Oh my God! Oh my goodness! And she comes to Tuckers!'

Amy was bouncing up and down with excitement. 'Isn't it just what you've been hoping for, you two?'

'It's perfect. Derek will love it, I know. Could you get us an appointment to view this weekend?'

'I've already fixed that, Babe. Saturday morning. Get your man to Selwyn Gardens at ten o'clock. Let's clinch this deal!' exclaimed Amy as if rallying forces.

On the Saturday, Julia and Derek walked across Cambridge to Selwyn Gardens. It was a lovely morning with a cloudless sky and unseasonably warm sunshine. The Colleges, whether red brick or stone, looked magnificent. Daffodils had opened on Parker's Piece and, along the Backs, blue, purple and white crocuses added to the spectacle. Derek and Julia walked hand in hand, keenly anticipating this first visit to the property, and excited at the possibilities it offered. Julia had not shown the photographs to Derek, saying only that it would interest him. At the end of West Road, they turned down Grange Road and took the next right into Selwyn Gardens. The house was located toward the end of this quiet cul-de-sac. Amy was waiting for them outside the property with a brochure hot off the press. She greeted Derek with air kisses and whispered encouragement into Julia's ear while giving her a hug.

'Hi guys. You couldn't have picked a lovelier day. The house faces south and west. So, if you want a second visit, come in the late afternoon. The garden will look its best then.'

They turned to the house, which towered to three storeys behind high front hedges. It was Victorian, built in 1870 in the Arts and Crafts style. The red brick walls had large multi-paned windows everywhere, each with thick white heavy frames and an arched top. A balcony in the same white joinery ran along the first floor on the west side, overlooking the garden. Amy led the way past a detached garage and up the gravel drive, which opened into space enough to park three or four cars. The house was L-shaped, and the front door nestled in the angle under a pretty porch. The owner preferred to let Tuckers show interested parties around and was out, as arranged. Amy opened the front door, neutralised the alarm, handed Derek the brochure and stood back.

'Go on, Derek. You first,' said Julia. He stepped into a double height hall filled with light. The staircase climbed up around the hall all the way to the second floor. In the hall, and in rooms off it, original features had been carefully preserved: deep moulded cornices, parquet and wood block flooring, picture rails and fireplaces accentuated the character of the house. The kitchen and dining room were on the north side of the hall. The two of them wandered from room to room, observing, noting, considering, rethinking and testing ideas one with the other.

'Julia, do you see the wiring has been done recently, and we could live with the appliances for a while don't you think?' asked Derek.

'I'd like to keep the Aga,' she replied, 'but it would be a good idea to add a modern electric oven. There's plenty of cupboard space and I quite like the rustic style. It complements the house.' Julia found a separate laundry room in which washing machine and tumble dryer fitted comfortably. Derek walked into the large room that came off the south side of the hall, opposite the dining room. He opened his arms expansively.

'This could take the piano and there would still be space for a small sofa and chairs. It could double up as a morning room and music room. Would you like that? And look! There's a conservatory coming off it, too.'

'This room would be full of light in the mornings. Usually, that's when I practise. Yes, it would make a lovely music room….Hey! look at this conservatory. I love it! We could breakfast here in the summer when you're home at weekends.' The west-facing drawing room had a splendid fireplace with a servant's bell beside it, which amused them. Its best feature was that it opened out through wide doors onto a large patio running along the entire west side and faced down the garden. It was just perfect for their own pleasure and for entertaining.

'Come into the garden,' called Derek, who had stepped outside, 'it must be all of half an acre and just look at those trees. What a sight they'll be in a month or two,' he added, bringing an arm up around Julia's shoulders when she stood beside him. I'll remember this moment, she thought: his excitement, his pleasure, the solidity of his body as he pulls me into him. The happiness she felt at his obvious pleasure intensified the feeling of being in love with him. He worked hard. He deserved a lovely home, and she knew just how to change this property from *an attractive house of character* into a stylish and sophisticated home. Really, the house was lovely, even nicer than the photographs and floor plans in the brochure had suggested.

They went upstairs. On the first floor there were four large bedrooms and a family bathroom. The bedroom on the north side and that on the south side had *en suite* facilities. Entering a large west-facing room, Julia remarked that it could be turned into a library and an art room. The light would be perfect, and she was keen to be creative again in a visual or tactile sense. Her music had rather pushed this side in recent years.

'Would you mind if your study was across the landing?'

Derek liked these ideas and added: 'I expect you'll move your easel onto the balcony and paint the garden. Just look at the view.' On the second floor, they found a self-contained flat with kitchen and bathroom.

'Don would love this,' said Julia. Derek laughed: 'Wouldn't he just!' They asked Amy to bring them again one afternoon soon, but they told her they would buy the property if they could sell York Terrace. Remarkably, it did not take long at all for this to happen. Within a week of putting number thirty-two on the market, a Hong Kong Chinese couple came to view the property, liked it, and offered to pay the asking price in cash. Julia and Derek learned that the imminent handover of Hong Kong to China was one of the key factors in the recovery of the housing market in certain areas of the UK, and investing in Cambridge property was regarded as one of the best ways of protecting, indeed growing, one's wealth.

Now, Derek thought himself blessed. He owned one of the largest houses in West Cambridge within a short stroll of King's Parade and Market Square. His wife was more beautiful than ever. Would Julia have remained so darn gorgeous if she had had children? Unlikely! Her body would have stretch marks; her nipples would have darkened; her breasts would dangle; she'd have run to fat. Would she still be interested in sex? Probably not! She'd be exhausted, sleep-deprived and stressed. Those nightmarish years of wanking woefully into the wash-hand basin would return. She wouldn't have the energy or the time to look after the house and garden as she does so magnificently, to put together a delicious dinner every night, to entertain. Also, there would have been hefty school fees to worry about. As things stood, they were going to pay off the mortgage so much sooner; and he'd been able to indulge himself. An electric blue Porsche sat on the drive.

Julia had not reckoned with every consequence. The most significant was the inevitable disengagement with the community around St. Barnabas. Frankly, there was no soul to Grange Road: no Hot Numbers, no Norfolk Street Bakery, no exotic Asian food store... no character! The Newnham Co-op and the city market were an easy cycle ride away; not the same! Nevertheless, she still thought her husband's happiness was worth the price. She made keeping in touch with the Jefferies her priority and ensured she saw Fiona on Thursday evenings at choir practice and at Sunday service. Instead of the post-choir practice glass of wine, Julia joined them all for coffee and biscuits on Sunday mornings while Derek, mistaking Cambridge's roads for those of Monaco on Grand Prix day, *Porsched* his way to the Gog Magog Club for a round of golf. He was happy now. She had been happier then.

7. FALLOUT

rancesca Cryan wanted to hear Stanley's version of
events at the inquest. She was a small thin woman
on whom even well-tailored expensive clothes hung
loosely. No one thought of her as ill because she was
extraordinarily active. She was tanned, not a little weather-
beaten, and had her grey-blonde hair cut expensively but un-
attractively into a practical short style that more or less held
its shape in or out of the wind. And she loved the wind, which
was surprising given the danger to one so slight. Francesca
was happiest windsurfing, sailing, walking on hills and jumping off them harnessed to an oversized kite.

Francesca was a full-time NHS pathologist and shared
responsibility for the diagnostic service to the neurosurgeons
with Stanley, until recently for two weeks to Stanley's one.
Six months ago, Stanley had pleaded for more time to do research: he was at a critical point, about to debunk the myth of
unconventional viruses, on the cusp of a radical new understanding of neurodegenerative disease. She had agreed to
take on the NHS diagnostic work for three out of every four
weeks to give him more time in his research lab.

Stanley thought of Francesca as a competent and ac-
commodating colleague. Her one irritating feature was a tendency to speak as softly as possible. The fewer the audience
and the smaller the room, the quieter Francesca became. So,
Stanley had to crane his neck toward her even when the two
of them were sitting side by side at the microscope discuss-
ing a case. He couldn't fathom why she did this. After all,
Francesca could address a lecture theatre audibly enough.
Stanley concluded that the tactic forced listeners to bend

themselves down toward her, giving onlookers the impression that Francesca commanded rapt attention.

This craning had its consequences. Once drawn into Francesca's personal space, Stanley's nose had picked up her subtle alluring and arousing scent and one thing had led to another, which is how Stanley learnt that Francesca could be just as hyperactive indoors. It was only about sex; never more. Stanley's mind was focused on his work; Francesca's on her career. In this regard, Stanley was a problem to Francesca, since she was forever in his shadow. He chaired the weekly business meeting despite the fact that she did more of the diagnostic reporting; the surgeons sought out Stanley when they had a particularly difficult problem; Stanley would be asked to give a second opinion on a case that she reported but never the other way round. No, she would have no problem fucking Stanley.

Fiona went down to the concourse, ordered two flat whites to go, stuck them into a cardboard tray, made her way back to the consultants' offices and knocked on Stanley's door.

'Oh hello, come in,' he said, surprised to see his colleague so early in the day.

'I thought you might need this,' she said, offering a coffee and a smile to Stanley, 'John Walker stormed into my office this morning before I had time to kick off my outdoor shoes.'

'Have you seen the morning papers?' asked Stanley, knowing the answer.

'Yes, I read the report on the inquest. John brandished *The Telegraph* at me. Steam is coming out of his ears.'

'Well, he did rather embarrass himself in the witness box yesterday. He had to retract his statement on *cause of death* under Hillman's questioning in front of several of our consultant colleagues.'

'John claims it is your fault that his evidence went pear-shaped. He says you didn't tell him about the findings in

81

the brain. He couldn't place the changes in the other organs in the correct context.'

'That's rubbish! John is being damnably disingenuous. My report was available on the Department's IT system, as you well know, and I authorised access to other clinical staff as soon as I had typed it in.' Stanley felt his ire rise at the realisation that Walker may be looking for a scapegoat. 'In fact, John didn't report his findings until after I authorised my report. I'm the one who had to examine the brain without having a chance either to look through the medical notes or to see what other changes were present in the body.'

'Shouldn't you have discussed the case with John before the inquest?'

'Look Francesca, I had not the slightest idea of the fuss the case had kicked up. No-one told me the relatives had complained about the care the deceased received in hospital; or should I say the lack of proper care, given what I've read in the newspaper! I'll have this out with John in a day or two, when he's calmed down. What most concerns me is that, if John is taking aim at me, Mitch and Julian might be even angrier.'

'Explain,' invited Francesca.

'The son and daughter knew that cerebral angiomas ran in the family. When the son took his dad to the Emergency Room, he told the admitting doctors and nurses about it. They made an entry on the family history in the case notes, but the neurosurgeons failed to note it and didn't enter the information on the scan request form to Julian.' Stanley took a swig of the cooling coffee before going on. 'Julian misdiagnosed the angioma as traumatic brain stem bleeding. Then, not unreasonably, Mitch wrote off the patient as irreversibly brain damaged. Worse, Gillespie's team ignored the relatives when they reported a lightening of their father's level of consciousness. I don't know how the Trust responded to the relatives' complaints, but it would surprise me if the Trust had been anything other than dismissive until the inquest.' Stanley drained the rest of the coffee. He felt irritable.

'What line did you take on the stand, Stanley?'

'What line do you think I took! I said it was a very difficult and unusual case, that the diagnostic error was understandable, that it was difficult to make the diagnosis on direct brain examination, let alone on the brain scan.'

Francesca picked up the empty coffee cups and tray. 'I'll get rid of these or your room will smell of coffee all day. Thank you for taking me through the issues. Keith Night wants to see me this afternoon. I don't know who else will be at the meeting. While he hasn't told me what he wants to discuss, it can only be about the inquest. I shall have to get away quickly afterwards. So, I'll tell you about the meeting tomorrow morning.'

'We've got the multidisciplinary team meeting tomorrow morning.'

'Yes, I'll be at the MDT. We can stay behind after the meeting and talk. See you then.' And off she went, quite content.

So the Chief Operations Officer has summoned Francesca but not me, thought Stanley with some consternation. Well, he'll get round to me. Meanwhile, best get on with the diagnostic work. After reporting the biopsies, Stanley prepared for the MDT meeting. This meeting was held every week in order to decide how best to manage patients who had undergone surgery and been found to have a brain tumor. Every section of the team had to be represented: a minimum of one surgeon, one radiologist, one oncologist, a senior nurse who managed the brain tumour care pathway, and one of the two pathologists. The point of the MDT was to ensure that management of the patient was undertaken by a team of specialists, not by any one individual, and that clinical decisions were evidence-based, critiqued and communicated to the whole team.

In the morning, Stanley walked into the meeting room

to find most people already assembled. Julian, Mitch, Fiona and the Care Pathway Nurse were cross-checking their lists of names. Stanley greeted them as he made his way to the projection microscope, but only Fiona acknowledged. When Francesca entered the room, she was greeted warmly by the others, as if to emphasise the fact that they were giving Stanley the cold shoulder. Generally speaking, case discussion and commentary did not prevent amiable banter and repartee. Indeed, this went on during the meeting on this particular morning, except that any witticism coming from Stanley was left without response. Have it your own way, thought Stanley, and he kept his contributions terse but professional.

After the last case, he collected his material and left the room without a word. He waited a half-hour, then walked round to Francesca Cryan's office. He knocked on the door, more aggressively than he intended, and went straight in. Francesca leapt out of her chair.

'Hey! You can't just barge in.' Stanley glared at Francesca.

'What the hell are you up to, Francesca? We talked. I explained. You understood. At least, I thought you did. The inquest has nothing to do with you. Why did you join in their little game this morning?'

'I really don't know what you're talking about. I didn't join in any game. I didn't notice any game going on.'

'How did the meeting with Keith Night go then?'

'Wait a minute, Stanley! You come in here and accuse me of playing some game this morning. Then suddenly, you change the subject and demand to know about a private meeting.'

'I'm asking what Keith had to say about the inquest.'

'I'm not privy to the Trust's view on the inquest. That subject was not discussed.'

'What *was* discussed, then?'

'I beg your pardon,' snapped Francesca. 'Did you not catch what I said. It was a *private* meeting.'

'Clearly, it was that, Francesca,' said Stanley with unconcealed bitterness.

The MDT meeting marked the end of Stanley's stint on the NHS service rota. So, he left the NHS Pathology labs and walked down to the University research laboratories in the same building. He settled into the glass-partitioned corner of his laboratory and tried to focus on the set of experiments needed to advance his research. He saw Conrad Conti pick up files and approach his office, but he wanted some time alone after the confrontation with Francesca. Stanley signalled *later* and Conrad retreated to his workspace near the door. To his surprise, Stanley saw Fiona Jefferies come into his lab and speak briefly to Conrad. Conrad pointed to Stanley's office, and she came over.

Stanley was attracted to Fiona, without being able to work out why until he noticed that their facial features were similar. She wore her straight brown hair in a masculine short style; its concession to femininity being the right-sided parting and the avoidance of tapering to the back and sides. They would look at one another when they spoke, in a manner that suggested surprise at the feeling of familiarity that doing so evoked. While Stanley could have lived with that face and loved it, inexplicably, he wasn't sexually aroused by Fiona. But he liked her. Fiona had been a specialty registrar in neuro-oncology at Bolingbroke's and had impressed everyone. When she completed her training and passed the specialist examination, she was offered a consultant post.

'May I come in?' she asked.

'Yes, of course,' replied Stanley while heaving a pile of scientific papers off the second chair in the room. 'Can you navigate through the mess to this chair?'

'No mess. Just evidence of a busy scientist,' she said with a smile and sat down. 'Stanley, I'm mortified at the behaviour of our colleagues at the MDT. I've picked up something of what has upset them. Well, there isn't anyone in the hospital who hasn't seen the papers or heard what's in them. I came to offer support, such as I'm able to give. I want you to know not everyone is against you.'

'Is everyone else against me?' asked Stanley, shocked at the possibility.

'I've heard that Mary Bowman and Keith Night summoned the Clinical Directors of Clinical Neurosciences, Pathology, and Clinical Medicine yesterday to tell them that the Trust is being sued by the relatives in the case. It's clear that the newspaper stories on alleged abuse of the *End-of-Life Care Pathway* are going to run for some time. *The Telegraph* says its reporters are committed to uncovering the scale of similar abuse across the NHS. Apparently, the Trust has *ordered* – can they do that! – ordered staff not discuss the circumstances of the case, neither among themselves nor with anyone outside the Trust.'

'Was my name brought up, do you know?'

'Yes. Bowman and Night hold the view that your evidence at the inquest was an exercise in one-upmanship. There's nothing in writing and no emails, but they have let it be known that they don't want you near Trust business. It seems to me they're scapegoating you to save face. I'm so sorry. I thought someone should tell you what's going on.' Rather than upsetting Stanley further, this confirmation of his unspoken anxieties settled him emotionally. He took some moments to digest things.

'Fiona, I can't tell you how much your visit means to me. I shall think of you always as fair-minded and generous of spirit. Now, promise me that you'll play the same game as the others.' Fiona was taken aback but Stanley gestured that she should hear him out.

'Here's why. Firstly, you've only recently been appointed to the consultant post. Secondly, you're a full-time employee of the Trust. Thirdly, you have to interact with the surgeons and radiologists on a daily basis to deliver optimal cancer care. You've your career and your patients to think about. So, I beg you, don't even think of stepping out of line, of expressing indignation, of arguing on my behalf. Show me as cold a shoulder as the others. Promise this.' Stanley could see his exhortation had upset Fiona. He stood up and she did the same. Then, she said:

'Stanley, ever since I came to Bolingbroke's I've been in awe of your diagnostic expertise, in awe of your teaching skills, in awe of your research. Now, I'm in awe of the man. I'll do as you say until you tell me otherwise.' Stanley held out his hand. When Fiona took it, he brought her hand up to his lips in the old-fashioned way and kissed it.

'This visit hasn't happened,' he said, but with an appreciative smile.

'Stanley, call on Matthew and me if you ever need to talk things over.' With that, Fiona left. If only I had that woman as my co-pathologist instead of Francesca, thought Stanley. He straightened up, looked at his reflection in the glass wall, and told himself: show some backbone! He stepped into the lab and went over to Conrad.

'Conrad, starting first thing tomorrow, we're going to sort out the programme grant application. If you're not in the middle of an experiment, could you drop what you're doing and use the rest of today to assemble the differential centrifugation and infectivity data?'

'Will do. Shall we meet at eight thirty?'

'I'll bring the coffee.'

Next morning, Stanley entered the lab to find Conrad had cleared all equipment off one of the benches, cleaned it down and taped down large sheets of white paper. As well as providing a clean surface on which to spread out the results, they could scribble notes on the paper as they threw ideas about. Conrad loved these jamming sessions with Stanley. Often, a new line of investigation would emerge. Midmorning, Conrad fetched more coffee. At lunchtime, Stanley picked up sandwiches, which they gobbled in his office in their rush to get back to the bench. At about four o'clock, they were done.

'Well, Conrad, as Sherlock Holmes would say: Once you eliminate the impossible, whatever remains, no matter how improbable, must be the truth...... Except Carleton Gallagher couldn't see it! Conrad met his boss' gaze with a mixture of incredulity and excitement.

8. PITIFUL (1957)

T he Great Barrier Reef could be seen out of the port-
side window, but Carleton Gallagher pretty much ignored the spectacular view. His mind was on the
opportunity that presented itself in the middle-of-nowhere
place to which he was heading; the opportunity to study an
entirely new disease and to work out what was causing it;
not to mention the chance to make his name. I'll name it
Gallagha virus if the cause turns out to be a virus, he thought.
Hey! how about that for a name! Carleton liked the idea
of emulating his boss. The scientific community had agreed
the name *Coxiella Burneti* for the causative agent of Q-fever
in recognition of Frank MacFarlane Burnet, director of the
Walter and Eliza Hall Institute of Medical Research in Melbourne. Carleton had been with Mac for just over a year. He
had impressed Mac with his technical skills, intellect and enthusiasm. A decade earlier, Mac would have jumped at the
chance of investigative fieldwork, but not now. This project
needed someone younger, fitter, hungrier, more courageous
even, than Mac was now – hence, Carleton.

   The Douglas DC-4 began to lose height as it approached
Port Moresby and circled over the Coral Sea. As land came up
on the port side, Carleton's gaze followed the rolling forest-
cloaked hills that rose higher and higher to the northwest
until they disappeared into the blanket of cloud draped over
the peaks of the Eastern Highlands. That's where the Fore
tribes are, he thought; up there, in the high valleys between
those mountains. Will they be friendly? He had been up to
Sydney to learn something about the tribes that lived there
from the University's Department of Anthropology and from

89

the Australian School of Pacific Administration.

In fact, none of the academics had actually been among these people. They spoke in general terms: a stone-age type of existence, small scale crop planting in the high valleys, hunting with blowpipes and bows and arrows in the forests. It's when they mentioned inter-tribal warfare that Carleton became anxious. On the positive side, Segal seems to get along with them, thought Carleton. Vincent Segal was AS-OPA's man out in Kainantu. He had been there for seven years and was the only medical officer in the Eastern Highlands. No one at the Walter and Eliza Hall Institute had heard of this guy before his letter to MacFarlane. Carleton knew nothing about Segal, but he would have to get on with him.

The airport was about five miles outside the harbour town, the largest of several airfields that had dotted the islands during the war. The humidity hit Carleton as he stepped down onto the tarmac and sweat was dripping down his back before he made it into the terminal. The other passengers were regulars: teachers, administrators and a couple of military personnel returning to their posts in Australia's external territories after some home leave. They grinned and offered good-natured encouragement as they hurried past Carleton who had stopped beneath one of the ceiling fans, dropped his bag, slipped out of his jacket and pulled a handkerchief from his trouser pocket to mop the back of his neck.

Vincent Segal was asking himself if the yank had made the trip when Carleton finally emerged into the arrivals area, tie loosened, collar open, his jacket over one arm and a suitcase in the other.

'G'day! You've got to be Dr Gallagher. I mean I hope you are, because that's who I'm here to meet and you're the last man out.' Carleton smiled in acknowledgment. They shook hands.

'Yup, that's me; but hey, call me Carleton will ya?'

'And you call me Vince, like everyone else. We don't do formality between ourselves out here,' he said and, pointing to the suitcase, asked: 'Is that all you've brought?'

'Yes. All the equipment is being flown here at the end of the week and the Administration people say they'll transfer it to Okapa by light aircraft.'

'Right, let's get a couple of coldies into you. You look like you need them,' suggested Vincent, thinking he could do with some himself after all the standing about.

The two men walked out of the terminal and Vincent indicated the green Land Rover with *Administration of Papua and New Guinea* painted in white lettering on the door. The two men were similar in appearance in some ways: about the same height, rather closely set eyes and ears that stuck out beneath their short-back-and-sides haircuts. Both had temple marks indicating they wore spectacles to work. Vincent was older by three or four years and had curly hair brushed back whereas Carleton parted his straight, light brown hair on the left. One striking physical difference between them was their smile. On the rare occasion that Vincent smiled he revealed a set of overlapping crooked teeth discoloured yellow by repeated courses of tetracycline antibiotics and nicotine, whereas Carleton would readily flash two perfectly complementary rows of white picket fence-like teeth. The most telling difference was in their bearing. Vincent seemed to carry the weight of a recently fractured world on his slim shoulders. Carleton, bronzed and more muscular, exuded the confidence and optimism born of the fact that the American dream had become reality.

Vincent took the palm-fringed coast road into town despite the fact that there was a more direct route. The sea breeze made the drive pleasant. They pulled into the United Services Club, in which everyone in the P&NG Administration was welcome. The Administration had its own Club where serving officers enjoyed reciprocal arrangements, but the United Services Club had a covered veranda with a seaview. Vincent reckoned this would be a good spot for them to take introductions further. So, they settled into comfortably cushioned wicker armchairs with a couple of ice-cold beers, and two more on order.

'Where's your accent from, Vince?' Jumping in with both feet, thought Vincent but he decided to make nothing of it.

'I grew up in Estonia. Thank goodness I got out in 1940 before the Russians turned up. I studied Medicine in Hamburg; another stroke of luck, I'd say, seeing as I avoided the Russians again. I guess you're hearing my German accent beneath the consciously acquired Aussie twang.' Carleton expressed amazement.

'Hamburg? Wow! You *are* lucky. I assume you got out before the place was firebombed in '43.' Carleton had not seen action in the war. He had been drafted into the US Army in '51. 'I'm relieved to have missed the fighting,' he offered sympathetically. 'The draft came while I was working on viruses in the research labs at Harvard. The Army sent me to their own research facility and told me to continue the work.' Carleton decided not to ask how or why Vince came to Papua New Guinea after the war.

'Good on you, Carleton. It's a top-notch virologist with access to top class laboratory facilities that I need here. Glad to have you aboard, mate!' said Vincent, happy to bring the subject round to the reason they were both there. 'Look, here comes the second beer. Right, shall I fill you in on what's going on?'

'Sure, Vince. I can't wait to see the sick natives, and if a virus is causing this disease, I'm telling you we'll find it. Mac's got the best lab set-up outside the States!' Vincent bristled. Sick natives! They're patients, and they'll be his patients. He took a long drink of beer while it was still ice-cold. Ease up, he told himself. Then he stretched out his legs, raised them onto the chair next to him, crossed them at the ankles, and began the story.

'I came out in 1950. This place seemed as far away from Europe as one could get, which suited me just fine. For the first couple of years it was all about snake bites, wounds, malaria and other fevers, and obstetric problems. The sick would have to come to the station because I didn't like the idea of venturing into the highlands. The highest peaks and high valleys of the southern part are not mapped, and the Administration hasn't got a presence up there.'

'While I was in Sydney, I was told the tribes are head-hunters,' interjected Carleton.

'The Catholic missionaries that came out with the prospectors in the 30s put a stop to that in the lower valleys. High up, though, the tribes are pretty short-fused and fight one another. About five years ago, the Administration decided to pacify the region. We sent regular patrols into the area south and east of Mount Michael to make contact with the tribes. That's where the epidemic was discovered, by the way. Now, police reinforcements are flown up to the valleys to settle any disputes.'

'Could you communicate with them?'

'Actually yes; we have Fore-speakers among our local policemen. I've learnt to speak it a bit myself, but it's safer to use interpreters. You don't want to be accidentally insulting anyone armed with a bow and steel-tipped arrows; and we've usually got forty or fifty drawn bows and raised spears to face down.'

'I sure hope you're kidding me!' Vincent grinned. He enjoyed inflicting momentary anxiety on the American. Then he checked himself. Don't assume the yank is wet behind the ears, he told himself. Melbourne wouldn't have sent him if they didn't think he'd measure up. He raised a reassuring hand.

'It's not quite so dangerous now. And we've spun them a tale. We've assumed you'll need to get as many autopsies done as possible. So, I've convinced the tribal elders that the evil spirit will enter another body if the person dies among them. Now, the tribes are happy for us to take away anyone in the final stages of the disease. It gets the evil spirit that's causing the illness out of their village; out of their valley.

There's cooperation, not resistance.'

'So, what do you make of the illness, Vince?'

'Well, here's the sum of it. I've documented almost a hundred cases and I'm sure there are forty or more natives in early stages of the disease. The brain rot must start in the cerebellum because trembling and unsteadiness are early features. Then the damage extends to other parts of the brain because it becomes a bit like Huntington's chorea and a bit like Parkinson's disease. Pretty soon the patient becomes mute, demented and immobile, apart from sudden involuntary jerks of an arm or leg. At this stage of the illness, the patient is placed on the floor of a hut outside the village and left alone to die in their own excrement from starvation.' This stark eponym-loaded report telegraphed a message of horrible suffering.

'No remissions? No recovery?' asked Carleton.

'Relentless and progressive. The illness is uniformly fatal in six to twelve months,' Vincent replied, raising his hands in abject frustration. 'I've tried sulpha drugs, penicillin, quinine; you name it, I've given it. Not that I expected any medication to work. There's never any fever, redness or swelling, no pus, no rash; really, no sign of infection at all.' Carleton got thinking about another feature contained in Vincent's original letter.

'Why does the disease strike women and children particularly?'

'I have no idea. I need someone to take a fresh look at the data and to examine those affected in case I've missed something. Could it be hereditary? Well, I've constructed some pedigree charts of some four generations to look for a clear pattern; again, I've drawn a blank'. The two men went quiet for a while, each in his own thoughts. Vincent always felt emotional when relating these experiences. Helplessness, frustration, pity, and horror were all that this damned *Kuru* brought him. He lifted his legs off the chairs and straightened up.

'Look, I should get you to the hotel. We've got rooms at *The Papua* for three nights. It's decent enough and the grub isn't bad at all. You freshen up and we'll meet for dinner in a couple of hours. We'll talk strategy and draw up a list of what we should get from the hospital in town.'

Over dinner, Carleton inquired about the hospital facilities at the Okapa Patrol Post, the frequency and times of flights to Port Moresby, and of connecting flights to Melbourne. A 'cold chain' of liquid nitrogen vats, fridges and freezers would be required so that samples of blood, cerebrospinal fluid and tissue from major organs could be kept frozen all the way from the field, via Kainantu and Port Moresby, to the Walter and Eliza Hall Institute in Melbourne. Vincent had already set up a Kuru hospital with its own mortuary and basic laboratory facility, separate from the main health centre. Carleton had come prepared with lists of test reagents for blood chemistry, specimen bottles, media for bacterial culture, glutaraldehyde fixative for electron microscopy. Vincent assured Carleton that everything could be arranged pretty quickly.

'We have an appointment with Leslie Bridges tomorrow morning. Les is the pathologist at Port Moresby General Hospital and very much a 'can-do' chap. He'll run most of the tests in his lab. We should get the tissue sections, stained and mounted, within a fortnight. So, we'll see the nature of the brain damage ourselves. The samples for metal analysis will go to Sydney and those for virus studies will be shuttled on to Melbourne. So, worry not, Carleton.'

'Hey! My mistake to think this place was the back of beyond. I'm impressed.'

'There is one other item," said Vincent teasingly. 'We need a police force! The day after tomorrow, you and I can inspect the local force and pick out men. I reckon sixteen men ought to do it. At least two of them must be Fore speakers. The older ones saw war service and are tough as nails.'

'So, it *is* dangerous work.'

95

'Put it this way. It's much less dangerous with local policemen to help us. Also, without them it would be impossible logistically. You and I will be getting about quite a bit. The terrain is rough. The valleys are about five thousand feet above sea level and covered in tall Kunai grass. The surrounding hills are upwards of seven thousand feet and forested. The medical station – that's us two and two orderlies – serves some thirty thousand tribespeople. While I haven't seen Kuru outside the Fore region of some fifteen thousand persons, it's important to check that the disease has not spread more widely, beyond the traditional boundaries of tribal inter-marriage. You and I will have to split up if we're going to complete the survey and fieldwork before the rains come in three months. The policemen are our guides, our porters, our interpreters, our photographers, our cooks, and our bodyguards.'

'OK! I get it, Vince.' Actually, Vincent didn't think Carleton had got it yet.

'There's more. As we go, we shall have to deal with the usual illnesses: whooping cough, measles, mumps, meningitis. On the plus side, there's no malaria at these altitudes. The point is we're doctors first and researchers second.' Carleton felt he had been rebuked. He thought Vince had been judgemental but chose not to rise to it. It's his territory, he said to himself, I'll cut him slack.

Vincent had laid the groundwork efficiently. So, the next morning their meetings went well. Les Bridges was hugely obliging and pretty excited that he would be the first pathologist to examine the autopsy brain tissue sections. The chief of police did not object when Vincent picked out several of his best men. And it wasn't all work. Carleton found time to get down to Ela beach for a swim, and the District Commissioner had them round to drinks the night before their departure. Carleton caught a sniff of why the Aussies called the place Paradise.

Once in Highlands the two doctors quickly settled into a

routine. They went out together a couple of times to establish and agree procedure. Thereafter, they separated, each leading a team of eight policemen in the field for ten days, returning to base for five days when they collated, studied and filed the information and specimens that had been gathered. In this way, the two men covered the territory in twelve separate treks. The teams would move out in four Land Rovers, taking the hard-baked tracks up to small hill stations, in which tents and basic camping gear were stored securely. The equipment would be packed, tied to poles, shouldered, and carried the rest of the way. On the approach to a cluster of villages, one policeman would go ahead to ensure the villagers would have the time they needed to prepare the traditional welcome. The tribesmen would quickly put on their finery, which consisted of the most gloriously colourful feathered headdresses Carleton had ever seen.

Apart from grass skirts, the tribespeople wore no clothing. Their faces and bodies were painted, and they had all sorts of body piercing: mostly sharpened and polished bones through noses, lips and ears. Necklaces provided additional ornament. The tall headdresses brought the otherwise short men up to Carleton's height. What concerned Carleton were the spears and bows and arrows with which the patrol was challenged as it came to a halt at the entrance to the village. The tribesmen would suddenly ululate, pull faces and dance aggressively around the patrol. It was much like a Maori Haka, designed to scare off enemies. The first time this happened, Vincent had placed a calming and restraining hand on Carleton's arm.

'Stare them out and don't flinch,' he had said. Indeed, this seemed what was required to gain the tribe's respect. Afterwards, the villagers would be cooperative and hospitable, as long as the patrol set up camp outside the village. In this, the villagers helped by easily assembling a grass hut to serve as a clinic, which was a useful supplement to the patrol's accommodation. Carleton and Vincent never turned up empty-handed. The village elders expected gifts, particularly hand axes and hunting knives. Sometimes, the villagers

97

killed a pig in honour of the visitors, which they cooked slowly in an earth oven. Delicious!

Carleton marvelled at the natural beauty of the Highlands. The densely canopied rain forest of the lower slopes seemed to have an extraordinary number of orchid species and butterflies, some the size of birds. Possums rustled around in the ferns. Tree kangaroos played about the buttress roots of the pandans and the climbing palms; and amid the towering tree trunks and high spreading branches, birds with plumage in amazing technicolour would squawk and beat their wings at the patrol's intrusion. Among these, the birds of paradise were the most striking. Higher up, in the saddles of mountains, moisture from settling clouds produced an abundance of mosses, lichens, and alpine flora.

This garden of Eden, which is how Carleton came to think of it, was a helpful counter to the misery and suffering of those afflicted by Kuru. He carefully noted the symptoms and signs of the disease in all its stages, recorded the age of onset and duration, asked about antecedent illnesses, investigated differences in diet, and mapped family trees. He had brought out one of the new Kodak Brownie movie cameras, which he used to capture their limping, lurching, teetering and tottering gaits. Some villages had almost no women without some sign of Kuru. That left several healthy, brown boys to chase excitedly after the American for the candy he pulled from his pockets. He photographed them too.

When the patrol came to a village in which a native was near death, the police interpreter would remind the chief of the need to remove the body so that the evil spirit would not enter another villager. As soon as the sick native died, the patrol would remove the body from the dying-hut outside the village and radio up a small aeroplane to take the body to the Okapa mortuary. One memorable day, Carleton's team came to a village in which the Chief was about to carry his wife to the dying-hut. She was so tremulous and unsteady that she could not sit up unaided.

The realisation that this woman was to be left on the

ground, out of sight, to starve to death over many days, horrified Carleton. Much to his surprise, the chief visited Carleton's tent that evening to say, through an interpreter, that his wife would be dead in the morning and should then be taken away. Carleton knew that the woman's agony would be long drawn out and he asked the Chief to explain himself. The Chief said nothing but the two men stood face to face, and after some moments the Chief blinked away a tear, then turned on his heels and left. Next day, as Carlton watched his policemen secure the woman's body on a stretcher, he noticed two puncture wounds of a snakebite on the neck.

9. SERENDIPITY (1959)

I n late April of 1959, as in almost every springtime, the rains swelled the streams sufficiently to cause the Pang and the Roden to flow through the Surrey village of Compton, rendering it particularly picturesque. On the day that Jim Jellison came to visit his good friend William Hadlow, the sun shone, and the pastures that sloped down to the village and away from it were full of ewes minding and feeding their lambs. Rams did not seem to be doing much, other than overseeing the general activity and bleating an ovine warning when a lamb wandered too far. William had driven up to Didcot station in the Institute's Ford Consul to collect Jim who had come to stay for a few days before flying back to Montana. Jim waved his hand at the white-speckled green hillside and said:

'I guess that this scene never fails to raise the spirit in a vet, Will'

'Absolutely, Jim! I can tell you it pleases my heart and soul no end to see hundreds of healthy new animals like this. It's a counter to the Scrapie work. That gets me down a little, you know. The ewes have a terrible time of it.'

They drove through the village and on toward the Institute of Animal Health, to which William had been seconded from the Rocky Mountain Laboratory. As they came up the drive, William pointed to a holding pen on the left, in which two sheep were isolated.

'There's a couple of them, Jim. See there how they get up to the fencing and rub themselves. Of course, that's where the name comes from: the ewes seem to have an uncontrollable itch, which makes them compulsively scrape off their fleeces.'

'Is it a skin condition?' asked Jim, who knew next to nothing about Scrapie.

'Nope. The pathology is in the brain. The animals become unsteady, hunched up, and liable to seizures. The illness is progressive.' Jane had seen the car turn into the drive and came to the door to welcome them.

'Jim dear, what a treat it is to see you again! Come in. I've got some tea and cookies ready for you. When in Rome, you know; particularly at four o'clock.' She gave Jim a hug, showed him where to leave his case, and led the way into the parlour. 'How was Vienna? I hope you didn't spend all your time in the conference hall and found time to sightsee.'

'You know I do that, Jane. It's your husband who takes his work over-seriously.' When Jane had served the tea, William asked Jim whether any new ideas on the cause of Scrapie had come up at the Virology Congress, which had been the reason for Jim's trip to Europe, but Jane insisted that the men should leave veterinary talk until after dinner.

'I want to hear news of Lucy and the kids; in fact, all the news from home, Jim.' So, Jim dutifully reported the happenings in Hamilton during the year that the Hadlows had been away. Then, Jane released him to freshen up and dress for dinner.

Jim didn't mean to bring work into the conversation during dinner. In fact, it was Jane herself who inadvertently led him to it. She asked how he had amused himself in London the past two days, hoping to be updated on the theatre and art gallery scene. Jim had been to see Richard III. He wouldn't miss a chance to see a Shakespeare play in London because, as he put it, only in England can one hear His verse fall trippingly, trippingly off the tongue. However, it was his visit to the Wellcome Medical Museum in London the previous afternoon that came to mind, given William's special interest.

'Now, you're a brain pathologist. So, I've got to tell you about this new exhibit at The Wellcome. An American from Harvard – Gallagher's his name – has discovered a new disease of the nervous system out in Papua New Guinea. I overheard talk about this Kuru, as it's called, in Vienna. They were excited by it and told me about the exhibit in London.'

'Is the brain damage unusual, then?' asked William.

'It would appear so. Gallagher has sent tissue sections from an affected brain to The Wellcome where they're set up on light microscopes for anyone to examine. I saw the sections myself. The brain seems full of tiny holes; you know, sponge-like.' To the amazement of Jane and Jim, William turned on his friend, pointing at him with his dinner fork.

'Good God, man! Did you say sponge-like?' Jim was taken aback.

'Now steady there, Will. Yes, spongy; kind of little empty bubbles in the tissue.' Jane, horrified by the discourtesy, was about to chastise her husband, but he waved her down.

'And what else did you see?' William asked excitedly.

'Apart from the holes or bubbles or whatever, do you mean?'

'Yes, apart from that,' urged William impatiently.

'Well, some protein accumulates in the brain tissue in blobs. Gallagher used the Congo Red stain to look for bacteria and these tissue deposits took up the dye. The red colour makes it easy to see them. The blobs are not bacteria at all; more like deposits of protein.'

'But this is extraordinary! Here I am studying the brains of sheep with Scrapie and you're telling me that in Papua New Guinea some natives have developed the same disease. My sheep have spongy brains, for Heaven's sake, and the same pink blobs.' Jim's jaw dropped.

'Wow! These guys don't know about Scrapie. There's no

mention of it. You have got to go see this exhibit and check it out, Will.'

'I'm stuck here with lab work for the next four days, but I'll get up to London straight after. Meanwhile, you could have a look at my sheep brains and tell me if the two conditions really are one and the same.'

The next morning, Jim Jellison confirmed that the Scrapie changes in the sheep brains looked just like the brain damage of Kuru.

'William, have you worked out how sheep get Scrapie?' he asked.

'I suspect the ewe gets the disease from the placenta. The ewes get Scrapie, not the rams; and it's the ewes that eat the placenta after lambing. I've looked so hard for bacteria or viruses in the placenta without success. This season, I've had teams grabbing the placenta before the ewe can get to it. Perhaps in time Scrapie will disappear from the flock.' Jellison was pensive.

'Gallagher may want to know that. His guess is that Kuru is inherited, not passed around through infection. Maybe there's Scrapie out in New Guinea and the natives are eating infected animals, you know, undercooked.' The plausibility of this proposal added to Hadlow's sense of urgency.

The two veterinarians travelled up to London together four days later. They parted affectionately at Paddington Station and William went on to the Wellcome building. The exhibit consisted of a poster that described the Kuru outbreak. Monochrome photographs showed affected natives, some requiring help to stand and others at a sedentary stage of the disease. There were mounted photographs of a Kuru-damaged brain removed at autopsy and four light microscopes with tissue sections from various parts of the brain on the microscope stages were arranged on a bench beneath the poster.

William read that Gallagher and Segal identified and

studied one hundred and fourteen affected natives over three months. During this period, sixteen affected natives died, and at the time of writing six others were in the terminal stage of the disease. He saw that, apart from the absence of compulsive rubbing or scratching, the symptoms and physical signs were identical to those in his sheep and he was struck by the fact that females were affected predominantly.

Gallagher had carried out an autopsy examination in eight cases. Observing one of the brain tissue sections at high magnification, William spotted a few nerve cells that appeared swollen by the presence of multiple vacuoles not unlike clear soap bubbles displacing the pink-staining cytoplasm. This curious vacuolation was the clincher as he had seen it in every case of Scrapie and in no other disease. The resemblance to Scrapie was extraordinary.

Carleton burst into Mac's office waving several sheets of paper in the air.

'What the hell, Carlton!' but Mac suppressed the rebuke when he saw Carleton's excitement.

'Mac, I'm sorry to crash in, but you've got to see this letter from England. We've been handed a new lead.' Mac took the letter.

'Hadlow? I've not heard of him.'

'He's not a virologist; not even a medical man. Hadlow is a vet; but read on.'

'Astonishing!' exclaimed Mac when he had read it through, 'Hadlow says that Scrapie was passed from animal to animal successfully some thirty years ago by inoculating a normal animal with brain tissue from an affected sheep. I assume you realise the implications of this, Carleton. Are those Highland tribes cannibalistic?'

'We never came across it, Mac. I can tell you Vince and

I would have been pretty scared to find ourselves among cannibals.'

'Did you ask how the Fore disposed of their dead before you convinced them to let you have the bodies?'

'No, we didn't. It didn't occur to us to do so because, on occasions when the local witch doctor was obstructive, we saw the natives take the body from the dying hut and bury it,' explained Carleton, but he added quickly: 'Nevertheless, we haven't been thorough. I'll telephone Segal. He'll know how best to convince the natives to be open about this.'

'You do that. Meanwhile, I'll organise the animal experiments to test Hadlow's hypothesis that Kuru, like Scrapie, is transmitted infectiously, not inherited genetically. I'll sort out the paperwork for the research licence and order the chimps. Right, crack on, man!'

Vincent Segal was far from thrilled to hear from Carleton. When developing the several rolls of film, he had come across too many images of the smiling American sitting among native boys; some showing them sitting in his lap. Experience of a groping schoolmaster had left Vincent with an aversion to homosexual men. After some reflection, he quieted his antipathy by reminding himself that Carleton had given no hint of any attraction toward him. Also, Vincent considered it extremely unlikely, assuming Carleton really did like boys in that unnatural way, that he would have had opportunity to do any more than have a fast fondle. And, anyway, what would the boys have made of that? he thought. So, Vincent took it no further but reassured Carleton that there was no need for him to come out to Papua New Guinea. Vincent would investigate the question of funerary rituals himself and report.

In fact, it took several weeks for Segal to negotiate access to a tribal funeral. He visited a village in which two women had quite advanced Kuru and asked for a meeting with the village chieftain and witch doctor. Through his interpreter, he told them that the tests he had done on the Kuru victims to date had revealed hugely malevolent spirits trapped in the bodies after death, and that these spirits were desperate to find a way into another living person. Vincent could see the chief and his medicine man were unnerved. He turned to the interpreter.

'Mambo, we've seen them bury bodies. Ask them if they dig them up again. If they do, ask them what they do with them.' The interpreter engaged in a long exchange, in which he did a lot of arm waving and face pulling.

'You are right, boss. They do unearth bodies and eat them. They say it is to return the good spirits of their loved ones to the village after the bad spirits that killed them have escaped into the ground.' Vincent considered the situation. If cannibalism has resisted past efforts of missionaries and present-day administrators, one should tread carefully.

'Mambo tell the chief that the villagers must not eat anyone who has died from Kuru. Tell him that he must help us warn the other villagers and tribes of the danger. Tell him too that we do not want to interfere in the customs of the village except to destroy Kuru.' The chief agreed to this injunction after he and the witch doctor had discussed the matter with the men of the village in council, but the witch doctor insisted that Vincent attend the next village funeral. Since Vincent had the ability to detect bad spirits, the village wanted him to assure them that bad spirits were not trapped in other bodies.

So, some six weeks later, Vincent witnessed the grisly ritual. The exhumed corpse was infested with maggots, having been interred for nearly a week. Despite sitting some distance away, the stench was unbearable. Amidst a great deal of ceremonial dancing and chanting, the corpse was dismembered and every part, including the brain, was served to the women and children related to the deceased. When Vincent asked why the men did not feast on the corpse, he was told that men who ate human flesh would be weakened in battle.

'Now let's prove Kuru is spread from person to person through consumption of body parts,' said Mac when Carleton showed him Segal's report. While Vincent was out in the field, Carleton had secured six two-year-old chimpanzees for the experimental animal house. 'The most important question to answer is whether Kuru brain tissue is actually infective. If we prove that, the possibility that it's inherited will be ruled out and we can concentrate on isolating the infective agent.'

'Okay, I'll anaesthetise the chimps, drill a hole in their skulls and inject liquified brain tissue from one of our Kuru patients,' said Carleton.

'Do that in three animals,' said Mac, 'but, in one of them, filter the suspension of Kuru brain through a virus filter beforehand. That way, we'll get an idea of what size of microbe we might be dealing with. If that particular chimp becomes infected, we'd know to concentrate the search on the smallest, filterable viruses.'

'I'll feed Kuru brain to a couple of other chimps,' added Carleton, 'and in the one remaining animal I'll smear the Kuru brain tissue over several small skin wounds.'

'Why so?' asked Mac.

'At the funeral that Segal witnessed, the women smeared some of the brain tissue over themselves and the children. Some of them had cuts and sores, which could be an entry point.'

'That's a good idea. Here's another one. In one of the two chimps getting the unfiltered Kuru tissue directly into the brain, heat the Kuru brain suspension beforehand to eighty-five degrees for thirty minutes. No known infectious agent survives that kind of heat treatment.'

'And if this monkey develops an illness along with the others, what then?' asked Carleton.

'Ah! Then you'll have a long career looking for something we know nothing about,' said Mac with a wry smile.

Once inoculated or fed the Kuru material, the chimps were isolated so that one could not infect another. Carleton examined the chimps every week. He had no idea how long the disease took to incubate in humans. So, he concentrated on the search for a virus in the human Kuru tissue that he and Vincent had banked.

Fifteen months after receiving the Kuru inoculum into their brains, the three chimps, Georgette, Daisey and Henry developed symptoms. Initially, the animal house technicians recorded apathy, but the chimps became increasingly unsteady, lurching about their cages. By the second month, Georgette became tremulous and stumbled frequently. She spent most of the day pulling herself around the cage in a seated position. Daisey and Henry progressed at a slightly slower rate but soon became similarly handicapped. Five months after the onset, Georgette lay huddled on the cage floor. She had difficulty swallowing and was obviously distressed. So, Carleton euthanised her. He did the same to Daisey and Henry two months later. At autopsy, all three brains showed changes identical to Kuru and Scrapie. It took a long while for the other monkeys to develop Kuru but develop it they all did.

Carleton was elated with the proof that Kuru could be passed from person to animal, and so from person to person. He set about presenting the experimental results at scientific conferences around the world and received considerable acclaim. But what was this germ that could ravage remorselessly the brains of sheep and humans? Neither Carleton nor others who sought desperately to discover the microbe got very far. The fact that Kuru had been transferred successfully after passing the inoculum through the membrane filter indicated the microbe had to be one of the smallest viruses. But was it a virus at all? Not only was Kuru infectivity preserved after heat treatment, ultraviolet light, which damages the DNA and RNA in the replicative core of viruses, did not prevent transfer of the infective agent.

Faced with physical and biological properties that no conventional virus exhibited, Carleton came up with the name *Unconventional Virus* to accommodate the agents of Scrapie and Kuru into the classification of disease-causing microbes. He spun this scientific supposition with vim and vigour, and in 1976 he was awarded the Nobel Prize for discovering *new mechanisms for the origin and dissemination of infectious diseases*. When he heard of the award from the evening news, Stanley Posner was more than a little annoyed. Carleton the charlatan, he hissed. I know he knows he's wrong. I'll prove it.

10. HER PRIORITY, HIS OPTION (2003)

Never allow someone to be your priority while allowing yourself to be their option'

Mark Twain

Once cocooned in first class, Derek would begin to relax. He never worked on documents on the train, but he did use the first twenty minutes to take stock of the day and to edit his To-Do list. Catching the 5:45 train back to Cambridge every Friday was one thing on which he wouldn't compromise. After sorting out which contracts required attention over the weekend, Derek would relegate work to the back of his mind and begin to look forward to the evening. His train would get to Cambridge at six thirty-five and, traffic permitting, his taxi would deliver him to Selwyn Gardens before seven o'clock.

Derek caught the six-fifteen train on other days of the week, but Julia insisted the weekend started on Friday and reserved the right to get tickets to a concert at West Road or a play at the Arts Theatre. He was not unhappy that on this particular evening the Endellion Quartet's concert had sold out, and that a play they had seen three years previously was being repeated at the Arts Theatre. Julia was disappointed but, as far as he was concerned, the prospect of a Friday evening at home with Julia to himself was something to relish.

The summer was best, of course. Julia would have the G&T ready and they would sit out on the patio together, from where he would enjoy the tall trees down the end of the garden, backlit by the low lingering sun. There would be invigorating colour everywhere. Julia's flowerbeds could compare with many National Trust Gardens and her forte was an extraordinary range of dahlias, which he held to be more imaginatively arranged than the prismatic crescent at Anglesey Abbey. Nevertheless, Winter's homecomings didn't disappoint because he loved the house. It was furnished luxuriously and tastefully, with every piece of furniture and wall-hanging just as and where it should be. It could feature in *Country Life* or *Home and Garden*. Yes, it had been expensive, and he had been stretched financially at first, but money concerns were not an issue now after seven years as partner.

The temperature had fallen rather suddenly earlier in the week. Until then it had been unseasonably warm for November. Julia came into the hall as he closed the front door behind him and put down his briefcase. She placed a hand behind his head and drew him down to the cheek she offered. He kissed it and the other, which was brought round after a brief pause. Julia eased her head back. Derek looked down to her mouth to catch the Mona Lisa smile before she lifted his chin for his lips to receive hers, always slightly parted. Julia called this ritual her 'dolce vita' kiss. As far as he had seen, Italians might touch cheek to cheek but simply blew kisses into the distance over each other's shoulders. This kiss, when he came home from work, left him feeling anything could happen.

While Julia refused to jeopardise her marriage by self-indulgent paranoia, she couldn't help herself from inhaling quietly but deeply for any trace of another woman's scent as she kissed her husband to welcome him home from work each evening. There was danger everywhere. Female colleagues, clients, even commuters on the Cambridge Cruiser were sure to target Derek. The increasing number of female employees in the London office whose marriages were breaking up worried her. *If another woman stole my husband, why shouldn't I go after another woman's man* might be the attitude. The stakes were high.

Julia was methodically proactive at keeping her husband. From four o'clock on weekdays, she began to arrange the house. Not just tidy it. Julia prepared it to receive her husband: she would open the windows for a blast of fresh air, build a pyramid of easily flammable coke pieces over a couple of firelighters in the sitting room grate, replace the scented candle of the previous day, wipe the furniture surfaces with a damp cloth so that not a speck of dust spoiled the gleam, smooth down the sofa fabric and pummel the cushions into shape, put the cans of tonic water to chill in the fridge and check on ice cubes, and she would distribute fresh flowers between the hall vase and that on the coffee table. Then, she would turn her attention to her own appearance.

Derek was ever thankful that he had married a beautiful woman. That face, that elegant neck, the hourglass shape with hips slightly wider than her shoulders, those full breasts that signalled arousal invitingly, that hair; especially that hair! How easily Julia's hair excited him! As he approached the house every evening, he would wonder how she would have dressed it. The simple but perfect rolled French chignon, with its top curl and not a hair out of place, was his favourite. Of course, the Autumn gold in her hair would no longer be natural, but Derek had never seen in Julia the off-putting grey bands at the roots on so many of the parted heads one encountered on the underground.

He shut his eyes and concentrated on the smell of her freshly washed hair as she offered him her cheek. Yes, he was quite content to be welcomed in the manner of the 'dolce vita' set. Derek wasn't at all surprised at his early erection. His desire had been mounting as his train approached Cambridge because of the reasonable expectation of sex, given the fact they were staying in that evening. Julia would have got dinner ready for him…hopefully, not too long afterwards?

Derek turned his mind to the preliminary pleasures of the preprandial fireside drink and Julia's delicious cooking. He kicked off his shoes, stepped into his carpet slippers and, leaving his briefcase in the study, he went up to their bedroom to change out of his suit. Ten minutes later, he settled into the cushions at the end of the sofa nearer the fireplace and reached for the large G&T on the table next to him, sipped it, then put it down again to await Julia. The appetising aromas that escaped into the hall as Julia left the kitchen to cross into the sitting room got more of his juices going.

Over dinner, Julia told Derek about her day. He was solicitous for her news and attentive despite not being particularly interested. He preferred this to taking questions about his working day and commute. After clearing the kitchen together, they went into the sitting room to listen to some Mahler with the remainder of the bottle of wine. Julia sat beside him, her feet curled up beneath her. As the last movement reached its climactic choral finale, Julia leaned into Derek and rested her head on his shoulder knowing well the effect it would have. Derek turned his nose and lips into her hair and spread his legs apart to give his now pulsating joystick some room.

'As we're confined to barracks, you wouldn't be interested in turning in early, would you?' she said, moving her fingertips lightly across his thigh.

Julia brushed her teeth, taking a little longer than necessary so as to heighten his anticipation. She sprayed a mist of *eau de toilette* ahead of her and stepped through it. While crossing the room slowly to where Derek sat naked in the middle of the bed, she pulled two hairpins from her chignon to let her hair fall about her shoulders. Never change the way you do this, thought Derek. He turned toward her, propping himself on an elbow, as she lay down beside him. He kissed her and brushed his free hand up Julia's thigh, onto her abdomen and up to her breast. That's when he discovered the lump.

I so wanted Derek to love me that evening. I love the way he lets me bring him on gradually: presenting him with my lightly perfumed neck, moistening his lips with my first kiss, touching him gently as I brush past him, letting clothes and hair fall away so that he wants me urgently, desperately, hungrily. All of it aborted in an instance and, in its place, worry, fear, uncertainty. When Derek found the lump, my heart sank, my throat tightened, my stomach knotted; his too. What's going to happen to me? Will it be cancer? Has it spread?

I couldn't sleep and went downstairs with a blanket to a sofa. I tortured myself with worry and cried a lot, but into the blanket so as not to disturb Derek. Actually, I don't think he slept either. He looked terrible in the morning, as did I. I tried to cover the bags under my eyes with some makeup. Derek didn't want to talk about possibilities. Wait till we know what we're dealing with, he said. He rushed to catch his train! Oh, how I needed him to stay!

At lunch time, thinking she would be between clinics, I called Fiona at work. I felt bad about intruding on her professional time, but I was desperate to talk to her. I know she was upset at the news from the catch in her voice. She made time that evening for me. At her home, I asked her to look at me, to examine me and tell me what she thought. She said my GP would fast-track me through the system and I'd be seen by a breast surgeon very quickly, and perhaps it would be better to get the expert's opinion. No! Even a week of not knowing is too long. But one can't know for certain without a biopsy, she cautioned. I guess not, but still...

In their bedroom, I stripped to the waist and stood facing Fiona, arms by my side, as she asked of me. She looked at my breasts, and again after I had raised my arms above my head. Then I lay down on the edge of her bed with a pillow under my right shoulder. Fiona knelt beside me and began feeling my neck, my armpit and then, more gently, my up-turned breast. All the while she looked at me, at my face, into my eyes. I saw her eyes narrow, the forehead frown, the tear spring up.

I took her hand from my breast and, holding onto it, sat up. Will I lose my breast? I asked. She was still on her knees.

She said that I was the most beautiful person she had ever met and that I would always be beautiful, with or without hair, with or without a breast. She must have seen my shock, my fear, because she pulled me down to her and kissed me. I felt her love through that kiss and drew on her strength. There is no right or wrong way to make this journey if you're called to make it, she said to me after some minutes, but there will be an end. It may seem a long way ahead at times, but it is there. I'm sorry I made you do this, I said to her, but thank you. Fiona thinks I'm strong enough to face whatever will come my way.

I was fast-tracked and saw the breast surgeon three weeks later, and even before seeing him the hospital sent for me to get a mammogram and scans done. My world spun so fast I thought I'd fall off. A diary helped me to cope with the dates for tests and doctors' appointments. It was our practice nurse who suggested this in case it came to complicated treatments. She told me I would be able to talk to myself through it. You know, like a *personal* diary in which I could express my thoughts and feelings. Other women told her they had found this helpful.

Derek came too and I asked him to make notes of the interview because I really didn't think I'd be able to hold it together, but it turned out he needed more support than me, like when the surgeon told us about a lumpectomy: an odd word for cutting out the breast lump. That would settle the diagnosis: whether or not it was cancer. He said he would also take glands out of my armpit to see if the cancer, if that's what it turned out to be, had spread to the glands. I listened. Thanks to Fiona's honesty, her patient explanation and her love most of all, I didn't break down. We've known each other nearly fifteen years; she's the older sister I never had.

Derek was beside my bed, holding my hand, when I came around from the anaesthetic. Behind him was a wall of flowers and a pile of cards. The flowers took up half the room. I was so glad to see him, and he was sweet. Ottie, Lottie and Dottie filled their card with love. Amy organised a card

115

signed by the gang at Tuckers; it was filled with sweet messages wishing me well. The card from Astons was signed by Lionel Aston himself, and another came from Derek's London office. The vicar wrote to say the congregation was praying for me, and the choir sent chocolates: good to have had this for the nurses. I was so surprised at just how many people cared.

Mum was staying at Selwyn Gardens to keep an eye on the gardener and the cleaner, and to see to the washing, ironing and Derek's dinner. She had become so grumpy over the years, so venomous toward Dad, that visiting her wasn't at all pleasant and I avoided calling on her if I could find an excuse. Yet, here she was. Pat and Don wrote to say they wouldn't get in her way but could be down to help at a moment's notice.

I was a little sore, in the armpit mostly, and my right arm was slightly swollen. When the dressing came off the first time, the scar looked enormous, at least three inches long, maybe four, and my breast looked smaller on the outside, like it lost the full round shape. I became upset and the nurse replaced the dressing quickly. That was nothing to what came next. When the surgeon came to tell us the result of the biopsy, the only good thing was that the lymph nodes were negative.

Everything else was bad: the lump was cancerous, it was three centimetres across, and the pathologist found tumour at the margin even though the surgeon thought he had cut out all of it. So, despite taking out quite a lot of my breast there was cancer still in there. I was devastated. I was heading for a mastectomy. I couldn't stop shaking, couldn't stop crying. Derek went white as a sheet. It was the nurse who held me and helped me settle. Derek didn't have anyone to hold on to. My worst nightmare; his too.

When the nurse said the surgeon was coming back the next day to talk about the next steps in treatment, I called Fiona. She'd be there, she said without hesitation. I guess she telephoned the surgeon to work out their schedules because they turned up together. Then Fiona took off her white coat and sat beside me, as if to say I'm your friend not your doctor. Derek couldn't be there. And then the words had been said, in just a few seconds: mastectomy and chemotherapy – awful, horrible words! meaning pain, disfigurement, amputation, scars, vomiting, hair loss and God knows what else!

The surgeon offered to do the reconstruction at the same time. Like, he's asking *me*. How do I know what's best? How can I think it through now? Fiona said that if I required radiotherapy the reconstruction might fail. So, not at the same time then, but what about reconstruction? What could be done? How would I look? He said I am slim. So, the only type they could do is cover an implant with muscle from the middle from my back: a *Latissimus dorsi* flap or something. The surgeon would have to remove everything from the areola under the nipple to where the lumpectomy scar is. The nipple would be cut off. This is because the scar from the lumpectomy had to be cut out as cancer cells were still in there. A skin graft would be necessary. He showed me photos from some other poor woman with a big circular scar, a ridiculously reconstructed fake nipple, and a coloured tattoo around it in place of the natural brown skin around the normal nipple. So, the skin on the breast would be ruined as well. I was traumatised. Fiona got him out of the room.

Fiona calmed me down, which wasn't easy. She told me that I'd find the strength to face this; she *knew* I was strong enough, she said. Look to your husband, your friends and family for support, she said. I do have family and friends; I'll know soon who among them love me. She said I must hold onto my sense of humour, of beauty, even when I'm feeling very low. My sense of beauty? Really? Breast cancer is going to steal my breast, scar my body, wrench out my hair.... everything that makes me beautiful, desirable, will be ripped away. I was shaking again, uncontrollably. She held me tightly.

That evening, I was told I could go home and return for surgery in a fortnight. Mum had been really helpful, but her consistently negative view of life depressed me even as I was trying to summon up courage for what lay ahead. So Derek told her he would appreciate it if he and I had some time alone before the operation. I think she was happy to get back to Ely. But nothing good came of the time we had alone. A three-inch scar covered with a dressing turned Derek off. I'm still me, I said. This is the same soft hair that would send you shuddering to climax before all this. Here are the same parts that you would willingly and lovingly kiss in return. But he wouldn't let me take off my top. He didn't want to see anything. He couldn't bring himself to touch my other breast. He couldn't keep it up. He pushed my hands away when I tried to help. Sorry, he said. Will Derek ever look at me naked again? If he couldn't bring himself to look at the lumpectomy scar, will he ever look at me when I have a breast on one side and, on the other, a circular scar and no nipple? Will he touch me again? Will breast cancer steal my husband?

I went to St. Barnabas to see David Richmond. Surgery was scheduled for the day after next. David was looking old, but not his eyes. They were bright as ever. We talked. He asked me if I would like him to pray with me. We went into the church and knelt side by side. He did the praying for me. I confessed that the breast cancer has shaken my faith and so I was finding it very difficult to pray. He turned to me and said that wasn't true, that I had faith, he knew it. He said that faith isn't about not having doubts; everyone has doubts. Then, he said something so helpful, I clung to it in the weeks that followed. He said the opposite of faith is despair. I should think of faith as hope. You have hope, he said, or you wouldn't have chosen to go through with surgery. Jesus is Love and Hope. It is how He was able to bear the passion asked of Him. He was right, I realised, at least about the importance of hope. I didn't want to die. The surgery, the chemo, radiation: these could save my life, and I wanted to live, hoped to live. I would have to bear up, to endure, but I decided that I was not going to be passive, absorb the knocks, soak up the punches. I was going to fight and scream and scratch whenever I had the strength. I will win. I will be a survivor.

There! It's done. I have lost my right breast. It hurt, but less so now. I've been given a soft prosthesis to put into my bra cup. I think it won't look too bad as long as I'm not wearing anything low cut. Don and Pat closed up their house and drove down a couple of days before I was released from hospital. They've settled into the upstairs rooms. I hope they can cope with the stairs. Don's hip is troublesome, but he insisted they come, and waved aside any concern. He says it's me that needs help and support, not him. Don cheers me up. He makes tea upstairs and brings it down to my bedroom, with biscuits. I can't hold up a book because of the discomfort. So, he reads to me. I love listening to his Yorkshire accent. If I dose off, he sits quietly in the chair. When I wake, he just starts up again.

While Don is with me, Pat sorts out the laundry and ironing, and cooks dinner. She has never shown me as much warmth as Don and I'm sure the fact I couldn't have children affected her deeply. But now she helps me bathe. She washes and dries my hair. My hair! We don't speak it, but we both think it. Apart from the surgeon and the nurses, Pat is one of only two persons to see my mutilated body; to touch it. I love her for doing so. She helps me feel I am still me. The other is Fiona. Not my husband. Derek has not been near me. Pat says he needs time to adjust.

I know that it's ridiculous to weigh hair loss against the chance of cure, but every time I think about going bald I just break down. I cant avoid chemotherapy. I have to face it. Don found me in tears. I cried on his shoulder and he told me that even if there wasn't a single hair on my body, my smiling eyes would stop anyone ever noticing. I'll soon find out as I've had my first dose of chemo. I felt nauseated for a couple of days, then started to feel a little better as each day passed. I am getting out and about. Well, I'm in the system now. For some reason, this makes me feel that I'm more in control. They say my hair will fall out in a fortnight or so. They arranged for me to get a wig on the NHS. The people at the wig shop were really lovely, kind and caring. I cried before they put one on me. I can't believe this is happening to me.

I had my hair cut short and, actually, it looks nice. If

anything, it makes me look younger. It's a bit weird having no weight and warmth at the back of my head. When I told Clarissa I wanted to cut my hair short, she was horrified that I should think of doing such a thing. I had to explain about the breast cancer. I soon realised dear Clarissa had heard this before. She told me she would do my hair after closing time, bless her. After letting me in, she closed the blinds, gave me a big hug and we had a good cry. Then, she brought out a couple of glasses and a bottle of wine. To help both of us, she said. We took some photos, before and after! I love her. Next, she fitted the wig - a nylon one! She cut it into a short pixie style. I was surprised at how good it looked; how good I looked. Amazingly, I can wash it easily and stick it in the airing cupboard to dry. My waiting wig helps me.

My hair started coming out in clumps. I called Clarissa and went around after closing time again. She shaved my head and I left the salon in my wig. Outside for the first time in my wig. Not easy! I wore make-up, which helped me feel feminine despite my baldness. At first, I was sure everyone was looking at me. I ran into Amy as she came out of Sainsbury. She said I looked lovely, bless her. She chatted away and at one point I found I had forgotten I was wearing a wig. This has been the hardest thing, but I'm over the hurdle thanks to Clarissa and Amy.

Chemo wasn't as bad as I expected. I wasn't actually sick though I retched quite a lot. Fiona told me to take the anti-sickness tablets regularly over several days even if I didn't feel sick. My *off* feeling lasts three or four days, and I let my body do the talking. I sleep on if I feel tired, but I do make myself get out and about. Funnily, the persistent metallic taste to everything is the most annoying thing. When I'm having chemo, I can't believe how much stuff they pump into me, but I just keep thinking *this is keeping me alive!*

Everyone keeps saying I look fine. I see my body every day unclothed. My husband does not. He moved a bed into the study weeks ago. It seems he couldn't get to sleep, and work was difficult as a result. I hate my body and dress as quickly as

I can. I look no different with clothes on. I want to return to normal life as quickly as possible. I won't have reconstruction after all. It's hard, but I am so lucky to be alive and loved by friends and family.

Eight weeks after completing chemo my real hair is growing back. Of course, it's grey. Strangely, it looks as if it'll be curly. It's time to put away the wig.

Julia's hair is growing back. She looks very different. The grey hair does go with her blue eyes rather well; attractive even. Will she colour it? Can this new hair actually take colour? I wonder whether she will keep her hair short or let it grow long. Long grey heads abound in Cambridge, usually untamed. Some feminist statement, I guess. I've no doubt Julia would get hers styled expertly. Dare I bring up the subject? I don't have the right after the way I've reacted to the cancer thing.

Beautiful hair has always been something of a fetish with me. I'm kidding myself. It *is* a fetish; a powerful one. I used to think it weird to have almost uncontrollable desire at the sight of beautifully cut hair. On the other hand, I think myself fortunate. Not in the sense that I'm pleased to have such a powerful sexual urge, but that it is directed at something safe, acceptable. Julia's hair drove me wild. I was stunned to see her with her hair cropped. The lovely forehead, the perfectly set blue eyes, that upturned nose, the cheekbones, the soft full lips, the slim waist, the shapely breasts and hips: all were unaltered, yet everything had changed.

I couldn't bear the thought of Julia's long tresses being cut away so savagely. Worse! Two weeks after that mutilating haircut, the remaining brush of her hair started to fall out. I have never seen Julia bald. The wig made it less difficult to look at her. She had painted on eyebrows and put on false eyelashes, which helped too. She tried so hard to look normal. I'll admit Julia's wig is so well styled that not infrequently I get an erection, but I'm terrified that the wig might slip off. So, what kind of weirdo am I that a nylon wig excites me!

Dad wanted a word with me before he and Mum returned to Yorkshire. We went into the garden. Julia's snowdrops were everywhere, and early daffodils were opening here and there. It was at this time in the year that Julia and I first viewed Selwyn Gardens, and were captivated by it. Dad asked how I was. Bearing up, I said. He looked up at me and said Who's having the worse time of it, do you think? You're about to make a point, I said. Then he came in hard. I haven't seen you hold Julia, hug her, kiss her. You couldn't look at her when she lost her hair. You didn't help her through the difficult decisions about treatment. Instead of offering her your love, giving her reason to endure and fight, you withheld it. You bottled it. Shame on you! I reacted defensively and with some irritation. Son, he said, don't be a fool, don't lose her, it's not too late. Then, he went out to the car and they drove off. What an indictment! He doesn't know the half of it.

Julia appraised herself in the mirror. She ran her fingers through her hair, now two inches long. Then she pushed it back, parted it on one side, then the other. She fingered her eyebrows. Eyelashes had grown back. She called the salon and asked Clarissa for an appointment Friday afternoon.

Julia had three days to put her plan into action. She dusted and aired the drawing room and her bedroom. She polished the furniture and set out vases, ready to receive fresh flowers. New candles were placed round the two rooms; unscented, as this wasn't about the candles! She devised a menu and stocked up with ingredients. Then, she sat down with hair and fashion magazines.

At two o'clock on Friday, Julia walked *into Hairworks*. Clarissa did a second take. Julia wore makeup, which was rather dramatic for the early afternoon, but it was designed for the evening. When Julia smiled, the bright red lips flashed apart to accentuate her dazzling white teeth. Her manicured hands had expertly shaped nails as red as her lips.

'Julia!' exclaimed Clarissa, 'is this a new you?'

'Not yet, but it will be after you've finished with me, I want to dazzle my husband tonight, Clarissa. Help me do it.' Clarissa gave her a supportive hug.

'Let's do it, love!' she said with her usual effervescence. They sat down together to look through some pictures that Julia had cut out of her magazines. Julia pointed questioningly to a model wearing sharply cut, short, blonde hair.

'What do you think, Clarissa? Does it say *I'm alive! I'm happy to be me. I'm going to be noticed. You're not going to take your eyes off me.*'

'Yes! And how! Just add earrings; ones that will make a statement with short hair; perhaps large, hanging gold rings,' said Clarissa clapping her hands. 'I'll give you a haircut that will turn every head were you to walk into a nightclub on a Saturday night'

'There's only one head I want turned my way.' Clarissa got to work. She coloured Julia's hair a platinum blonde so that it bordered on silvery. Then she used a scissors-over-comb technique to cut the hair on the sides and back ever so close to the scalp, but without any hard edge to the hair-line. Clarissa graduated the cut to leave the hair longer as she brought the comb up towards the crown. Then she cut the top hair to the height of one finger, while leaving it a little longer at the front so that the front hair could be quiffed up gently with some gel. When she had the length just right, Clarissa used a point-cutting technique to add texture. The finished look was stunning: a sharp style with softness all over.

'Are you ready, then?' Clarissa asked. The other hairstylists had gathered round.

'It feels so right. Let me see it.' Clarissa pulled the cape away from the mirror with a flourish. Julia couldn't believe the transformation. Gone were the slate grey chemo curls. The woman who looked back at her oozed confidence. There

123

was no hiding behind tumbling locks. The beauty was in the long neck, in the shape of the head, in the small ears flat against the head, in the eyes and lips, framed in platinum blonde.

'Oh, Clarissa. You're such an artist. This is just what I'd hoped for; much more, actually. I was afraid I might end up looking rather cheap. You've made me mysterious. I'm amazed that less than an inch of hair is the difference between feeling dehumanised and feeling empowered.' Julia rose from the chair and hugged Clarissa.

'I'm so pleased you like it. Truthfully, I felt a little nervous doing it. I hope it will do the trick.'

That Friday evening in midsummer, Derek stepped out of the taxi, walked through the door and caught a light, floral fragrance that was new to him; the scent of night-blooming flowers like jasmine, orange blossom and frangipani. Then a drop-dead-gorgeous cropped blonde walked slowly into the hall toward him. She wore a fitted white shirt blouse with the top two buttons undone and super-tight leather trousers that sat low on her hips. She stood tall in high-heeled ankle boots. Apart from rings in her ears and on her finger, her only accessories were a silk neck scarf round her neck and a mother-of-pearl belt. She reached him, put a hand over his breast and ran it upwards slowly under his jacket and onto his shoulder as she moved in further, her soft breasts pressing into his chest and her red lips almost touching his. Her fragrance was intoxicating. He swam in the blue of her eyes.

'Julia!' softly, breathlessly, was all he could say. She kissed him fully on the mouth, softly at first, then with a little more pressure, then with the tip of her tongue.

'Where have you been, Derek?' she said softly and her lips, glistening with moisture, came back again. Julia brought her left hand round onto Derek's bum. She held him steadily as she swivelled her hip against his groin, and he grew large and groaned with pleasure, and she was thankful. With not a little anxiety, Julia took hold of Derek's right hand and brought it up to her breast. He felt her erect nipple and moved his thumb against it while cupping the breast. 'It's up to you, darling' she whispered as she reached to his crotch, now rock hard. 'Before or after dinner?'

'You look so utterly ravishing. I'll explode if you keep your hand there.' Julia pushed her hands up Derek's chest onto his shoulders, lifted his jacket off them and let it slip to the floor behind him. Then she pressed him against the wall and kissed him hard on the mouth. Derek reached up and brushed his fingers lightly over Julia's cropped head. She undid his belt, unhooked and unzipped his trousers, put one hand onto the front band of his boxer shorts and pulled outwards, reached in with her other hand to grip his penis, and stroked it back and forth a few times, drawing the skin further back with each stroke. Derek began to rock his pelvis backwards and forwards as Julia clutched him. At that point, she pulled the penis free of his shorts, stroked him hard while letting the head rub against her, and when his groans got louder and his rocking more forceful she pulled the scarf from her neck, wrapped it over his penis and with her other hand reached down between his legs and grabbed his balls. Derek exploded! He sank to his knees and Julia went down with him. He held her hands in his and noticed the nails.

'Blimey! No wonder your stroking brought exquisite ecstasy... I'm afraid your scarf is ruined.'

'It served its purpose perfectly.' Julia smiled bewitchingly. She touched his face. 'I have missed you so much, Derek.'

Derek showered. Then he pulled on his chinos and a polo shirt and slipped into moccasins. Appetising aromas greeted him as he came downstairs. Julia called out.

'In the drawing room, Derek. I'm coming through in a minute.' The patio doors were wide open to the summer evening. The last of the sun cast orange beams through the trees. Lanterns hung from some of the near branches. The lights over the patio were on but the drawing room was only candlelit. Derek saw that the opened card table, placed just inside the room from the patio, was dressed in a white tablecloth and laid out for two with their best China and crystal. The new perfume lingered in the air.

Julia came to him. She had arranged her hair differently again. Now it was parted on the right and combed flat in the manner of Twiggy in her heyday. She had freshened her lipstick and a short string of pearls drew attention to her neck. God almighty, he was getting aroused again. He took the glass of wine she offered, and they stepped out onto the patio. She put her arm through his and they stood side by side for a while, looking at the fading colours and listening to the final movement of the dusk chorus, thinking different thoughts.

'Come in now,' said Julia when the sun set, 'dinner will be ready. Will you shut the patio door? It will get chilly very soon.' Derek did so, then sat down. Julia brought in a starter of hot goat's cheese drizzled with balsamic vinegar and salad. Then, she handed him the bottle of wine, from which he filled their glasses. She looked up at him as he put a forkful into his mouth. 'Just for a moment, I think, you didn't recognise me.'

'Your metamorphosis is as dramatic as anything Ovid dreamt up,' he said, raising his glass. An alarm sounded in her head. He didn't use language like this when they were intimate.

'In Ovid, metamorphoses don't end well,' she said.

Derek put down his knife and fork and put his hands in his lap. 'I see a nymph, not a laurel tree.' Husband and wife sat looking at one another.

'And which of Cupid's arrows has struck you, the golden one or the leaden one?' The long pause that followed filled her with dread.

'I have met someone else,' he said without averting his eyes. She did not move except to hold onto the table edge to steady herself. She did not look away though tears welled up and spilled over to run down her cheeks, smearing her makeup. She did not wipe the tears away. He thought, this is how a heart breaks.

'Can't you find your way back, my love?' she asked in a voice cracking with pain, hoping against hope. He looked down, perhaps at his hand about to turn the knife. 'She's pregnant...I'm sorry.' Julia gasped, her hand moving reflexively to her throat. No, not that! I can't win against that, was all she could think. She rose from the table unsteadily, as if the wound were physical. If only; she had learnt from experience that *physical* pain could be borne. The room became stifling, oppressive even. She had to get out, had to get away. Without another word, she staggered out, and up the stairs to her bedroom, packed a small suitcase, grabbed her handbag, and almost ran from the house that seemed to be the vanity of vanities.

11. A FRIEND IN NEED

Who on Earth, could it be at this hour? Fiona asked herself when the doorbell rang. She went to the door, switched on the porch light, slipped on the chain, then opened the door cautiously. In the yellow lamplight, she saw a pathetic clownish face: yellowish hair topped a sad face on which black mascara ran down sallow cheeks to a downturned red mouth. Fiona did a double take, then cried out.

'Julia! hang on, I'll take the chain off.' In her urgency, Fiona fumbled with the chain, but then got the door open and stepped out to hug the pathetic, quivering figure, and held on to her, knowing she might otherwise break down. This is not the cancer, she figured.

'Hold on, love. Whatever has happened, we'll sort things out.'

'Oh, Fiona! I'm so sorry to do this to you. You're the only one I can turn to.' Fiona took Julia's hand, urged her indoors and shepherded her into the sitting room. She called out to Matt, who was in the kitchen stacking the dishwasher.

'Matt, we need a drink; anything, but make it a large one.' Fiona sat beside Julia, put an arm round her shoulders, and kissed the side of her head. 'Wait until you've had a drink before you tell what has happened, darling.' Fiona took the very large gin and tonic from Matt, who had appeared in the doorway in no time, and handed it to Julia. Then, she waved him away. Julia took a gulp, only to splutter at the strength of it. 'It'll help, sweetheart. Just now, tell me what you need most urgently,' invited Fiona.

'Your sofa for the night? I can't go back.'

'Right, just wait here. I'll sort this out and be back in five minutes.'

'You'll stay here as long as you like, Julia. Ottie's bedroom is yours,' said Fiona reassuringly when she returned. Julia was mortified.

'No, I couldn't do that. Lottie was so looking forward to having a room to herself during Ottie's gap year. Dottie too. The sofa will do, honestly.'

'The girls are awake. All I had to say was that Aunt Julia needs help. Do you think for a moment that they hesitated? I had to stop them running downstairs to comfort you. I promised they could call in on you tomorrow morning before they go off to school. Now, just have another sip of your drink, while I get one for myself.' Fiona poured out a drink, picked up a box of tissues and sat beside her friend. 'These are for me. I may need them,' Fiona said. 'I don't know what's coming, but clearly it's going to be upsetting... And don't worry about taking your time because Matt has things in hand.'

'You are both such true friends,' began Julia, 'thank you. I won't dramatise things because I've done my crying. Well, you can see that, can't you. I must look a mess...' Fiona waited. 'I wanted Derek to be attracted to me again. We haven't been intimate since the awful day we found the cancer, you know. Then I thought, my hair might be just long enough to style; time to lose the chemo curls. Clarissa made me look like a model and I surprised him when he got home. I swear he didn't recognise me at first. And then we had sex again. I thought: At last! I've got him back. We've saved our marriage... But it was all for nothing, all too late... He told me he is having an affair... It crushed me.' Fiona's own emotions, confused by ambiguity initially, turned to anger.

'That man is spineless, self-centred and cruel. He's a right bastard!' she hissed contemptuously. 'I daresay tomorrow he'll say he's sorry, and couldn't you forgive him? And couldn't you make a fresh start?' She intended to add *don't fall for it* but checked herself. There needed to be anger in the room but better not from her.

'He said sorry; *sorry that he hurt me,* I think. Perhaps, sorry as in *he feels ashamed.* Sorry as in *will I forgive him* even. But I know it isn't the sorry of *It was just a mistake, meaningless, I love you, can we start again?* Everything has changed. It can't be undone. His mistress is pregnant.' This news silenced Fiona for some moments. She buried her face in her hands. Hypocrite! If a child mattered so much to him why didn't he say so all those years ago. Julia would have given him his child. She just needed to hear him say he wanted one badly and wanted her to bear it. When Fiona raised her head, it was clear she was fuming with rage.

'Why isn't *he* on the streets? Why is it you that's out of your home when he's the one who has behaved despicably, atrociously?'

'The moment he told me, I knew that no matter how hard I fought, I couldn't win; not against the mother of his child. I knew our marriage was over. Then, I don't know quite what came over me. I couldn't breathe. I couldn't bear to be in that house a moment longer. I had to be away from it. Do you know, what flashed before my eyes were the years I spent making his perfect home and garden, preparing myself to please him, waiting on him, washing and ironing his clothes, feeding him, giving up my own ambitions, giving up my job at Tuckers, distancing myself from my friends; and in that instant I thought *I have been a fool.*' Neither of them said anything for a short while and, perhaps because of that, Matt popped his head through the door.

'Can I get you anything, girls? Everything is sorted out here. Do you need me?'

Julia went over to him. 'Matt, I'm so sorry to have intruded like this.'

'Think nothing of it,' he said, giving her a hug. 'Anyone can see it's an emergency. Now, you stay here as long as you need. I'd be pleased to have four girls in the house again to love.' Fiona blew a kiss.

'Thanks, Matt. You get to bed. I'll sit with Julia for a while longer; at least until we get through these drinks. Then I'll make sure she has everything she needs. I'll come up quietly.' Matt walked round the sofa, leaned over to kiss Fiona, then Julia. He wished them goodnight and turned off the centre light as he left the room. Fiona raised an arm to invite Julia to her side and into her embrace. She kissed the top of the head that snuggled into her breast and stroked her hair. She just held Julia against her, and they sat like that. Fiona felt her anger dissipate. Julia felt love's comfort. Not once did he hold me like this during my ordeal, she thought. How much harder he made it. Did he ever truly love me?

Julia did not get much sleep, which was hardly surprising given the complex emotions associated with the inevitable review of her marriage through the long night. Of course, this scrutiny changed nothing. She knew this. Her marriage was over, and she would not agonise over what might have been. She was not to blame for the breast cancer. Shit happens, Amy had said, doesn't mean you deserve it. Unexpectedly, the feeling that dominated all others was that she was free. Free to work out what she wished to do with the life she had wrested back from cancer's grabbing claws and free to live it as she wished. She had no short-term anxiety. Fiona had made it clear that she could stay with them for as long as she needed. It was not only refuge that the Jefferies offered. Julia knew that they would also be her primary source of reliable and trustworthy advice on how to move forward.

At a quarter to seven, Julia brushed her teeth, combed her hair and put on just enough makeup to mask the effects of the sleepless night. She slipped into Ottie's dressing gown and went downstairs to the kitchen. Fiona was already showered and dressed for work. She stood by the toaster expecting the toast to pop up any second, knife and butter dish at the ready. The kettle came to the boil. She turned to Julia.

'Come here, you!' she said, leaving everything and opening her arms. 'I don't suppose you got much sleep, did you?'

Julia stepped into the hug.

'I got some sleep… enough to survive the day, thanks to you and Matt. The treble G&T helped too.' Fiona pushed Julia's shoulders back to look at her.

'My compliments on your new hair. In fact, I'm flattered that you're imitating my style,' she said with a wink.

'I am, aren't I? When I saw the style in a hair journal, I thought of you and how much it suited you. I think I've gone too far with the colour, though.'

'Nonsense! It's a bold new colour with which to go boldly forth. I *love* it.' The toast popped up. Julia stepped in and buttered it while Fiona finished off the four mugs of tea. 'Would you like to get the girls up, Julia. It's seven fifteen.'

'I'd love to, and I'll hurry them into getting ready; don't worry.' Julia took the tray up to the girls' room. When she whispered to them that breakfast had arrived, Lottie and Dottie jumped up excitedly. The girls wanted to know how long she would be with them, whether they would have the chance to do stuff with her. She assured them she would be staying for a few weeks. 'There is a downside for you,' she said with a smile. 'Your mother wants me to supervise your piano practice.'

Back downstairs, Julia asked Fiona what work was needed around the house. She would figure out the routine in a couple of days but thought it more useful to find out what would be best done first. When Fiona insisted that there was nothing more required than clearing up the breakfast things, Julia said she would look after dinner.

'Matt's not dining at College tonight, is he?'

'No, he isn't. We're here tonight and neither of us will be bringing work home. We thought we would eat early, straight after the girls' piano practice. They'll have homework to do afterwards, which will leave the three of us free to enjoy a glass of wine out back.'

'Right, I'll get something that can be put together easily after piano practice. I'll aim for dinner at six.'

'Are you sure about doing this. Oughtn't you to be taking as much time as possible to work out what you want, what you need?'

'I'll have time. There's all morning and afternoon. I don't want to brood, so I'm going to walk around the neighbourhood. I have missed the Mill Road community.'

'Then, if you're sure you'll be alright, we're going off. Don't hesitate to telephone me. I can always take time to talk, even if I can't leave the hospital. I've left the spare key on the kitchen table.' They hugged. Then Fiona first, the girls next, and finally Matt cycled away.

When the front door shut behind the last of the Jefferies, Julia sat on a kitchen chair in the silence to think. It was eight fifteen. Normally, she would already have emptied the washing machine and dishwasher, hung out the clothes to catch the morning sun, ground coffee beans and got the coffee percolator going, watered some flower beds, prepared Derek's buttered toast, eaten breakfast with him, made sure the taxi was on its way while he got his things together, and waved him goodbye feeling, really and truly, grateful to him for working so hard. Bloody hell! What a mug I've been! she thought.

Julia started her new life by washing Derek out of her hair and enjoying an indulgent soak in the bath. After drying herself, she applied moisturising cream to her chest and worked it into the scars. These were looking less red with each passing week. The cream softened the scar tissue. She massaged it into her skin while seated in front of a mirror as a way of facing up to things, of guarding against self-disgust. When she had rubbed in the cream, Julia stood naked in front of the mirror for a while. She had remained slim into her forties and still wore size eight. However, there was less shape to her, less contour; nothing to do with the missing breast, but everything to do with the cancer and chemotherapy. I'm more thin than slim, she thought, and my body looks battered. It occurred to her that she had not exercised for many months.

There and then, she decided that she would get fit again, which suddenly thrilled her. It struck her as peculiar that setting herself such a simple and straightforward objective as getting fit should raise her mood, her morale, so quickly. Acting on the impulse, she began some stretches, then tried some push-ups. She couldn't manage the latter. So, she limited herself to half-pushups, lifting only her upper body off the floor. She could manage a few sit-ups. This left Julia breathing hard, but she enjoyed the adrenalin surge. There, that's one item for my list of things to do, she thought. She showered again lightly to remove the sweat, pulled on a T-shirt and jeans, and left the house to breakfast on croissants and coffee at Hot Numbers, thinking how much she had missed this place.

The rush-hour traffic had slackened by the time she finished breakfast but not by much. The city was so clogged up by traffic that Julia decided to get away from it. She took the back streets to Stourbridge Common, cut across the Common to the bridge *by The Green Dragon,* crossed over to the Chesterton side and then followed the route to the tow path beside the Cam. It was a beautiful Saturday morning and several boats from the City clubs were already out. How delightful to hear the rhythmical splash of water as the crew of an eight glided past, and to see the small herd of brown cows on the other bank engaged in ceaseless chewing while their tails flicked frequently to swat away flies. Anglers sat on canvas seats at regular intervals, alert to any tug on their lines but without much in their nets yet. She walked past Fen Ditton and under the A14 to Baits Bite Lock, the point where boats turned around and headed back to the boathouses by Midsummer Common. Julia walked on and soon she was alone under a blue dome of Fenland sky.

Much as she wanted to look forward, Julia continued to gnaw at the reasons for the breakdown of her marriage; specifically, whether she had sown its seed all those years ago by passing up the opportunity of giving Derek his child. She knew now, from her feelings toward her goddaughter, indeed toward the three Jefferies girls, that she would have loved the child. Would Derek have gone to another woman and had a child with her if he had a family? She had judged him materialistic; would he have been so obsessed with more money, a grand house, a fast car, if she had given him a child... or two. Her ovaries did not work but her womb did, her breasts did. Why, oh why had her heart not worked? So, it wasn't simple, she thought. It's all too easy to blame Derek, to say he didn't love her. Perhaps she had not loved him enough. At no point in this self-examination did Julia think her marriage was salvageable but that didn't make the deliberation pointless. It brought her to the conclusion that apportioning blame was tricky and that both of them had made mistakes.

Julia was not fit enough to stride along for miles, but she got as far as *The Bridge* at Clayhithe, where she treated herself to a cold cider seated on the riverbank. The exercise, physical and ruminative, had freed up her thoughts. She was now able to pose another set of questions: what do I most regret not having done? what do I most enjoy? what do I most care about? and where do I want to live? The last of the questions was the easiest to answer: the upper Mill Road neighbourhood, to reconnect with St. Barnabas' community and rekindle relationships and friendships that she had neglected in recent years. She knew too what she most enjoyed: art, craft and music. This chimed with the choice of where to live as the neighbourhoods around the Mill Road were home to lots of music teachers, musicians, painters, sculptors, potters, textile artists and so on, not least because it was the more affordable area of private housing in the City.

The remaining questions needed closer examination and the answers crystallised over several more days. Nevertheless, Julia returned from her walk with a notion of what they might be. Her greatest regret was that she had not been to University and she wanted a second chance. Of course, she may have to start with another A level or two to meet entrance requirements although a foundation year might be an alternative. She decided to inquire at Anglia Polytechnic on East Road and, if they weren't able to help her, the Open University.

In one respect, she knew well enough the answer to the final question; she cared about cancer. Rather, she cared about other cancer sufferers. While she was grateful that surgeons and oncologists had battled with her cancer to save her life, the experience had been bewildering, frightening, draining, humiliating, impersonal and, in the case of her marriage, destructive. Need it have been so? Would things have turned out better if she and Derek had received psychological support or counselling. As a cancer survivor, could she help? Could she make a contribution to the support and well-being of people diagnosed with cancer?

Well, no time like the present. So, Julia returned to the City along the river as far as Elizabeth Bridge, then along East Road to Anglia Polytechnic. The entrance was covered in purple balloons and banners advertising the forthcoming open day in early July. She stepped inside and went up to the reception, where she asked for prospectuses for courses on Art or Music. She was handed a copy of the main prospectus and several pamphlets about courses on Art and Music. One in particular caught her eye: a BA Honours course in Fine Art, starting in September. It seemed to combine both practical and academic approaches; a requirement to create art as well as to study the history and context of art. She was confident that she would cope well with the practical creative course work and told herself this should counter possible weaknesses in the academic components. Having nothing to lose, she registered for the Open Day.

Julia turned down Norfolk Street in hope and found The Old Bakery was still there with freshly baked custard tarts piled high in the window. She bought half a dozen tarts for tea and one to eat immediately. It was as delicious as when Derek served them up on her first visit to York Terrace all those years ago. Surprisingly, the memory was not painful. Quite the contrary, she wanted to savour thoughts of a time in her marriage when she had been very happy. So, she decided to walk on to York Terrace. As she approached number thirty-two, she noticed a small red and white sign hidden behind a hanging flower basket. I don't believe it! Can it really be true? she said out loud. There was no doubt at all - number thirty-two was up for sale.

Lottie and Dorothy went up to their room to prepare for the next school-day and Julia rose to clear the table.

'Oh no you don't,' said Matthew, getting to his feet quickly. 'You've looked after the girls since four o'clock *and* prepared dinner for all of us. So, off you go to the lounge, and take Fiona with you. Take the bottle of wine too. It won't take me long to clear the table and load the dishwasher. I'll catch up soon.' Fiona had had a difficult day and looked tired. She was glad to do as Matt suggested. When Julia inquired, she said it was a mixture of things. They were coming to the end of a week in which every brain tumour biopsy came back with the worst diagnosis possible – *Glioblastoma*. There wasn't anything she could do for her patients. All these people would be dead within a year. The thought depressed her.

'It's disheartening when there's no break from bad news all week,' she said when Julia expressed concern. 'We try several things, but they buy the patient little time. In fact, the survival rate for *glioblastoma* has remained essentially unchanged for forty years. This will change because new research is coming through all the time. Meanwhile, it helps if the week brings a mix of cases; you know, some patients to whom I can say *your brain tumour is not one of the bad ones, we have drugs or radiation that will keep you well for several years, we can help.* This week wasn't one of those.' Fiona held her hands up. 'Enough of cancer and my day. Look, here comes Matt with his dessert.'

'Hey Julia, the girls have had a lovely time with you. They keep mentioning the delicious custard tarts. I think I'll find out what the fuss is about.' He took a bite out of his *Pastel de Nata.* 'Yummy!' he remarked, 'how have I not come across these creamy wonders!'

Fiona turned to Julia. 'How did it go with the girls? You look good this evening; maybe being with them helped?'.'

'They were lovely! It was fun being with them and, you're right, they cheered me up. But, you know, I've had a good day. No, a *remarkable* day actually, if I consider the co-incidences and the opportunities it has brought. It's surreal.' Matt looked questioningly at Fiona, but she signalled that she didn't know yet.

'We're intrigued,' said Matt. 'Go on, tell us your news.'

'I went for a walk to clear my head. It has been the perfect summer's day and I couldn't resist going down to the river and then walking along the tow path as far as *The Bridge.* Well, I worked out what was important to me, what I'd like to do, where I'd like to go from here. So, one idea is that I want to go to University.'

'And the coincidence? the opportunity?' asked Fiona, too curious to wait for Julia to unfold her story.

'Well, here's the amazing thing. I saw that Anglia Poly-technic was advertising an open day and I popped in for a prospectus. They have a three-year degree course in Fine Art. It isn't just academic. There's quite a lot of hands-on practical art that is assessed for the degree.' Fiona clapped her hands.

'This is terrific, Julia! What a find! You are so artistic, and you've been reading about Art ever since I've known you.'

'The other thing I've decided is to exercise. I don't just mean go to the gym a couple of times a week. I want to get very fit. Actually, I want to run a marathon to raise funds for cancer research. Now, I'm not being as selfless as you might think. This is very much for me. You see, I have to learn to like my body again.'

'You have taken big steps forward,' said Fiona with a sense of relief at this progress.

'Ah, but there must be more. There is more, isn't there?' said Matt. 'What you've said so far is marvellous, but you talked of coincidences and opportunities, in the plural.'

'You'll think the next thing a little crazy, I expect' said Julia, '*crazy* as in such a strange coincidence and *crazy* as in the snap decision I've taken' said Julia, feeling both nervous and excited. 'I went to York Terrace in the afternoon and found, to my astonishment, that number thirty-two is up for sale. Well, I seem to have been in *carpe diem* mode, because I rang the bell. The people selling are the same ones to whom we sold it nearly fifteen years ago.'

'Are you thinking of buying it?"

'I don't know if it that will be possible; but yes, I'd like to do just that. Probably, you think it a bad idea for me to return to our first home, but I really did love that house. I still do. We only moved to Selwyn Gardens because Derek was obsessing about a grand house and garden. Of course, whether or not I can get number thirty-two will depend on how the divorce goes.'

'Explain the *carpe diem*,' said Matt, half impressed and half amused. 'Ringing the doorbell doesn't quite cover that. What have you done exactly?'

'Oh, I told the sellers I could meet the asking price and asked them not to decide on any other offer for a week,' said Julia, blushing a little at the thought that she very likely wouldn't be able to honour the claim.

'And can you?' asked Fiona.

'Actually, I have no idea. On the other hand, I don't know that it will not be possible. All will depend on Derek. I guess I'll have to contact him.'

'Julia, you really have had the most remarkable day,' said Matt, 'I knew you would dust yourself down and pick yourself up. In fact, this brings us to the question of a lawyer to handle your affairs, your divorce, *if* it comes to it.'

'Dear Matt, it *will* come to it; it *has* come to it,' said Julia. 'Today wouldn't have turned out as it did, had I not been so absolutely certain that Derek would not come back to me. I saw it in his face, yesterday. I couldn't give him a child. Now, he is going to be a father. He's forty-eight. One might say that's too old to enjoy a son or daughter, but Derek has worked hard and made a significant amount of money. He may be in a position to retire early or reduce his hours in order to be around as his child grows. In fact, the thought of how happy he will be to have a child has helped reduce my pain and sorrow. The only questions are the divorce settlement and the time it'll take.'

'And you've given this some thought, Julia?' asked Matt.

'It isn't difficult to work out. I've had cancer. While I may be cured, one can never tell with cancer, can one? I may have only a few years. I've told you some, not all, of the things I want to do. I also want to engage actively in cancer support, beyond just fundraising. I don't want to go back to work to support myself. Anyway, from the stories one reads in newspapers I imagine I'm entitled to half the house and half our investments and savings. I don't know if Derek's adultery counts against him when it comes to financial settlement or whether I'm entitled to maintenance. Obviously, I'll need a lawyer and I was hoping you could suggest a good one.'

Fiona interrupted: 'Julia, would you like Matt to have a word with Derek on your behalf? You may want to collect more of your clothes and personal belongings from Selwyn Gardens without running into him. Anyway, it may be in your best interest not to see Derek until you see a lawyer. Matt could sound Derek out about when you could access the house.' Julia turned to Matthew.

'Would you, Matthew? It would reassure me to know that Derek is able and willing to help me settle into a new life quickly and without fuss. I could go round for some things on any weekday afternoon. I just need to know if he ever intends to work from Cambridge, which he hardly ever does.'

'Of course, I'll do that. I'll telephone him tomorrow morning and ask if he could see me tomorrow evening or the next.' The three of them wanted to move the conversation on to a lighter note so as not to head for bed with heads buzzing about the best way forward. So, when Julia brought up the music practice she had done with them, Lottie and Dottie became the very pleasant subject on which to end the evening.

Before leaving for work next morning, Matthew gave Julia the name of the solicitor that Fiona and he had been using for some years. Later in the day, he telephoned Derek at his office and arranged to call round at Selwyn Gardens on Friday evening. Derek welcomed him rather stiffly. He's on the defensive, thought Matt. Derek led the way through the hall into the drawing room. As the curtains were drawn back, the last of the evening light reached into the middle of the room.

Derek went over to the drinks cabinet, looked back at Matt and asked what he would like. He shrugged his shoulders at Matt's refusal of a drink, poured himself a Scotch and then carried it to a sofa and chairs off to one side of the sunlight. He pointed to the sofa by way of indicating where Matt should sit and dropped himself into the armchair. They sat at right angles to one another and Derek turned on the table lamp between them. Its lampshade kept his face in shadow. An empty glass sat on the table. Derek said nothing immediately, preferring to sip his whisky, and the large house was disconcertingly silent.

'How is Julia?' he asked.

'She's resilient... And forgiving, I think. She will get through this.'

'I don't think I could have forgiven her if the positions were reversed.'

'Do you think for one second that Julia would ever have betrayed you?'

'*Touché*'

Matthew signalled a truce. 'I apologise. I spoke out of turn.' Derek waived the apology aside.

'Fiona and you are Julia's closest friends. You speak out of concern and love for her. I take your rebuke in that context. Nevertheless, it would be more helpful to Julia if we could address the present and future positions, rather than the past.'

'Well, Julia wishes to agree the divorce settlement quickly. The question is will you facilitate this? Julia hopes she will not need to engage a lawyer other than to register an agreement, reached amicably and rapidly.'

'Go on.'

'She's been advised that in broad terms she should expect half the assets, including property, investments and savings. She knows that Selwyn Gardens means a lot to you and she hopes you will not have to sell it. On the other hand, she needs a home of her own, and quickly. Remarkably, your first home in York Terrace is back on the market. Julia wishes to live there again and asks if you could anticipate the financial settlement so that she can purchase it. From Selwyn Gardens, she wants one thing only: the piano.' It seemed to Matt that the last request affected Derek, who looked down at his hands for some minutes. Then, Derek cleared his throat.

'Tell Julia I agree to her requests. In addition, reassure her that I shall continue to pay her health insurance. Tomorrow morning, I'll ask a colleague at Astons to draft an agreement based on a 50:50 split of our assets. I'll send the lawyer's contact details to her at your home address, if I may, and Julia or her solicitor can feel free to contact him about any further changes. While it'll take several weeks to obtain valuations of the house and portfolio, to organise transfers and payments and so on, Julia isn't going to have to make final payment on any house any time soon. I expect our savings can cover the deposit easily enough, so she should feel able to make an offer for York Terrace, if that's what she wants.'

'I'll pass that on. Oh, there's another thing, Derek. Julia asks when she could call round for her personal effects, perhaps when you're at work?'

'Yes, I see. Tell her she may call round any weekday afternoon in the next month to collect her things. I'm assuming that Julia is staying with you and Fiona in the short term?' Matt nodded agreement. 'Well then, it may be that she'll have to rent somewhere until she can take possession of York Terrace, or wherever. I'll instruct my lawyer to cover any short-term lease she takes up, until she moves into her own home or the date of the divorce, whichever is sooner.' Matt was not quite sure what Derek was getting at and showed it with an involuntary lift of his brow. 'Ask Julia to leave the house keys behind her by this date next month, would you? There'll be someone else in the house after that.' Much as Matt strove for clarity, precision and economy in speech and writing from himself and his students, this matter-of-fact attitude of Derek compelled him to bring some emotion into the space between them.

'Derek, Julia loves you and wants you to be happy. She realises the centrality of your child, perhaps children, to such an outcome.' In response, Derek got to his feet with a noncommittal grunt. He thanked Matt for coming and began walking to the door, obliging Matt to follow. He waited until Matt had got into his Hi-Vis gear, donned his helmet, mounted his lights, clipped his trouser bottoms and cycled out of earshot. Interfering prat! he said under his breath.

Derek returned to the armchair in the corner of the drawing-room where he sat for a while with his whisky and his thoughts, the latter in the form of variations on a basic theme: Here I am, then. Forty-nine today. The same age as Clementine's old pater, but where's the wisdom that comes with age. Dreadful sorry, Julia. The truth is that the very thought of your mutilated, once-perfect body horrifies me. I can't get past it.

Jane sniffed me out: the self-pity and pent up desire. I helped her into her coat. Before she turned around, she pulled a comb out, and her shimmering blonde tresses cascaded over her shoulders. You know what that does to me.

143

Jane knew. She wasn't wearing underwear; none at all. Flawless breasts... two of them! The recollection brought the same rush of blood that had driven him desperately into her. He leaned back in the armchair, opened his fly and comforted himself.

On the side table next to Derek, two cards lay face down. One card brought birthday wishes from his mother; she had penned Don's name herself. The message inside the other, also a birthday card, read:

Dear Derek,

Happy birthday!

I have been able to make a new start. I wish you every happiness with your child. You know how much I regret not being able to give you one.

I loved you yesterday. I love you still, always have, always will.

Goodbye,

Julia

12. FOLLY

I'm back, called out Don as he came through the front door with the Sunday paper. As usual, he and Pat had gone their separate ways after Sunday worship; he, to the newsagent and then to *The Black Magic* for a pint or two with a dwindling number of lifelong friends; she, home to hear from her son and then to prepare lunch.

'How are they, then?' asked Don.

'Sit down, Don. Lunch isn't ready. I've been on the phone with Derek for some time. I'll grill the chops now. Give me fifteen minutes. Then, we'll talk over lunch.'

'What's up then? Is Julia unwell again?' he asked, suddenly anxious about his daughter-in-law.

'No, she's not unwell and Derek is alright, but there is a problem. Best leave it till we're at table.' Right, have it your own way, thought Don not a little irritated by this condescension. First she says there's a problem then she doesn't say what it is; like it's their special relationship.

'Right, Pat,' said Don after he had finished the soup and Pat had brought the meat dish to the table, 'what's going on down South?'

'Do you want the good news or the bad news first?' asked Pat.

'Is this comedy club? Come on, out with it, woman.'

'Derek and Julia have separated.' At this, Don slapped his hand down on the table, bouncing the cutlery and crockery off the table, spilling food.

'Bloody fool of a man! I warned him.' He was full of mixed emotions; disappointment and anger featuring strongly. 'I take it that's the good news and the bad news will be Julia is taking him to the cleaners. Well, he deserves it. He didn't support her. He didn't care for her. He just thought of his own precious self.' Don could feel his blood pressure rising. Pat could see it too as Don became more and more flushed.

'Don, please calm down. Your outburst doesn't help. Anyway, that was the *bad* news.' She reached for a cloth to wipe the table clean.

'So, the good news is that he realises how stupid and selfish he is and that he intends to fight for Julia, is it? I can't think of any news that I can call good unless it's that.'

'Well, the good news is that we're going to be grandparents.'

'Grandparents! Is this a joke?' shouted Don. Then the penny dropped. 'Oh, I see! He's gone and got another woman pregnant. So, this is what it comes to. The boy gets to Cambridge, becomes a lawyer, shows he's got a brain, but chooses to think with his dick! A fifty-year-old man; it's obscene.'

'Don don't be crude! I'll not have you talk like that in this house,' said Pat.

'I'll tell you one thing, Pat. He's breaking up my family. I've had a loving daughter these fifteen years. Derek may be prepared to give her up, but I'm not. I don't want to lose her.'

'Derek will marry the mother. He said her name is Jane. We'll have a daughter-in-law *and* a grandchild,' said Pat, thinking this would help.

'That bloody fool may want to start a new family at the age of fifty. I'm nearly eighty. I don't want a new daughter-in-law. I want to keep the one I have.' Don got to his feet and walked out of the kitchen.

'Where are you off to, Don?' asked Pat anxiously.

'I'm going to call that son of yours.' Pat leapt after him, faster than she thought possible, and disengaged the telephone before Don had finished dialling.

'Just wait a minute, Don. You can't act on impulse in something as serious as this. There's nothing to stop you calling Derek later on. He isn't going anywhere. First, though, we need to talk it over.' Don hesitated. 'Come on back to the table and finish lunch. We'll talk there,' she urged. When they were seated, Pat said:

'Now just let me have my say and don't go choking on your food. I know you love Julia, Don. I do too. She really has been a daughter to us. She knows that we love her and you know my heart goes out to her for what she has been through with the cancer. It's the cancer that has wrecked their relationship.' Don was about to take issue with this thesis when Pat silenced him firmly. 'Now, don't interrupt me! I'm not saying it's Julia's fault. Derek wasn't strong enough to handle the cancer. He is the weak one. He's the one who has made a mistake. Now, try and set that aside for a moment because we're in a new situation. Derek is going to marry a woman who is pregnant with his child.'

Pat paused for effect. She wanted Don to understand exactly how she felt about things. 'You know I've never thought any less of Julia because she is barren. Still, just as she will have yearned for a child, I have yearned for a grandchild. I want to hold my son's baby. Everyone else around us became grandparents long ago. Their families have grown. Our friends have more people to love and cherish. Do you think that having to watch everyone else with grandchildren while having none of my own hasn't hurt me? In the early years, I even used to go down to the local school to see the children come out. I would imagine myself picking up my own grandchild, just as I used to collect little Derek. Now, out of tragedy, comes a chance to hold my grandchild. I want to be a grandmother. That means, I'm going to stay on the right side of Derek's new wife. As for Derek, he's ashamed of what he's done. However, when all is said and done, a child is on the way and it needs parents. There, I've said my piece, Don. Just think carefully before you lose your son and grandchild.'

'Then, we too are to betray Julia.'

'No. We can show her that she means a lot to us, that we love her. We'll visit her whenever we're in Cambridge and she will be welcome here, always. The question is: will she let us?'

'I don't doubt that for a minute.'

Jane and Jessica met outside Angel tube station, as they did every Thursday lunchtime. Jessica worked in-house at *Expedia*. She offered to get down to Old Street on alternate Thursdays, but Jane would have none of it. Where could we go in Shoreditch that's half decent, she would say, I wouldn't be able to stand the place were it not for the fact that business is booming. Jane and Jessica had been firm friends since Freshers Week at University. They both read Law, lodged together and partied together.

They were there for one another when relationships blossomed and when they faded. They had been maid-of-honour to one another when they married. Jessica's marriage was happy; she and her husband were thinking about having a baby now that they were settled in their jobs and Jessica was eligible for full maternity benefits. On the other hand, Jane's marriage had lasted fifteen months. She had left her ex-husband in the law firm where they had started as associates and joined Astons & Kentwell.

'Jane, you're got a smile a mile wide,' said Jessica as she embraced her friend.

'I have news. Come on, let's find somewhere nice for lunch. It's so good to get away from Old Street. It may only be one tube stop along, but Islington is a world away.' The two friends walked up to The Green and decided on *Bellanger*. They were just ahead of the lunchtime rush and didn't have to wait more than a few minutes for a table. They ordered.

'Come on, Jane. Don't keep me in suspense any longer,' said Jessica.

'Well, my love life is about to become less complicated. Derek has proposed marriage!' Jessica couldn't hide her surprise, which rather deflated Jane. 'Aren't you pleased for me, Jess?'

'Oh, Jane! I'm sorry. Of course, I'm happy for you. It's just that I thought you weren't serious about this relationship because he's much older than you... Oh, no! I've been insensitive again.'

'He's forty-eight, going on forty-nine. I'm thirty-five. Amal Alamuddin is about to marry a man sixteen years her senior.'

'Is your Derek a George Clooney?'

'He's attractive, Jess. He's fit and good-looking. He's got nice teeth and he's kept his hair. We're good in bed. And, he's senior partner.'

Jessica laughed. 'Almost as nice a package as George Clooney! So, how come he isn't married?'

'Actually, he was married. His wife has just agreed to a divorce.' Jane caught the slight wince in Jessica's features triggered by the thought of someone being hurt. 'But I'm not the cause; their marriage broke up for other reasons,' she added defensively. Just then, their food was brought. Jane took the opportunity to turn the conversation away from Derek. She was a little miffed that Jessica wouldn't just be happy for her. It was alright for Jessica. Everything always worked out just fine for her. However, Jane's small talk didn't have the desired effect.

'Jane, is there a rush to marry? This relationship is only five or six months old, isn't it?'

'Well, I have been trying to tell you the good news, Jessica. I'm pregnant with Derek's child.' Jessica was obviously shocked.

'Jane, please tell me this isn't an Infidelity-pregnancy-entrapment plot-line.'

'Hey! Hold on, Jess. I told you the breakup is nothing to do with me. Derek's wife had breast cancer...' Jessica gasped.

'I'm really sorry, Jane. I'm not feeling very well.' She pointed to the door to the ladies' loos. 'I'll just be a few minutes.' Jane was annoyed. She knew her friend inside out. She's moralising right now, thought Jane, like adultery is some sin. I mean, look at the law, there's no penalty for the unfaithful partner when it comes to splitting assets. No one is to blame. Stuff happens. Relationships form and break up. That's life. Left to Jessica, we'd be like *if your right eye cause you to stumble, pluck it out and throw it away from you.* Jessica would be the only one with two eyes. Honestly, if she weren't my best friend...

Jessica returned to the table just as their order came. She said that she was feeling better and turned the conversation to mutual friends, but intimacy was missing and soon afterwards they made their way back to their respective offices, neither feeling the situation had been handled well.

Jane had no difficulty renting out her apartment in Barnsbury. She moved into Selwyn Gardens two months after Julia had left it. Julia had taken every personal item from her bedroom, including her favourite framed photographs. Derek had packed away the many others from the other rooms. So, there was no trace of Julia that Jane could find. Derek saw her everywhere; in the furniture and soft furnishings, in the subtle lighting of the drawing room, in the stylish but pragmatic kitchen and, especially in the garden.

Not surprisingly, Jane loved the house. So did her mother, Amanda, to whom Jane bore a remarkable resemblance. Jane's father would scrutinise his daughter's features for some evidence of his contribution without success. Jane could have been cloned from her mother in Dolly-the-sheep fashion. Amanda had no intention of letting time diminish the likeness. She used a sizable part of her divorce settlement on plastic surgery. There were additional regular expenses: regular timely hairdresser appointments went into her diary before anything else, for instance. The investment returned significant dividend. Evenings at the theatre and opera, excellent dinners and stays in posh hotels cost her nothing except for some action in bed. If there was any difficulty in this, it was in continually having to ward off proposals of marriage from so many older men. Amanda had no intention of going beyond the wooing phase of a relationship, having not especially enjoyed the aftermath on the one occasion when she did.

Jane dispersed her personal effects around the house. Then, with Amanda, she set about organising the wedding. They made straightforward arrangements and kept the guest-list short: a civil wedding in Cambridge City Hall followed by a champagne reception and dinner at DoubleTree by Hilton. Restricting numbers helped them get the hotel. The offer to double the fee encouraged an authorised official in City Hall to give up his lunch break and insert their wedding ceremony into an otherwise full schedule. So, Jane and Derek were married when the bump was still a respectable size.

Jessica was one of the witnesses. The two friends had put the scene in *Bellanger* behind them. Jessica had called Jane as soon as she had returned to her desk. She had been judgmental and couldn't forgive herself for spoiling everything for her closest friend. Jane had been bursting to share the news. If criticism were to be directed at all, it ought to be aimed at the man. A true friend would warn Jane that a man who was unfaithful to his wife when she was most in need of support could not be trusted. However, Jessica bit her lip and kept to the apology that she felt sincerely.

Don and Pat drove down from Yorkshire before the wedding to meet Jane and Amanda. The best that can be said is that all parties survived the meeting. Real feelings remained unexpressed. Jane realised very quickly that her mother was rubbing Don the wrong way and she stayed beneath the radar. At the sight of the two elderly, frumpish northerners, Amanda began to speak as if she was at one of her former cocktail parties in Weybridge, which induced Don to turn up the Yorkshire. By the end of the first evening he was incomprehensible to everyone except Pat. The next morning, he was up early and disappeared until lunchtime. He left a note in the hall: *Gone to the Scott Polar Museum.* Derek suspected that his father had gone to see Julia, but he said nothing.

Pat did her best to mitigate the damage. She paid handsome compliments to Amanda and expressed genuine concern that all was well with Jane and the baby. Pat sensed that Jane was not a little anxious about the prospect of labour and motherhood. She assured Jane that she would be there for her when the time came if Jane should wish it. Pat also assured Amanda that she recognised Jane would prefer to have her own mother by her when the time came, and Pat wouldn't get in the way unless needed.

Derek and Jane honeymooned in Porto, which was a success considering the morning sickness and tiredness that had overcome Jane. They had taken an apartment through Air B'n'B. This gave them space and freedom. The hosts were keen to welcome then warmly. They made a daily delivery of fresh bread and croissants, and stocked the fridge with ham, cheese, eggs, butter, juices and coffee for a reasonable charge. As Jane slept in, Derek breakfasted alone. Then, he sat out on the balcony and worked. Reliable Wi-Fi had been a precondition.

Jane was ravenous when she surfaced around lunchtime. Derek was amazed to see her eat for two, given that she had been nauseous all morning. The apartment was in the Ribeira, just a short walk from the cafes and bars along the North bank of the Douro. This is where Jane and Derek relaxed after lunch and in the evening, usually with some sightseeing nearby in the late afternoon.

Jane did not make an effort to look her best at the time. She would emerge from the bedroom with uncombed hair, teeth not yet brushed and no makeup. Derek told himself that it would be unreasonable to expect otherwise given the fact that she was having a hard time of it. Anyway, Jane had youth on her side and the sight of breast, bum or thigh through a loose nightdress would set Derek's penile pulse racing. If Derek had to have sex, Jane preferred to get it over with before she showered. So it was that Derek did have sexual intercourse every day, which kept sexual tension from building up. However, the thought did occur to him that he was making love to Jane, whereas Julia had always made it seem as if she was making love to him.

At eighteen weeks, the ultrasound scan showed that Derek and Jane would be having a daughter. When the obstetrician announced the fact, the first uncontrollable thought that flashed through his mind was *Oh, bugger!* But he pushed the negative thought away and soon warmed to the idea that it might be rather nice to have a daughter. Neither Derek nor Jane believed that naming the child would be tempting fate. They came up with Rose. Once named, Derek felt connected to Rose.

While the morning sickness abated, the tiredness persisted. As the pregnancy progressed, Jane became a somewhat reluctant sexual partner, not that she had been enthusiastic on the honeymoon. She read a magazine article that claimed semen contains a chemical that stimulates uterine contractions, increasing the risk of miscarriage or premature labour. Derek didn't argue the point. He wasn't keen on the changes in Jane's body. The pendulous breasts with prominent nodules in the increasingly pigmented area around the nipple, the blue veins in the stretched skin of her abdomen, the puffy ankles; these changes were unattractive. Jane's pubic hair had overgrown because she couldn't easily trim it. In the other scale, pregnancy had thickened Jane's hair and made it lustrous, and the skin of her face was more strikingly pink and soft. The effect on Derek's libido was confusing. He was strongly attracted to Jane when she was fully clothed and freshly groomed, but desire would leave him during foreplay on the occasions when Jane acquiesced.

Derek and Jane intended that Rose's room would be next to their own. Jane and Amanda had fun designing it. Of course, the baby would be placed in a Moses basket in Derek and Jane's bedroom to start with. However, she would be moved out as soon as a regular sleep pattern could be established. The room across the landing became Amanda's room. She intended to move in a fortnight before the expected date of delivery and stay as long as she was needed. Pat and Don had a few personal things in one of the second-floor rooms. Selwyn Gardens could accommodate them all easily.

Rose was born at Bolingbroke's Maternity Hospital. Labour had been rather prolonged. So, Rose was extracted using a Ventouse suction technique, which gave her scalp a peculiar conical shape. Jane had to have quite a large episiotomy for this procedure and required several surgical stitches. Derek did not attend the delivery. He had given advance notice that this was something he simply could not do, no matter how much expected this was of a modern husband. Instead, Amanda stayed by her daughter's side throughout.

Derek was becoming concerned at the length of time it was taking. He was relieved when the midwife came with the news that all was well and the explanation for the delay. He called Pat; she was thrilled to hear she had become a grandmother. Then, when everything that could possibly distress him had been removed, he was shown into Jane's room. Amanda had done her best to tidy Jane up before Derek was let in. She washed Jane down with a flannel, brushed her hair and applied a hint of rouge to her cheeks and pink lipstick.

Derek entered to find Jane propped up with pillows and Rose asleep in her arms. He kissed Jane, told her she was marvellous, and thanked her for the gift of a daughter; then, he sat in an armchair to receive Rose. He did the things most men do: admire her tiny hands and feet, count her fingers and toes. Also, he fell in love with his daughter from that moment.

Jane couldn't fault the midwife and nurses and felt that the two of them were in safe and capable hands. So, she urged Amanda and Derek to go home and freshen up. Derek promised to return early next morning to see how Jane felt about coming home. Jane couldn't think that far ahead. She just needed a good long sleep but feeding got in the way. There was not a little stress until mother and child worked out a mutually agreeable breastfeeding method at some point in the night. After that, both slept better and longer.

From the hospital, Derek and Amanda drove to Waitrose in Trumpington. They bought ready-to-roast lamb shanks, oven-ready potatoes and root vegetables, and a bottle of wine. When they got to Selwyn Gardens, Amanda turned on the oven, stripped off the packaging and popped the food in to cook.

'It will be ready in forty minutes, Derek. I've set the timer. Now I'm off to shower,' she said. Derek laid the table for two, opened the bottle of wine, then went to his room to clean up. He was back downstairs first, just as the oven buzzed to signal the end of cooking time. He served the food, poured the wine, threw out the foil trays, and voilà: a delicious dinner with no effort at all and no mess. Bless you all - Waitrose, M&S, Gastropub, whatever, he thought.

'Ooh, I'm looking forward to dinner,' said Amanda, breezing into the kitchen. Derek turned around.

'You look terrific, Amanda,' he felt compelled to say, because she did look good. Amanda had washed her hair and blow-dried it freely. It was full, wavy and slightly damp, which added appeal. She was wearing a full-length skirt that fitted her hips before filling out. A lace top with thin shoulder straps left her arms bare. Obviously, she was not wearing a bra. Amanda walked up to Derek, kissed his cheek and said:

'Congratulations again on a lovely daughter. Let's drink to her.' They sat down opposite one another, clicked glasses and began the meal. Rose was the subject of conversation for a while with some discussion about whom she resembled more. 'I wouldn't be surprised if Rose ends up the spitting image of Jane,' said Amanda.

'The spitting image of you then, Amanda," said Derek, finishing off the last of the bottle.

'And would you like that, Derek? Do you find us attractive?'

'You are very attractive, both of you.'

'Then, I wonder if I may say something… You know, as one adult to another.'

'Do go on, Amanda. I'm intrigued.'

'I've noticed you have had a difficult time of it lately. A man needs attention. Understandably, pregnancy isn't a state that fills a woman with desire. Then there's the discomfort from all that stretching, cutting and stitching. It will be some time before Jane can take you comfortably. I know desire is a powerful urge in a man and I wouldn't want you to look for satisfaction elsewhere; not when I could help you. Just ask, won't you.' Amanda stood up, came to Derek's end of the table and bent to remove his plate. He caught her hand, pushed back his chair and rose to his feet. Amanda reached for him.

'I thought so. Let me help.' Derek opened his fly and let his engorged member loose. Amanda backed toward the kitchen island and pulled up her skirt. She had nothing on underneath. Derek all but charged into her, lifting her off her feet. He thrust into her, deeply, severally, and shouted out in pleasure and relief as he came. 'I guessed right, didn't I? You were at breaking point. I'm glad I got to you in time.' Amanda kissed Derek, savouring the red wine on his lips and tongue. 'I would quite like a slower ride on that pole of yours if you think you could get it up again in a little while. Shall we go to my bed?'

Derek took one week of paternity leave. It was as long as he could bear. He was exhausted at the end of it. Jane and Amanda were astonished at the extent to which he engaged with Rose. He would get up the minute he heard her cry and bring her to Jane for feeding. Then, he would take over and pat her little back gently with two fingers until he was rewarded with a loud burp. He changed Rose's nappy and bathed her. All the while, he talked to her and sang to her softly, close to her ear. If men bond biologically with their newborn children, this certainly seemed to happen to Derek. Rose's scalp swelling receded by the end of the week, which left her looking adorable.

Jane was more than happy to see Derek engage in this way. She thought fatherhood had effected a dramatic change in him. He might be tired from the disturbed nights, but he was calmer. She was especially grateful for the several short sleeps she could get between feeds at the breast and for the bottle feed that Derek administered at three in the morning. Amanda encouraged Derek not to keep Rose in his arms after she had been winded and cleaned up; far better to get her accustomed to sleeping in her cot, she advised. She helped Jane with repairing her body: the warm salt baths for her perineum, the nipple care, and the expression of milk for Rose's middle-of-the-night feeds.

Jane felt positively scruffy, especially when her mother was around. Amanda seemed to be taking particular care with her appearance. She wore perfume and makeup; getting it spot on for the time of day. She wore her hair down during the day and dressed it up in the evening, when she changed into a fresh outfit. To encourage you to do the same, as soon as you feel up to it, darling, she would say to Jane. Derek oscillated between feelings of *higher love*, as Eric Clapton put it, and the amatory pleasures provided by his concubine.

Don and Pat arrived at Selwyn Gardens a fortnight after the birth of Rose. Jane and Rose had settled into a workable routine by then. Amanda had made a tactical withdrawal to her London apartment the previous day. So, Pat slotted in nicely. Rather than stay in the second floor flat, she asked to move into the room that Amanda had occupied. She was prepared to take the night calls and had to be within earshot of Rose. Don remained upstairs. His nights were not disturbed. So, he took the first call of the mornings, between half past six and seven o'clock.

Pat handled Rose efficiently, effectively and lovingly. Sensibly, she made no attempt to wrest control. She bonded with Rose very easily. Jane appreciated Pat's help, which extended to managing the washing machine and dryer. Don put sandwiches together for lunch and made cups of tea on demand. Derek had arranged for domestic help to deal with cleaning of the house and with the pile of ironing. The Portuguese woman who took the job also prepared a dish for dinner each weekday. So, the logistical aspects of the household went well, and Derek returned to work happy in the knowledge that his parents were connecting with his new family. Pat and Don returned to York after a fortnight, content with the way things had gone.

Now that Derek was sleeping through the night, he felt vigorous. This vigour was manifest both in his work and in his assignations with Amanda, which took place on Wednesday evenings. Derek tried to get back to Cambridge at a reasonable time on other weekdays. He might not make bath time, but usually was home to catch Rose during one waking period before he went to sleep.

Jane's episiotomy wound healed a month after childbirth. Over the next fortnight, she tested for soreness by inserting one, two, then three lubricated fingers. At six weeks, there was no discomfort at all. In fact, the act excited her. Her libido returned too. Jane reckoned it was time to divert some attention to Derek. He had been so understanding, so undemanding, and she appreciated his sensitivity. She went to the hairdresser one Friday afternoon, for the first time in twelve weeks, and asked for the split ends to be trimmed away. The hairstylist had not been given the opportunity to be creative all morning and, reassuring Jane that her oval face could cope with a shorter style, suggested a completely new look. Jane was nervous at the thought of losing any length at all but agreed on a blunt, chin-length bob that came to the jawline, with a feathered fringe down to the eyebrows.

For a second time in his life, Derek stepped into the hall of his home to be accosted by a sexy woman whom he didn't immediately recognise. Long, short, blonde, brunette, it just didn't matter as long as the hair was expertly cut and styled. Then, there was that distinctive just-out-of-the-hairdresser smell as he nuzzled into her neck. Irresistible! The new style really did suit her, and Derek liked the fact that it muted Jane's close resemblance to Amanda significantly.

'You do like it, then' said Jane, pleased at the fact that Derek was aroused. 'I'm sorry to have taken so long, but I'm soft and smooth again down below, and ready for you.' Well, if she was ready, so was he; and in no time at all he was reminded of the wild woman who had come at him in his office that first time. Gone was the reluctant but acquiescing honeymooner. Yes, she could rock; with just as much energy as Amanda. He lay beside Jane, spent, and hoped nothing would disturb his little arrangement.

Jane stayed on maternity leave for nearly a year. She had made new acquaintances in Newnham through the Cambridge branch of the National Childbirth Trust and kept in touch with them after childbirth. She soon realised how much easier it would be to balance family, friendships and work if she could transfer to Cambridge after maternity leave. Astons obliged.

Rose did everything all babies do. She learnt to hold her head up, to sit unaided, to crawl, to climb down and up a step, to stand and walk, first with helping hands, then without, to say *mummy, daddy, Pa Don, nan and grandma.* These may be usual milestones, but the adults around Rose regarded them as singularly spectacular achievements worthy of applause, in which Rose promptly learned to participate. Derek found Rose's development even more dramatic; commuting meant that he played with Rosie and read to her only at weekends, which is when he would notice change, but at weekends he gave his daughter much time and attention. He loved her to bits.

Rose grew into a very pretty child. Big loose curls

covered her head, some dropping irritatingly across her face. Neither parent could bear to cut Rose's hair. So, Amanda did it when the time came for Rose to start nursery. Amanda stayed at Selwyn Gardens on alternate weekends. Pat and Don came down every month and would stay for four or five days. Don would disappear quietly to see Julia, but never told Derek how she was getting on. He reported to Pat on the drive home. Not that Pat seemed interested any more.

Toward the end of summer, just before Rose's third birthday, the main preoccupation in Selwyn Gardens concerned preparations for Rose's first day at school. She would love it once she settled in, though there was some anxiety about possible tantrums on the threshold at first. This wasn't a major concern because nursery had been a success and because Rose got on well with other children. She had a couple of little friends who were going to make the great leap forward with her. Jane and Amanda were talking up the fun and excitement of *big school* and Rose responded enthusiastically. One afternoon at this time, the Monkey Music class was cancelled unexpectedly. The teacher took a bend badly, slashed a car tyre, and had to sit it out until the RAC breakdown truck got out to her. Jane returned home early with a disappointed Rose to find her mother being jollyrogered by her husband in the drawing room.

This sort of behaviour really does seem to occur. Perusal of Agony Aunt columns reveals articles such as this:

> *Correspondent: My mother is an interesting, slim and attractive woman with fantastic dress sense. Recently, I found out that my 36-year-old husband (of 13 years) has been having sex with her. When he told me, I found that I was not upset at all, except by the fact that it didn't bother me. He's a good father to our children, a good provider, and he fulfils my emotional and sexual needs. I should be upset. I should feel betrayed. Actually, I don't. He will stop seeing my mother, if that's what I want. However, my mother and husband*

> *are happy in their affair. Since I feel neither anger nor jealousy, I'm inclined to let their relationship continue. Is this wrong? Am I being weird?*
>
> *Agony aunt: Congratulations! You've found what so many seek: True love, unconditional love. Spite, disgust, sadness, bitterness and revenge would be understandable reactions, but they are destructive emotions. You have adopted all that is best about the human condition: the ability to love deeply, spiritually and unconditionally, free from anger. This is as far from being wrong or weird as it is possible to be.*

Well, Jane may have found herself in the same situation as this Correspondent (and others?) but not having quite achieved a state of spiritual, unconditional true love with Derek over the three years of their marriage, her emotional response certainly included spite, disgust, bitterness and revenge. Jane filed for divorce and won a substantial settlement. When Jessica heard about the breakup of Jane's marriage, she was not surprised, though quite shocked to hear how it had come about. It was not an easy phone call. Jessica recoiled against Jane's acrimony and spleen. She tried to be sympathetic but found herself unable to give emotional support. She stopped calling and found excuses to cut Jane's calls short. The friendship died.

Derek was forced to sell Selwyn Gardens. He retained access to Rose, but Jane made this as difficult as she could. Neither Amanda nor Don and Pat were allowed to make contact. She thrashed Derek's reputation at Astons. Derek moved in with Amanda who made it clear this could only be temporary. What use to her was a man clearly on the way down and anyway there would be absolutely no chance of a reconciliation with her daughter as long as Derek was around. So, he ended up in an apartment in Barking with the small mercy that he could get into work on the Hammersmith & City line without changing trains.

When, on the weekends allotted to him, he journeyed

up to Cambridge to pick up Rose, he found her clinging to her mother, too scared to go with him. He could not bear to see her so distressed and let her be. He lost the one person whom he had truly loved. Don made it clear he never again wanted to see his imbecile son. He wouldn't stop saying *I knew it! I told you so!* For Pat, the pain of losing her granddaughter and her son was just too great and she became depressed. Her general health deteriorated, and she suffered a fatal stroke within the year.

Julia came to appreciate the care her solicitor had taken with her own divorce settlement. Much to her relief, the money was legally ring-fenced and secure from Jane's grasp. Whereas Julia had been unable to raise Pat's spirit, she was a great help to Don. It became clear that he would not manage without Pat. So, she found suitable sheltered accommodation for him in a new complex in Rowntree where she visited him regularly. When he died from a heart attack Julia missed him greatly, but she was in a different place entirely by then. She had moved on and with Don's death the Blacks became her past.

13. BENEFACTION (1982)

'Well, Conrad, as Sherlock Holmes would say: Once you eliminate the impossible, whatever remains, no matter how improbable, must be the truth... Except Carleton Gallagher couldn't see it!' Conrad met his boss' gaze with a mixture of incredulity and excitement.

'Are you saying it isn't a virus particle? Not nucleic acid at all? How's this possible?'

'*How?* is what we ask next. We have to work out how it is possible for a protein molecule to invade a nerve cell in the brain, how it comes to be replicated and how it spreads from nerve cell to nerve cell leaving devastation in its wake.' Stanley gestured to the reams of experimental results strewn over the bench and said: 'But these results are conclusive: the transmissible agent is a protein, not a virus or any other kind of microorganism. A protein is all that remains.'

Stanley first encountered a patient with Creutzfeldt-Jakob Disease in 1972 at the start of a residency in Neurology. He was deeply affected by the disease that could kill his patient in eight months by destroying her brain while her body remained unaffected by the process. There was no fever, no rise in the white blood cell count, no rise in blood immunoglobulin levels to indicate activation of the body's immune response. Only four years earlier, after Igor Klatzo reported the similarity between CJD and Kuru, CJD had been transmitted from humans to chimpanzees by inoculating the chimp's brain with a homogenate of brain tissue from a patient who had died from the disease. Stanley was taught that Kuru and

163

CJD were caused by an *unconventional slow virus.* He wasn't convinced, not even when he heard the news of Gallagher's Nobel Prize.

'The problem with our work is that it all takes so long and it's so expensive,' said Conrad. Every hypothesis we formulate requires an animal experiment to get an answer, but each experiment requires that sixty laboratory mice are inoculated with our Scrapie homogenate. It takes six months for the mice to develop Scrapie and a further twelve months for us to investigate the results from the mouse brains. So, we take almost two years to get an answer to one question and only then can we work out what the next question should be; and so on, using sixty mice at a time.'

'That's the practical problem, exactly!' said Stanley. Then he whipped a journal out of his briefcase, turned to a page, and handed it to Conrad. 'Here's the answer: the Syrian hamster!' Stanley gave Conrad a few minutes to scan the paper. 'Last year, Kimberlin and Walker transmitted Scrapie to the hamster. Just look at the incubation period: only seventy days! Then there's the number of animals required to yield the infectious fraction from the hamster brain: four animals! Only four! If we switch to the Syrian hamster our research will accelerate a hundredfold.'

'Bingo!' exclaimed Conrad, 'I think that works out at one twentieth of our current animal house costs. It could be a game-changer.'

'It is a game-changer' said Stanley, reflecting on the opportunity before them. 'So, here's what will go into the research application to the Medical Research Council. We'll switch to the Syrian hamster model, refine the Scrapie brain purification protocol, work out the amino acid sequence of the purified protein, and use optical spectroscopy to determine the conformation of the protein. We have a great chance of finding the *real* cause of Scrapie, Kuru and CJD.'

'This sounds like you'll be asking for a lot of money, Boss, and that's not including my salary. What are our chances of getting such a programme grant from

'Carleton Gallagher got the Nobel Prize for ⟨
cause was a new type of virus. We've got experin
that the cause is no virus at all but a protein, and we're offering the MRC an experimental route map that will take us to
the protein at a fraction of current costs. Come on, Conrad!
I think you could say your salary is guaranteed for another
five years.' Conrad took heart from Stanley's optimism. Living
from one five-year research grant to the next did not make for
a sense of security, but the body of work that Stanley had just
outlined would make the difference. If they were successful, he would have his name on a ground-breaking scientific
paper and a tenured academic post would surely follow.

Things did not improve for Stanley where his NHS colleagues were concerned. During weeks when it was his turn
to do the diagnostic work, several request forms from the
surgeons would come marked *For the attention of Dr Cryan*
and similar labels were stuck onto referrals for examination
of brains removed at autopsy by the General Pathology consultants. Stanley had been all but frozen out. He was hurt
and occasionally felt depressed. The experience was very
unpleasant. Yet, he was determined to be stoical. The silver lining was that Stanley and Conrad had more time to
write the programme grant application. It was ready in good
time. Geoff Minson, the Head of the University Department
of Pathology, himself a virologist, was fully supportive and
promised whatever laboratory space was necessary. Cambridge being a small place, Minson had heard all about the
goings-on at Bolingbroke's.

'Stanley don't let anything get in the way of your
research,' he said, after they had gone through the draft
grant application. 'The University will support you. If it gets
uncomfortable in our Bolingbroke division, I'll relocate you
here in Tennis Court Road, assuming this programme comes
through, which it can't fail to do.' However, fail it did. To Geoff
Minson's utter amazement, Stanley's incredulity and Conrad's desolation, the MRC made no award of research funds

to Stanley. Minson picked up the telephone and called Trevor Sparrow in Psychology, on the other side of the Downing site. Sparrow chaired the Neuroscience Board of the MRC. In answer to Minson's inquiry, Sparrow explained:

'Geoff, I'm as surprised as you are. Posner's proposal looked first class to me, but the referees cut his protein-only hypothesis to shreds. Given the competition, we couldn't make an award without endorsement from the referees.'

'Trevor, you'll have heard about the trouble at the Trust. Have Stanley's colleagues got to the referees?'

'We can't have this conversation,' Sparrow retorted sharply, 'the referees are not imbeciles. They produced reasoned argument. Now, you know as well as I that these things can be a matter of spin. I won't say more than that.'

'I understand, Trevor. Thank you.' Geoff Minson ended the call, leaned back in his chair and thought: What next, I wonder. I bet they'll do another assassination job on Stanley if he applies to the Wellcome. So, he called Terrence French.

'Master, good afternoon. It's Geoff Minson here.'

'Cut out the Master bit, Geoff. You're not a St Ursula man.'

'Seriously, Terry. Congratulations on your election. I think St Ursula's have made an inspired choice. I hope Lady French is well?'

'That she is, Geoff. Now, how may I help you?' Terrence French had only recently retired as Director of Transplant Surgery at Bolingbroke's Hospital. He knew the background. So, Minson got to the point. He explained the science in Stanley's grant proposal.

'Terry, this work could transform the field of neurodegenerative disease. It's not about CJD. Nor is it about the economics of the sheep farming industry. The implications are far wider. If Stanley could develop his ideas, the results could open up new lines of research for Alzheimer's disease,

Parkinson's disease and more. Without money he's stuck; we'll all be stuck.'

'And you're calling me because…?' interjected French.

'Because his only chance is a benefactor. Stanley is one of your Fellows. I've called to ask you to talk to your wealthiest alumni. The programme grant application requested a million pounds. Actually, we kept costs as low as possible to help the grant get through. All I can manage is fifty thousand from Departmental Funds, which will keep Stanley's post-doc in post for a year.'

'Geoff, in my view the NHS Trust has treated Stanley abysmally, and from what you say the MRC hasn't got it right either,' said French. 'Rest assured the College will do everything possible to help, but that kind of money is beyond us. Nevertheless, your benefactor idea is a good one. I'll explore it.'

Stanley felt pretty low. He had come to the end of the money from the Department's bridging fund. This fund was intended only to buy time between research grants from the major grant-awarding bodies. Immediately after the disappointment of his failed grant application to the Medical Research Council, he submitted an application to the Wellcome Trust. On Geoff Minson's advice, he did not list the same three scientists as referees whom he had nominated in the MRC application. However, the result was the same: a perfunctory dismissal of his main scientific hypothesis and, consequently, no award.

Conrad was applying for every Senior Research Associate post going. One couldn't blame him. Stanley had failed to secure his salary, which had been written into the grant proposal. This preyed upon Stanley's conscience. He felt responsible for the difficult position in which Conrad found himself. Conrad's wife had just started maternity leave. If things went as expected, Connie would deliver in a fortnight.

In retrospect, Stanley saw he ought not to have reassured Conrad that things would work out after the MRC application collapsed. He should have appreciated the extent to which malevolent former colleagues could wield influence.

With this on his mind, Stanley hoped that the Master's summons was not going to add to his worries. Terrence French had e-mailed him late on Saturday night, asking Stanley to meet him in the Master's Lodge on the following Thursday at eleven o'clock concerning a private matter. Stanley thought it odd that Terrence had fixed date and time. The usual form would be to ask when it might be convenient to meet. Nevertheless, he e-mailed back to say he could make it. The fact that he could make it irritated him further. Prior to the fallout from the Marshall inquest, Stanley's schedule had been jam-packed with NHS, research and teaching commitments. Having been frozen out of most clinical work and with no money to retain his research staff and to conduct experiments his availability or lack of it was no longer an issue. At eleven o'clock precisely, he rang the back doorbell to the Lodge. Terrence came to the door.

'Hello Stanley, do come in. You're one of only a few to be punctual always. We're in my study.' Stanley followed Terrence into the large and comfortable study. A couple was seated on one of two Chesterfield sofas. They rose for introductions and smiled at Stanley. They look familiar, he thought... Of course, it's Paul Marshall and his sister. They could almost be twins.

'Ah, perhaps you don't recognise these good people, Stanley" said Terrence. 'Let me present Katy Price and Paul Marshall, the daughter and son of the late Mr Charles Marshall.' Stanley extended a hand to both of them.

'I do remember you; from the Coroner's Court. I'm pleased to meet you, but also a little surprised that it should be here.'

'Do sit down,' said Terrence. Stanley sat on the opposite Chesterfield and French took an armchair between the two.

'Let me explain, Stanley. It appears that Mrs Price and Mr Marshall have been trying to find you for several weeks. Of course, they knew that you are a pathologist at Bolingbroke's Hospital, but they did not wish to come to the Hospital, nor to telephone and locate you through the Hospital switchboard. Some three weeks ago, I received a letter from them, in which they asked whether the College could arrange a meeting. They had looked you up on the internet and saw that you hold a Fellowship here. Naturally, I asked for more information. Forgive me for not filling you in, but I think you will understand.' The Master gestured to Paul and Katy: 'Would one of you like to take it from here?'

'Doctor Posner,' said Katy, 'my brother and I admire you for your expertise, your professional integrity and your courage. Your evidence at the inquest against the Trust and several of your colleagues was brave indeed.' Stanley interrupted.

'Mrs Price, I have to correct you. My evidence was not intended to be for or against anyone. The coroner set me the task of establishing the chain of pathological events that led to the death of your father and I simply reported the facts.'

'Yes, Doctor; and my brother and I have learned that doing so has come at a great personal cost,' said Katy. 'When Paul contacted the Master, it was to ask if it would be appropriate for us to visit you here to thank you personally. Now, having heard about the trials and tribulations that you face we wish to do more than just say thank you.' Paul Marshall took over.

'Doctor Posner, thank you for not shying away from the facts of the case, for speaking the truth publicly when, as we could see quite plainly in Court, you realised the significance of your evidence. In an instant, you lifted a heavy weight off our shoulders. Katy and I no longer felt alone. Here was an expert saying, as we had been trying to say for so long, that serious mistakes had been made. When Katy and I complained, the Trust had been defensive and patronising, and eventually had become aggressive.'

'That doesn't surprise me.'

'The Trust changed its tune after the inquest,' said Katy. 'Their lawyers contacted ours the very next day to settle out of Court. We can't give you details because the Trust insisted on a non-disclosure agreement. Paul and I thought this ridiculous, given the publicity on the case in the papers and the relentless exposure by the press of bad practice in end-of-life care in hospitals across the Country. Nevertheless, my brother and I agreed, but it cost the Trust dearly.'

'Please don't think of us as being interested in the money, Doctor Posner,' said Paul. 'We took it because making the Trust pay a large sum in compensation is the only way to improve care in the system. Also, because we want to do some good with it. Understand, please, that we don't want it for ourselves.'

'Really, I am pleased to hear you are able to move on,' said Stanley. 'The circumstances of your father's death shocked you, I know. I'm sorry any of it happened and very much wish you had your father with you still.' Stanley assumed that what these people had come to say had been said and moved to get to his feet.

'Stanley, wait a moment,' said Terrence, 'hear these good people out.' Stanley sat back again, somewhat perplexed at what might come next.

'Doctor Posner, I should come to the point,' said Paul. 'My sister and I have learnt that your research funding has dried up; very likely because you spoke the truth at the inquest. We wish to provide you with the funds necessary for you to complete your research. How much do you need?'

'Goodness me! Are you serious? Oh, forgive me, I didn't mean that. Of course, you are,' said Stanley clumsily. Terrence stepped in.

'If I may, Doctor Posner has applied for a programme grant of one million pounds. These awards are usually made for a five-year period. They cover the salary of one or two research associates, the cost of laboratory animals, instruments and consumables necessary to conduct the experiments, and the University's costs. The figures are checked and vetted by the University's Research Division. I have no hesitation in recommending Doctor Posner's work to you for support. He is on the verge of a breakthrough in medical science. If you are able to provide the funding that Doctor Posner has been denied so unfairly, you can be assured your generosity will be rewarded by a most significant contribution to knowledge with implications for Alzheimer's disease and similar neurodegenerative diseases.' Then, Katy rose from her seat, crossed the room and sat next to Stanley.

'Doctor, we want to hear more, of course, but we have been told enough by the Master and by Professor Minson to make this offer. Paul and I wish to give St Ursula's College two million pounds. The College will name the gift after our late father. One million pounds is for you, through a *Charles Marshall Senior Research Fellowship*. The only condition is that you acknowledge *the Charles Marshall Fellowship* when you publish your results. We have been assured that the breakthrough that may come from this support will ensure that no grant awarding body will deny you research funding in the future. Should it prove necessary, however, the College may allocate further support from the second million. If it is not needed, the remaining money will become the *Charles Marshall Access Fund*, which will help bright students from underprivileged backgrounds come to St Ursula's. Please say you'll help us remember our father in this way.'

'Paul, Katy, if I may, I'm lost for words. Your generosity is overwhelming. I accept your gift with much gratitude, and I shall do everything in my power to justify your confidence in me and my work. The stakes are high. Bless you and thank you.' The Master stood up. He patted Stanley on the back and said:

'Try to do it with one million, Stanley, won't you. We want to keep Charles Marshall's memory alive in the College for centuries to come. Now, take these wonderful people to lunch and tell them more about your work.' Stanley took the Master's hand, clasped it tightly and mouthed *Thank You.* Then he led Katy and Paul out and across Main Court to Hall for lunch. They entered a large, panelled dining hall with a raised floor at the far end, where two long tables were set for several places beneath two large three-quarter-length portraits.

'That's the founder, Robert Poldark,' said Stanley, 'and this is Mary Rampton, our principal benefactor after the founder.' They stepped up onto the high end. 'The longer table is for Fellows. Many of us take the opportunity at lunch to connect about students or College business. When one of us brings in guests, this second table is used. So, we'll take this end. Now, let me show you how it works.' Stanley indicated the soup tureen, the counters of hot and cold food, the vegetarian option and the cold cabinet on the side with desserts. 'We help ourselves and then, when finished, we take our plates over to that table there.' They filled plates with soup and were the first to sit on the guests' table. Stanley saw the President come in. Instead of heading for the Fellows' table, he came over to them.

'Hello Mrs Price; hello Mr Marshall. How nice to see you again! May I join you?'

'Peter! You know these good people? Excellent! Yes, please join us.' Then the Law Fellow came into Hall, spotted Stanley and came over too.

'Fleur, do you know Katy and Paul too?' asked Stanley, rather perplexed. Peter and Fleur sat down, grinning.

'Stanley, ever since Katy and Paul contacted the Master and told him they wanted to help, we have been working with them as fast as we could to draft the legal agreements and a new ordinance. It remained for them to meet you, and for you to agree,' the President said with a smile. He gave Stanley a pat on the back. 'Presumably, as you're here together, we have lift off! Fleur will bring the new ordinance to the meeting of the Governing Body this Friday. Once it's voted through, the Senior Bursar will take over.' After weeks on the receiving end of animosity, Stanley felt deeply moved, as much by the enthusiastic support from the College as by the overwhelming generosity of the donors. He turned to Katy.

'Katy, would you tell us about your father? We would be honoured to know something about the man whom you are commemorating with your gift.' Katy flushed with emotion.

'Thank you, Stanley. Yes, please think of him. I won't tell you what he meant to us as a father and how dear he was to us. That's not necessary, I'm sure; but I would like you to know that he was a very successful and much-loved headmaster. I believe the secret behind his success was his love of the classroom, its fun and excitement. He knew what ingredients make up the cocktail of great teaching and successful learning.' Paul came in.

'Just so, Katy. To make sure classrooms sparkled, Dad created a culture of excellence across the whole school. While he developed secure systems and values, he retained the flexibility to seize innovation. It won't surprise you to hear that he was single-minded in rooting out mediocrity, but he would always encourage his staff, dwelling on the positive, and applauding success.'

'In fact,' said Katy, 'his approach with students had similarities to the approach with staff. His mindset was that it's never too late. Not everything can be achieved at the same time, but staff and students can shift gear for a sustained period, from time to time. It was about creating a sense of urgency at the right time. What was needed was a collective ambition to improve.'

'Clearly, Charles Marshall was an impressive man; a successful leader, I should say,' said Stanley, 'but you have chosen to commemorate him through an access scheme. Why is that, Katy?'

'That's because Dad believed that every student with intellectual talent should be encouraged to consider an application to Oxford or Cambridge. He worked tirelessly to support students with potential. He wanted a partnership in which the Schools would reach up and the Colleges would reach down. So, we're asking that our donation be used to fund an Access Officer, based at St Ursula's, but linking with one or two other Colleges, to develop a programme of outreach to schools in the Anglian region.' Peter came in here.

'Katy, I assure you that the Admission Tutors and Fellows in every subject look forward to supporting this initiative. Everyone wants the most deserving students from the point of view of intellectual potential. The College will use your donation to seed a development campaign aimed at increasing the number of scholarships we can offer to students who are financially underprivileged.'

'That's terrific news, President,' said Paul. Then, Katy turned to Stanley

'Your turn now, Stanley. Would you tell us something of the work you'll be doing?'

'Oh no!' exclaimed Fleur in mock horror, 'not while we're eating! He'll mention the cannibals! *Please*, do it over coffee when we've gone.'

After lunch, Stanley took Katy and Paul up to the Senior Common Room for coffee. Fellows were seated in groups of three or four, drinking coffee, one or another peeping over and around newspapers to engage momentarily in the conversation. The three of them went to the far end of the room, where a sofa and armchair were positioned in a large bay window. When they were settled, Stanley began.

'Universities are beginning to establish professorships in the public understanding of science because most scientists, the people that actually do the science, are incapable of explaining their work in straightforward terms. I'm afraid I fall into this category. When this happens with me, please challenge me to explain more simply and clearly.'

'Don't worry, we will,' said Katy.

'Then, here's the problem: what is the cause of a group

of diseases in which the brain rots away to the point where, down the microscope, it seems full of small holes? Pathologists have called the appearance spongy change. Believe it or not, Spanish shepherds observed the first of these diseases in Merino sheep sometime in the 18th century. The sheep behave oddly, become unsteady on their legs, and appear to itch so intensely that they rub against fences, scraping off their valuable coats. Because of this, the disease was named Scrapie. It is still prevalent today. Now, the second disease is named CJD for short after two German scientists, Creutzfeldt and Jakob, who described a fatal paralysis in humans in the 1920s. Remarkably, the same spongy brain damage was found. It's a rare disease in man but reports of it affecting several generations of a family followed, which suggested a third version of the disease; this time clearly inherited.'

'Is the sheep disease inherited, Stanley?' asked Paul.

'Probably not. The disease affects sheep born from affected parents, but sheep in the flock without affected parents are also affected if the affected sheep are not isolated. So, the conclusion is that some germ carries the disease from affected ewes to their lambs and also to other sheep. In other words, Scrapie can be transmitted through some form of contact.'

'Is it spread through coughs and sneezes?' asked Katy.

'That's a good question, Katy. Most infectious diseases are transmitted through coughs and sneezes, by bloodsucking insects or by poor food hygiene, which is to say the microbes pass out in a patient's stool and then contaminate food. However, in the case of Scrapie, it seems the disease is passed on when sheep lick or eat the placenta from an affected ewe after she has delivered. Of course, the ewe may not have shown signs of disease at the time that she gives birth. This brings me to the fourth spongy brain disease: Kuru. This was recognised some twenty-five years ago. It affected indigenous people in a remote part of Papua New Guinea.'

'This must be where the cannibals come in?' said Katy

with a shiver.

'Yes, it is,' said Stanley. Not wishing to upset Paul and Katy with gruesome detail, he changed the subject. 'Perhaps I had better leave the detail to your imagination. Look, I'm obliged to say that my work has to involve animal experiments too. You may not be comfortable with this unless you understand how necessary they are and what is at stake. May I go on?'

'Yes, of course,' said Katy

'I'll be using laboratory mice. The first important experiment used primates – chimpanzees. Samples from the spongy brains from sheep affected with Scrapie, from a patient with the spontaneous form of CJD, from people dying from the inherited familial form of CJD, and from natives dying from Kuru, were injected into the brains of live healthy chimpanzees. Although the time from injection to the onset of symptoms was months or years, all the chimps became ill and died with spongy brain damage.'

'So, coming back to the cause,' suggested Paul, 'whatever it is, whether it's passed between animals by eating diseased tissue or passed down from one generation to the other in genes, the cause is in the brain, yes? Presumably the germ spreads round it until the entire brain becomes reduced to a sponge.'

'That's almost it,' said Stanley. 'I have found the cause. It's a protein, not a germ at all. Now, that might not strike you as remarkable, but crucially it is *only* protein. I have purified the spongy brain tissue from diseased animals and humans to such an extent that only one protein is left in the material. There is no nucleic acid at all, neither DNA nor RNA. I have injected the pure protein, only one molecule of it in fact, into the brain of a healthy mouse and the mouse has developed the spongy damage throughout its brain. So, a single molecule of the disease-causing protein, which I've christened *prion,* can spread around a normal brain and damage it inexorably.'

'And do you know what this protein is, what it does,

how more of it is made once it gets into a brain?' asked Paul.

'Katy, Paul, those are the great questions that your research fellowship will help me answer. My research associate and I are finalising experiments that will identify the linear sequence of amino acids that make up the prion. Throughout known life, there are twenty-two amino acids that form the building blocks of proteins. By snipping off one amino acid at a time from one end of the protein and identifying each one in turn, we can get to the primary structure. This sequence will give us a clue to the manner in which this chain of amino acids is folded on itself.'

'How does that help?' asked Paul.

'The folded structure of a protein gives a clue to function. Now, in the case of this disease-causing protein, it isn't a helpful, life-sustaining function. On the contrary, it causes terrible brain damage. However, here is where the inherited CJD comes in. The disease-causing prion gene is being passed from one generation to the next. The information for all the proteins in the body is held in genes, which are composed of DNA. In the CJD families, the DNA code for this protein has gone wrong leading to the substitution of just one amino acid for another. This may be sufficient to misfold the protein, preventing it from carrying out its normal function, endowing it with an abnormal function, or causing it to interact with other normal proteins to cause harm.'

'Can you look for the critical gene?' asked Katy.

'That is an essential step, Katy. Instead of going from protein sequence to protein conformation, we'll go the other way, from amino acid sequence to gene. You see, once we have the amino acid sequence of the disease-causing protein, we can predict the RNA template which the cell's protein-making ribosome reads to determine which amino acid should be placed next on the growing protein chain. From the RNA, we can produce the DNA sequence, because the DNA and RNA are complementary. When we know the DNA sequence for the gene that makes the disease-causing protein, we can scan DNA on the chromosomes for a match. We'll identify the gene in one of the persons who had inherited CJD and then, crucially, in normal animals or people.'

'And, if you find a gene for the protein in normal people, what then?' asked Katy, more than a little perplexed now.

'If there is an equivalent gene in normal animals and people, we shall determine if it is switched on or off normally. Then, we'll ask: Does a non-harmful version of our Scrapie-cum-CJD protein exist? How is it folded? What is its function? Does the brain damage in Scrapie and CJD arise because the normal protein is lost or silenced, or does it arise directly from positive effects caused by the abnormal protein?'

'How do you answer these questions, Stanley? Can you do it in a lifetime? Advances seem to come so slowly. You said Scrapie had been known about since the eighteenth century, but you are the first person to have isolated the protein that causes it' said Paul.

'Genetics is advancing at an extraordinary pace. Once we have found the *human* gene for the Scrapie protein, we shall identify the equivalent gene in *mice*. Then we can knock out the gene and create mice that do not have any normal protein at all. Will they remain healthy or develop scrapie? If they remain healthy, we can inject the Scrapie protein into their brain. Will the Scrapie protein cause disease in the absence of the normal form of the protein? When we identify the abnormal change in the gene in the families with inherited CJD, we could insert the abnormal gene into a mouse embryo instead of the normal gene. Will it then develop the same CJD brain changes?' Stanley checked himself. He had lost them. 'I'm sorry. I've gone on for too long, I think, and tired you. I wish I had the gift of putting things so much more simply. I just hope you managed to follow some of it.'

Katy reassured him: 'I haven't followed all of it, Stanley; but we've both been listening. What one hasn't quite understood, the other might have grasped. I assure you, though, that you've given us a sense of excitement of your work and an appreciation of the challenges you face. But there is one more thing. Back in the Master's study you said the stakes are high. What did you mean?' Stanley hesitated. The enthusiasm that had been evident throughout his account of the research questions that faced him, and which Katy and Paul were making possible, was replaced by a cautious, almost sombre tone.

'Paul, Katy, something is amiss. From my contacts in the veterinary field, I have heard that two dairy cows have become ill. The cows have become agitated, unsteady and seem to have uncontrollable itching.'

'Oh no!' exclaimed Katy, 'surely not Scrapie in cows. Cows wouldn't lick or eat the placentas of sheep, would they?'

'They would not, Katy. The problem has arisen from commercial pressures to increase food production. In an effort to increase productivity, whether for the dairy or beef market, farmers feed their cows protein supplements. In this country, the protein supplement is called bonemeal and it's made from ground-up animal carcasses. If the cows' brains end up showing spongy damage, the most likely explanation will be that Scrapie brain tissue from affected sheep has been incorporated into bonemeal. We can't predict how many cows could become infected.'

'So there could be any number of cows, already infected with the Scrapie protein through their feed, who don't yet show signs of the disease,' proposed Katy.

'Yes.'

'Meanwhile, we've been eating them!' Katy was aghast. 'Has it been passed from cows to people?'

'That's where the cannibal story gives information,' said Stanley wryly. 'The average time from the ritual cannibalistic feast to the onset of the disease was ten years. It may take that long before a human case emerges.'

'What are you saying, Stanley?' Katy asked.

179

I'm telling you that your gift is not only generous, but timely. It's essential that we find out everything about the infectious protein as soon as possible. The discoveries we make may place us in a position to develop a vaccine or a cure for the disease; and in a few years' time we may have a great need for them. This is what your gift could achieve.' Katy and Paul were dumbfounded.

'I must ask,' said Katy, looking directly at Stanley, 'I have two children.'

'Don't eat processed meat,' said Stanley, 'no sausages, no burgers, no offal. I think good quality steak should be fine. In the Kuru experiments, feeding the chimps muscle didn't transmit the disease.'

'From this moment, I'm a vegetarian,' said Katy, 'and so is my family.'

Katy and Paul thanked Stanley. Stanley made it clear that it was he who would be forever in their debt. After showing them out, the first thought to enter Stanley's mind was to tell Conrad Conti the good news. His second thought was: how peculiar that this should be my first thought! Stanley had enough insight to know his first thoughts were always about himself. Nothing so crude as self-gratification; rather, about how and when he was going to get on with his scientific research and how could he shortcut his other obligations to get to it. Francesca Cryer, Conrad Conti, Javed Iyer and many others were means to this elevated end. If he had to make an early start, work late, unburden him of routine work, he expected them to oblige, to be there, to have prepared everything, to follow-up on his directives without fail. That his demands might cause them inconvenience or worse wouldn't have entered his head.

It occurred to Stanley too that he had no one who could help him extract the potential for joyful celebration from this morning's remarkable rescue. There was no one who loved him; because there was no one he loved. The words of welcome to Freshers from the College's Senior Tutor came to mind: that there are three important things new members should remember; the first is to be kind, the second is to be kind and the third is to be kind. I have not been kind, he told himself. He resolved to change and made the call to Conrad.

14. STRIVING AND DOING

For suffering and enduring there is no remedy but striving and doing.

Thomas Carlyle

J ulia enjoyed every moment of the Fine Art degree course: every lecture, every tutorial, every set-piece of creative work, every essay that she was required to write, every trip to art galleries and museums. She had an aptitude and talent for the subject, and she excelled. She enjoyed campus life too. Her fellow undergraduates, all in their late teens or early twenties, cheered her up no end. Julia did not tell them about her personal circumstances. Her classmates assumed she had a husband, perhaps a family, which prevented her socialising in the evenings and at weekends. In fact, Julia had no wish to burden her young carefree classmates with the unpleasantness life can throw at one when the business at hand was an appreciation of beauty.

Fiona and Matt, Don and Pat, and Sylvia Ellison attended the ceremony at which the first-class degree was conferred on Julia, which was her proudest moment ever. They couldn't help but admire her achievement and convened at York Terrace to celebrate it with champagne brought by the Jefferies. Sylvia, Don and Pat had done the shopping and cooking, and served up the celebratory dinner. Soon after this happy occasion, the tragicomedy of Selwyn Gardens unfolded: Pat and Don never returned to Cambridge.

Julia's preferred medium was acrylic paint and she

quickly became known in local Art circles. Through an exhibition at St. Barnabas Church Hall, Julia discovered *Cambridge Open Studios* and saw that one of her former lecturers was a member. He sponsored her application for membership, which went through at the first time of asking, on the basis of work that she submitted for the purpose. She found herself in a community of some five hundred artists, sculptors, and artisans who open their studios to the public over the four weekends in July. Julia was ready to exhibit the second summer after joining the group, when she sold several paintings.

Modest commercial success was gratifying, but it was never the point. When Julia painted, she set aside the narrative. The appearance of the finished canvas, after the paint dried, was not essential to her. Naturally, she was pleased if it was well regarded, but she painted to experience the emotion evoked the moment fluid paint touched the canvas and metamorphosed. Whether she captured the sparkle of light on the river in paint or, for that matter, played Chopin the act was at once creative and cathartic. Julia had heard of music and art as therapy. Indeed, some of her fellow students at Anglia hoped the qualification might give them the opportunity to have just such a career in the NHS or in Education's Special Needs Sector.

These last three years, Julia had used music in a similar way. She had kept in regular touch with two women with whom she had shared the chemotherapy suite. The three of them met once a month at York Terrace. They talked about their lives after surgery and chemotherapy, about their fears of recurrence, about the effect cancer had had on their families. Then they gathered around the piano and Julia played for them, intimately; sometimes a soothing piece, other times a playful scherzo to cheer everyone up. One could listen to music by way of therapy but playing music for this purpose was not widely accessible. On the other hand, Julia believed that self-expression through art did not have a similar requirement for at least a moderate degree of technical skill. The practical side of the degree course had shown her how, in a few steps, one could acquire sufficient basic technical competence to derive personal benefit.

Julia's own experience taught her that cancer sufferers would feel much better if they could quite deliberately cease being passive patients and actively engage with life instead. A person with cancer was alive, and so must do something, anything; must engage and enjoy, as well as endure. Julia began to wonder if the hospital might allow her to support cancer sufferers by volunteering to take them for classes in drawing and painting, and also to make music for them; perhaps with them.

These ideas led Julia to ask herself where such activities could take place. It would have to be at the hospital, but she could not recall any available space in the Oncology Department. If she were to pitch for space in which to place a piano and to set up an art class, couldn't more be done with such a space? The more one could reduce anxiety, the better one would feel, which would enable one to cope better with pain and be less distressed by side-effects of medical treatment.

Since a great deal of anxiety came from not knowing what to expect, from not knowing enough to make informed choices between alternative and complementary treatments, from not having the opportunity to talk to people who have experienced cancer surgery and chemotherapy and come through it emotionally intact, Julia came to the conclusion that cancer sufferers needed a dedicated space for themselves: a Caring Centre, at which people could receive psychological and emotional support, learn stress-reducing strategies, meet other people in similar circumstances in a relaxed environment, and obtain information so as to become knowledgeable participants in their own medical treatment. Such a Centre would significantly improve the cancer journey. What cancer sufferers needed was a welcoming place near the hospital, with an office, a library and meeting rooms. Julia decided to sound out Fiona.

On entering Bolingbroke's Hospital, Julia immediately felt a mixture of conflicting emotions. It took only a few steps into the building, away from daylight and fresh air, to remind her acutely of the trauma of mutilating surgery, of debilitating chemotherapy and of the consequent destruction of her marriage. However, these emotions were counterbalanced. Julia was on her way to a conference with Professor Crowther, who was Director of the Oncology Service and Fiona's Chief, with Mary Bowman, Chair of the Trust, and with Keith Night, Director of Operations.

Fiona had discussed Julia's ideas with Professor Crowther; he was keen to hear more at first hand. Cancer services were subject to Department of Health scrutiny at the time. So much so that targets for screening programmes, for shorter referral times from GP to consultant, for patient satisfaction with hospital care, and for improved outcomes had been established. The Trust was under some pressure to consider new initiatives; now here was one from a former patient who had been sending in significant cash donations.

Everyone was punctual, arriving in the boardroom just in time for the ten o'clock start. Mary Bowman was in the chair. She was good looking, wore her hair in a classic bob and dressed expensively in a blue, boardroom-style, skirt-suit. She introduced herself to Julia and then invited the others to do the same.

'I think you know Dr Jefferies, Ms Ellison.'

'If it isn't inappropriate to do so, please call me Julia.'

'How right you are. I'm so used to one formal meeting after another that I've forgotten that this isn't one of them. I'm surprised I haven't asked for apologies for absence. Julia, we are delighted to meet you. Call me Mary. Now that we're going to dispense with formality, why don't you take the lead and take us through your idea?' Fiona had warned Julia that Bowman did not do small talk, not at a business meeting anyway. So Julia had rehearsed her introduction.

'Thank you, Mary. Well, I have been married to a lawyer

and that has made me aware that, with busy people, it's best to get right to the point. I believe there is a local need for a Cancer Caring Centre to help in three ways. Firstly, by providing information. At such a centre, people would be helped to find out what they want to know about their illness and their treatment. They would be advised about ways of minimising side-effects, should they arise. They could find out practical information about benefits. The centre would have a lending library, videos, access to the internet, and regular courses to join. Secondly, the Centre would offer a range of well-researched activities to help people learn to relax. Individual relaxation sessions could be booked, or one could join a group for yoga, tai chi or meditation. Music therapy and art therapy would be available too. The third aim would be provision of psychological support, both individually and also in weekly support groups, which would be led by a clinical psychologist. It is all too common for people with cancer to feel vulnerable and painfully alone. Meeting other people in the same predicament helps those who are feeling isolated to see that they have hopes and fears and experiences in common.'

'You have put that very clearly and very well,' said Mary Bowman, 'but tell me more about your own experience when you joined the cancer care pathway at this hospital.'

Julia considered this request. 'I think Michael Lerner captures the experience well in his book *Choices in Healing*. He likens a cancer diagnosis to a parachute jump behind enemy lines without a map. There you are, the future patient, quietly progressing with other passengers towards a distant destination when a large hole opens suddenly and inexplicably in the floor next to you. People in white coats appear, help you into a parachute and – no time to think – out you go. Aaaiiiieeeee! If you're lucky the parachute opens. You descend. You hit the ground. You pull yourself upright. You are surrounded by a thick fog through which a crowd of indistinct figures call and gesture *Here! This way!* But where is the enemy? Who is the enemy? What is it planning? And which way is home? There's no road. You've no compass, no map. You've had no training. The white coats are up above, in the plane, strapping others into their parachutes. Occasionally they wave but, even if you ask them, they don't know the answers. They are focusing on the parachutes, not on holding your hand until you find your way home. It is true that recently some of the parachute-makers have been asking new questions, which are revolutionising the process: monoclonal antibodies, oncogenes, vaccines, gene editing – all this research is leading to cures for a lucky few, and longer remissions for others; but can you promise me the magic parachute in a year? In two? In five? Meantime, I am down here in the war zone, lost.'

'That's a powerful metaphor. Doctors and nurses may overestimate the effectiveness of their explanations and reassurances. What about your experience of the hospital environment?' asked Mary Bowman.

'I could start at the beginning, I guess: the waiting room. Waiting areas in hospital can finish you off! I'm afraid hospitals are not particularly patient-friendly. Illness shrinks one's confidence and arriving for the first time at a huge hospital is often a time of unnecessary anxiety. Simply finding your way around is exhausting and the circumstances in which you have to wait matter very much. Overhead neon lighting, interior spaces with no views out and miserable seating against the walls or in back-to-back rows all contribute to extreme mental and physical enervation. Patients who arrive relatively hopeful soon start to wilt.

'In fact, waiting could be used positively. Sitting in a pleasant, thoughtfully lit, room with a view out to trees, birds and sky, and with chairs and sofas arranged in various groupings could be an opportunity for patients to relax and talk, away from home cares. An old-fashioned ladies' room – not a partitioned toilet in a row – with its own hand basin and a proper door in a door frame, would give privacy for crying, water for washing one's face, and a mirror for getting ready to deal with the world outside again. There could be a tea and coffee machine, and a small cancer library for those who want to learn more about their disease.

'More ambitiously there could be a TV with a small stock of cancer-informing tapes and a video laughter library. Norman Cousins' book *Anatomy of an Illness* makes a good case for laughter not only as escape but as a therapy to relax the patient physically, leading to less pain and better sleep. It seems to me that most hospital environments say to the patient, in effect: *How you feel is unimportant. Fit in with us, not us with you.* With very little effort and money this could be changed to something like: *Welcome! And don't worry. We are here to reassure you, and your treatment will be good and helpful to you.* Why shouldn't the patient look forward to a day at the hospital?'

'Yet more valuable insights," said Mary Bowman. She checked her notes: 'Julia, the first point in your introduction was *Information*. Would you like to enlarge on that?'

'Information eases fear, as I'm sure you'll appreciate. Few patients hear anything much the doctor says after the word *cancer*. Nor do the family or friends who have come with them for support. The next doctor's appointment may be a week or more away and meanwhile ignorance breeds fear. Information is what most cancer patients cry out for – at many different levels. A guide to some questions you might want to ask your doctor could liberate those who are too timid, too conscious of taking the doctor's time or too fearful of the answers they might get. A guide would indicate an openness on the physician's part to let the patient participate actively in their own treatment. New patients could be given an information pack with a hospital plan, the names of the doctors and specialist nurses, the telephone numbers and a friendly introduction to Macmillan Cancer Link and other support organisations. This would help a lot. So would the addition of a simple sheet, with space to write the answers and a pencil, called *Questions you may like to ask your doctor* – not just for the information itself, but because the act of a nurse or carer giving me this would have indicated a support system out there, ready to help. Feeling alone numbs the mind and lets in despair.'

Professor Crowther shifted in his chair; perhaps Julia's account had made him feel a little uncomfortable. 'Julia, did you use relaxation techniques? How did they help you?'

'Yoga and guided relaxation have helped me, Professor, though they were not available during my treatment. I have also spent ten days at a retreat learning Vipassana meditation, a technique that, by passing the mind continuously down and up the body to observe dispassionately all its sensations *as they are, not as you would like them to be*, can bring one into a remarkably positive and relaxed state. I find it greatly helps my confidence; when hit by fear or despondency, I have something to fall back on. However, I would encourage general physical fitness too. I've learnt that patients who eat healthily and keep active feel fewer symptoms and less pain, even in the final stages of their disease.'

Crowther took Julia in another direction. 'Tell me how you see the Caring Centre link up with the Hospital; with the Oncology service in particular.'

'I think the Cancer Caring Centre should be fully independent, financially and administratively, from the hospital. Nevertheless, it should have the closest possible links with it. The hospital environment is not conducive to a sense of well-being. In hospitals we are patients, and hospitals depend on us behaving like patients; otherwise, the complex systems cannot operate efficiently. Our Centre should not be just another hospital department. It has to be small and separate enough for the people who use it to identify it as their own place'

'I see,' said Crowther, 'and where do the doctors come in?'

'Oh, I regard it as absolutely crucial to the confidence of anybody using the centre that they should do so knowing they are not going behind the back of their doctors. Any way that they choose to help themselves at the Centre must have the full support and approval of their medical team. The medical team will know that any service offered at the

Centre has been approved by a Professional Advisory Board.'
Then, Keith Night said he wanted to know more about Julia's
personal experience at Bolingbroke's.

'Mr Night, I don't want to give the impression that the
negative experiences are the fault of this hospital. They're
inherent in the disease: in the implications of the diagnosis,
in the complexity of information, in the choices one has
to make. Ignorance fuels fear and helplessness. Most people
diagnosed with cancer know very little about the disease.
All that they are likely to know is that it is potentially life-
threatening and that treatments are horrible. I was over-
whelmed by information and by helpful and unhelpful advice. It is difficult to know what questions one wants to ask,
difficult to know who to ask and where to go to find answers.
Then, it's difficult to gauge the accuracy and usefulness of
the information one accesses. The second enemy is anxiety.
Anxiety aggravates physical symptoms. If one is anxious, and
who isn't, one is more likely to have sleep problems, to be more
sensitive to pain and to be less resilient psychologically. It
would have helped me so much to put problems that seemed
huge and unique into a shared context and to exchange ideas
about how to deal with them. It helps to learn that there are
things you can laugh about, and that you can offer support to
other people as well as be supported by them.'

Mary Bowman turned to Fiona. 'Dr Jefferies, you
brought Julia to us. I assume you see the proposal as a helpful
complement to our service?'

'Without doubt, Lady Bowman. One can't deny that the
demands on the service force us to organise appointments,
scans, surgery and chemotherapy on the model of an assem-
bly line. This centre would provide the counterweight of the
personal approach. Each person visiting the centre would be
helped to find his or her own best way of coping with the disease. It is about coping, and this applies to loved ones as much
as to the cancer sufferer. There would be no right way. The
centre would be a haven, where the range of use would extend from a cup of tea you could make yourself in a friendly

kitchen to attending weekly support groups led by a clinical psychologist. The proposal extends the care that could be given, and it is entirely appropriate that it should be in the hands of those who actually have cancer.'

Mary Bowman turned to Julia: 'Julia, are you aware of the commitment required to deliver this sort of project? It takes a lot of time and a lot of work. You would have to dedicate yourself to it.' Julia sensed that things might be going her way and she was determined to show her own commitment.

'I believe that it would make a huge difference to people with cancer and to their loved ones. Yes, I would give it everything,' she said.

'Thank you, Julia. We'll consider your proposal in formal committee and at Trust Board level. I can say that, unless Keith raises operational issues, I shall give it my support. I hope to be in a position to write to you soon.' Mary Bowman stood up, and the others with her. They congratulated Julia and then Fiona walked Julia out.

'Hey, that was an impressive pitch. Well done!'

'I couldn't have done it without you. Thank you for encouraging me, for rehearsing me, and for backing the idea.'

'Nothing but good can come out of it, darling. I'm backing you all the way.'

Six weeks later, Mary Bowman wrote to Julia to inform her that the Trust Board had approved the proposal in principle. The Board offered a small building, close to the Hospital Staff Recreation Centre, for development. There was also an offer of access to the Trust's lawyers to help Julia set up a Charity. Keith Night would be the senior administrator to liaise with her. The Trust offered to pay the legal fee for establishing the Charity and the cost of producing an architectural plan for conversion of the building into flexible spaces from which the Caring Centre could operate. The design would be left to Julia and the architect. Thereafter, Julia herself would have to raise funds for the construction and for running the project.

Julia discussed her plan with directors of the main cancer charities in the community, starting with Macmillan Cancer Support and Marie Curie. Both organisations were extremely supportive. They saw the value of a hospital-located, but independent Cancer Caring Centre, with which their Nurses could connect. Julia began to plan a programme of activities to raise funds. This included time set aside to paint. She intended to take advantage of every exhibition in the region. When Julia mentioned the project to other members of Cambridge Open Studios, the response was overwhelming. They proposed to dedicate one of the summer exhibition days to fundraising. One member contacted Julia and offered his services to design a website for the Charity, which would help raise awareness of the project and enable donations to be made.

A fortnight after the first letter from Lady Bowman, Julia received a second. This letter was written on private notepaper and it was a personal one. In it, Mary Bowman wrote of her own experience with cancer and how all that Julia had said at the meeting had resonated with her deeply and powerfully. She ended with a pledge of fifty thousand pounds to the Charity. Julia was deeply moved. She decided she would invite Lady Bowman to become patron of the Charity. She understood immediately how important such an early donation would be to seed her fundraising campaign. Lady Bowman's generosity and involvement would attract additional support and stimulate further donations.

15. CHANCE EN-
COUNTER (2007)

After adding a paper napkin, sachets of salt and pepper, and cutlery from the cupboard to the tray on which she carried her lunch of quiche, salad and coffee, Julia surveyed the room. Not one table was free in The Friends' Meeting Room of The Royal Academy. Three chairs in the room were unoccupied but with coats and bags settled on them. That left one empty chair at a table for two. Stanley occupied this table. He caught her eye, smiled and signalled for her to go over. Seeing her hesitate, he stood up and gestured toward the chair.

'Madam' he said, 'I've almost finished. Please take the table. I'll leave you to your lunch.'

'Thank you,' Julia replied. Then, noticing his coffee cup was half full, she added: 'but I should be embarrassed if you were to leave your coffee on my account. Let's share the table.'

'Alright, let's do that.' They sat down. Stanley did not introduce himself, perhaps to maintain the impression that he would be away in a moment and so she should feel at ease. 'I came down to eat at noon and people were queueing already. The last week of any exhibition always is very busy because of the FOMOs.' In answer to her questioning look, he added: 'Those with a fear of missing out.'

'Ah, I see. I confess I'm one of them. I would have been very disappointed to miss it.'

He pointed to Julia's quiche. 'I should let you make a start lest it get cold.'

'Do tell me what you think of the exhibition while I eat,' said Julia meeting his eyes, 'that is if you've already been in.'

His blue eyes twinkled. 'I have; I will' he said, 'but don't stop eating.' Stanley had noticed Julia in the exhibition. He liked to walk back through exhibition rooms, against the flow of visitors, to consolidate his visual memory and perhaps to rearrange the shortlist of his favourites. He had noticed her in the second room standing at one end of a group, viewing one of these favourites. When she moved to walk round the back of the group to look at the painting from the opposite side, He had been struck by the almost perfect symmetry of her face, by the pale blue eyes, by the sculpted cheekbones and by her silvery grey hair, cut in a short but sassy style. She's probably in her late forties, he thought, and isn't she beautiful!

Julie ate carefully, putting down the fork and returning Stanley's gaze between morsels. She listened attentively to his opinion. Apparently, he had neither read the printed captions nor taken the audio guide. His observations were exactly that: his own. He talked about details in the paintings that had caught his eye: some extraordinary use of paint here, anatomically incorrect abdominal musculature there, some not quite accurately placed vanishing point. Julia did not dissect a painting in this manner. Rather, she felt a painting - moving from face to face, from gesture to gesture, from light to shadow - and sensed the interplay of emotions. Whether she liked a painting or not depended on this emotional connection.

Looking at him over the rim of her coffee cup, Julia thought he may have a cold analytical eye, but his manner and features suggest softness too. A full head of smartly trimmed white hair, neatly combed with a side parting, blue eyes that can smile, regular and unstained teeth, closely shaved face and not a single hair poking out of ear or nostril may have been what she saw; but she thought in terms of kind, engaging and sensitive. He's in his early sixties, she thought.

'The agreement was that I would finish the coffee and surrender the table,' Stanley said, getting to his feet. 'Forgive me for over-staying. I've enjoyed our interlude very much, but I had better be off.'

Julia rose too. 'I've finished lunch and others need the table.' Stanley bowed slightly, said goodbye and left ahead of Julia. I talked too much, he thought, discourteous of me! foolish of me! Why on earth didn't I introduce myself? I would have her name. We didn't introduce ourselves, thought Julia with regret when Stanley left. She couldn't follow him out. So, leaving her tray to be cleared, she went to the Ladies'. Then, collecting her coat, she set off on foot for The National Gallery, where she had a timed-entry ticket to another exhibition at half past two.

Stanley read biochemistry prior to graduate medicine. While well-equipped as a result to make the most of the scientific opportunities that were to present themselves, he had envied his graduate school contemporaries who had majored in Humanities. At retirement, he decided to withdraw from *doing science* and to indulge instead in the study of European History. He would spend his *young* old age immersed in the art, architecture and archaeology of Europe. He began to lay the groundwork some fifteen months before the date of his retirement. Some of the Art and History Societies had membership waiting lists of several months. The Cambridge branch of NADFAS was one of the local groups to which he applied; a decision that proved serendipitous. It was at a NADFAS lecture on Late Gothic Architecture of France that Stanley and Julia met again.

People were chatting away in small groups over coffee, which was available before every lecture. Julia was talking to two other ladies, each a little apart from the other because of elbows and coffee cups. Stanley walked in the direction of the coffee table, taking the route that brought him behind Julia's companions, and turned his head to look straight at her. She noticed him and saw his smile, which lit the spark of recognition.

'It *is* you then, *Incognita*' said *Stanley*. 'Forgive this intrusion,' he said to the others who had moved apart and turned toward him. 'We met briefly in London almost a month ago,' he said indicating Julia. Then addressing her directly, he said: 'How nice to run into you in Cambridge! But I'm interrupting; so perhaps we could reconnect after the lecture?' To his relief, she agreed. Stanley took a seat in the back row and when the lecture ended he was first out. He moved to the far side of the foyer, thinking that he ought to give Julia the opportunity of walking out of the building should she wish to avoid him, but Julia emerged from the lecture hall without her earlier companions, looked about the room and, spotting him, gave a wave and walked over.

'Julia Ellison,' she said, extending a hand, 'to remove the sense of mystery.'

'And I'm Stanley Posner; recently admitted to the membership.'

'Welcome to NADFAS, Stanley. I hope very much that you enjoyed the lecture. I'm the Programme Secretary.'

'I recall that I indulged in a monologue the first time we met, and I really don't wish to repeat the discourtesy, Julia' said Stanley, finding her name rather delicious to utter. 'Look, they seem rather keen to lock up here. May I offer you lunch at *Fitzbillies* over the bridge? Do you have time for it?' Julia accepted and they set off together. She talked about the difficulty of finding a regular venue for the Society's meetings. It had been peripatetic until a Magdalene Fellow and Society member arranged the regular monthly booking in the new Cripps Building. This made her job much easier. It was late November with the temperature holding up around eight degrees despite the clear sky. The walk towards St. Giles wasn't pleasant because traffic was held up by temporary lights near Kettle's Yard and the air was full of petrol and diesel fumes.

Once they turned left onto Magdalene street and

crossed over the bridge, it was a different world. The last lectures of the morning had just ended. Students and staff piled out of lecture halls, laboratories and libraries onto streets filled with early Christmas shoppers. On foot or bicycle, they moved up, down and across Bridge Street to get to their College Hall for lunch. While the main tourist season had ended, hordes of Chinese continued to descend on Cambridge. The oriental restaurants around Quayside and in St. John's Street enjoyed their custom, but it was too much for some Cambridge residents. Instead of some meaningless reference to the weather, less sure-footed Emeritus Fellows would seat themselves at high table and complain that they had been shoved off the pavement by the snapping jabbering tourists.

The most congested part of the city was the route from The Backs, where coaches disgorged them, along Silver Street and up King's Parade. At the other end of the city centre, Julia and Stanley weren't so pressed. They sat at the front end of a long, shared table in *Fitzbillies*. The winter sun flooded the front of the shop and caught the two of them in its unexpected warmth.

'This is a nice spot,' said Julia.

'A greenhouse effect to our advantage. Now what would you like, Julia?' She chose avocado on toast. He ordered the smoked ham, hash and eggs. Turning to her again, he asked: 'Have you been here before?'

'Do you know, I haven't. Nor have I ever sat down to eat in the original *Fitzbillies* on Trumpington Street. Of course, I've been in to buy Chelsea buns a few times; who hasn't? My father-in-law used to love them; the stickier, the better he would say. He would lick the syrup off his fingers, not to miss out on any of it.' She smiled at the memory.

Stanley couldn't quite hide his disappointment at the mention of an in-law. 'Your husband isn't interested in Art, then?'

'I'm not married anymore; but, no, he wasn't. Actually, to be fair, he worked long hours and we had only occasional evenings free. Music and theatre were his thing, which I also enjoy. So, that's what we went to.'

Buoyed up again, Stanley said: 'We do pretty well for culture and entertainment in this little City, don't we? What with the Arts Theatre, the ADC, Corpus Playroom, the Corn Exchange, the West Road Concert Hall, not to mention the Colleges; and then there's the convenience of only a fifty-minute train journey to London. We're fortunate.'

'Do you sketch or paint?' asked Julia.

'I don't think I have any talent for either, though I've not actually tried. Like your husband, I have been rather absorbed in my work. However, I'm recently retired and very keen to do different things. Which is why I came to be at the Royal Academy the day we met.'

'There's plenty of opportunity to learn. That's another way in which we are lucky to be living here.'

'Have you taken up anything?' Julia leaned forward, secretively.

'Just a few years ago, yes. I paint; not badly, I'm told.'

'That's terrific! You really would be the perfect companion at an exhibition.' Just then, their food was brought to the table. Julia took the opportunity of the interruption to deflect the conversation away from herself.

'So, when did you retire?'

'At the end of September, which explains how I'm able to indulge in visits to London galleries and NADFAS lectures on weekdays. I didn't have much free time while I was working.'

'What was your work, if you don't mind me asking?'

'I was in Medicine, both practice and research. Rather more research than clinical practice.'

'That sounds more hospital-based, rather than general practice. What was your specialty?'

'Ah, now! Mention of my specialty almost invariably kills conversation. I would hate that to happen with us,' said Stanley with a smile.

'A friend of mine is a doctor. Sometimes, she talks to me about her work, especially if it's been a tough day at the hospital. I'm sure I can cope with hearing about your specialty, even on a full stomach.' Stanley leaned forward, mimicking Julia's earlier gesture. He tapped his head. 'I was a neuropathologist.' Julia clapped her hands in self-congratulation.

'I have a supplementary question; so the conversation need not die. Would you be the person who looks at brain biopsies? The one who makes the call whether a brain tumour is a *glioblastoma* or something less horrible?' Stanley was surprised and intrigued.

'Yes, that was a significant part of my clinical practice. How do you come to know about such a rare species as neuropathologists?'

'The friend I mentioned treats people with brain tumours. She's an oncologist. She talks of pathologists making the diagnosis by examining tiny bits that the surgeon removes.'

'I expect I know her, then' said Stanley.

'Her name is Fiona Jefferies. She's my best friend. Do you know her?'

'Fiona! Your best friend! Then you have as true a friend as a friend can be.' Stanley was visibly moved. He had not seen Fiona for a long time, though they had corresponded. 'At one time, and in particular circumstances, Fiona was my only friend,' he said. He said nothing more for a while. Julia thought that the conversation may have awakened some unpleasant memory. 'I would like to meet her again, someday,' he said, rather abstractedly. Julia did not feel she was being asked to arrange it. Soon after this exchange, they left *Fitzbillies.* As they parted, Stanley said he planned to attend the next NADFAS lecture and asked Julia whether she might like to meet again afterwards.

'It's the Christmas lecture next. Yes, you can treat me to brunch again. I'll look forward to it. Thank you.' He wondered if he could make something more out of this encounter. She wondered if she dared let more come of it.

16. UNFOLDINGS
(CHRISTMAS 2007)

S t. Barnabas' choir was beginning to take practice seriously. The director of music wanted it to be at full strength for several services over Christmas. So, Fiona made a special effort to attend, despite an increasing workload at the hospital as a result of sickness among staff. Julia was pleased to see her. When practice was over, Fiona invited Julia home.

'The carols have put me into a Christmassy mood. Let's make more of it with some mulled wine. I've been given a bottle by a patient and there's no need to faff about as it can go into the microwave.'

'Ooh yes, I'd like that. In fact, I hoped we would be able to chat after choir. I have some news that may interest you.' Matthew was keen to join them. He hadn't seen Julia for some time.

'Hello you,' he said affectionately to Julia as they came through the front door. 'Where have you been. I've missed you.'

'Hi, Matt. I've missed you too. I've been so busy. The run-up to Christmas is an important time for Charities, as well you know. We've lots of fundraising activities on and many of these are evening events: recitals, dinners and auctions, that sort of thing.'

'Now, let's get the mulled wine heated up,' interjected Fiona. 'Search the larder for nuts and crisps, Matt, would you? I'm sure there's a packet of walnuts tucked at the back of the shelf. The girls would have had to stand on a stool to find it. I hope it hasn't disappeared.' Once they had glasses of hot mulled wine nestled in their hands, and bowls of nuts and crisps on the sofa between them, Fiona and Matt were ready to hear the news.

'Well, I've met someone who knows you, Fiona. Actually, that's not at all adequate. I've met a man, probably a former colleague of yours, who thinks the world of you. He said you were a true friend.'

'Who can that be?' asked Fiona.

'He's Stanley Posner.'

'Stanley!' cried Fiona. 'Oh my God, you met Stanley! This is amazing. Two people whom I love in this world have run into each other.'

'Wow! So, he's OK, then?' said Julia amused. 'I haven't found out much about him. Do tell me.'

'You go first; tell us about your meeting,' insisted Fiona. Julia told her tale. Although, she didn't think there was anything of particular interest in the account, it seemed to set Fiona's eyes twinkling and her lips twitching into a smile.

'It sounds as if Stanley is attracted to you, Julia.'

'Oh, don't be silly. He just wanted company over lunch. Anyway, tell me about him.' Fiona laughed mischievously.

'Do you know, I don't think I will. You're going to meet again, and I don't want to deny you the pleasure of discovering him.' Julia protested, but Fiona insisted. 'Darling, let things unfold. I will say, though, that he's honourable *and* he's an interesting man. Really, I think the two of you will get on very well. He's an accomplished cellist, you know. No, no.... I won't say more, except to encourage you.'

Julia was intrigued, but she decided not to press. 'Do you know, Fi, I think you're right not to tell me. Stanley will be coming to the next NADFAS lecture and he has already asked whether I'd like to do lunch afterwards. I don't want to know more about him than he does about me. Do you agree that Stanley is interesting, Matt?'

'He's certainly that, Julia; and so are you, don't you forget.' They left it at that and moved on to talking about the girls. Julia wanted to know how they were getting on in their jobs. The three of them were in uncomplicated relationships. So, it was fun to get news of the boyfriends too. However, it was quite late, and Julia soon got up to go. Fiona walked her to the door. There, she touched Julia's arm tenderly and asked:

'Do you miss being intimate with a man?'

'I do, but I don't know that I could do it again. More to the point, I don't know whether a man could bring himself to be intimate with me. It's irrelevant, though, because I couldn't deal with the possible, no likely, rejection. I don't think I could bring myself to try.'

'Do you find Stanley attractive? He's probably ten years older than you, but he was pretty fit the last time I saw him.'

'He is very good looking; a bit Paul Newman. You know, the grey-white hair, blue eyes, strong jaw; and he is vigorous. More importantly, he seems kind.'

'Well then, of one thing I'm sure. If there's anyone with whom it's worth taking a chance, it's Stanley. Goodnight, Darling.' They hugged and Julia walked back to York Terrace. Am I strong enough to be hurt again? she asked herself.

The last lecture of the year for the Cambridge NADFAS was held on the nineteenth of December. Miranda MacDermot-Haig spoke on *The Christmas Story through paintings at The National Gallery*. She attracted a good audience despite the weather, which had turned bitterly cold. Members were unrecognisable until hats, earmuffs, scarves and heavy coats had been peeled off. Julia's work for the Society was much appreciated and she was liked. So, most people brought her a gift. After everyone had left, Julia found she had so many Christmas presents that she simply couldn't carry them home. Nor could they be left for later collection as the building was to be locked until the new term.

'I've a solution,' said Stanley. 'I live just across the river in Portugal Place. You wait here. I'll fetch my car and we can load your well-deserved presents into the boot. Then, we'll drive out to Grantchester. We should be able to get a table in one of the pubs. We might be lucky enough to get a seat by an open fire. How's that for a plan?'

'That'll be a great help; thanks. And if it brightens up, we could walk on the meadows after lunch.'

The Rupert Brooke has rather lost its charm from the outside because the original building has been opened into modern extensions on all sides. Inside, however, the spaces work very well; at least for people who prefer a café-cum-lounge atmosphere. The Red Lion and The Green Man haven't come quite as far, in modernisation terms, and The Blue Ball is the most authentic of all. Four pubs might seem over the top for a small village, but in the summer months one wouldn't be able to get a table anywhere without booking well in advance. The meadows drop down to the Cam from these pubs. An asphalted path follows the high side of the meadows from Newnham to Grantchester, ending just behind the pubs. In the warm months, locals, students and tourists stroll out of Cambridge *en masse* along this path or punt on the river to picnic on the riverbanks at Grantchester.

Being more café-cum-lounge in their taste, Julia and Stanley picked The Rupert Brooke and were pleased to see a couple of armchairs and a sofa free by the fire. They soon felt snug, removed the extra woollens, and settled into conversation. Anyone in the pub that afternoon would have seen an attractive late-middle-aged couple, seated together on the sofa, clearly at ease with one another. They talked about the paintings that had formed the spine of the Christmas lecture, without affectation. They shared knowledge and insights. Julia realised that the conversation with Fiona had led her to drop her reserve.

They went into the restaurant area for lunch. At table,

Julia said: 'I was with Fiona the other day and mentioned that I've met you.'

'And what did she say about that?'

'Fiona decided to be enigmatic. She told me you were worth getting to know, but she refused to tell me about you. Well, there was one thing that slipped out.' Oddly, Stanley looked a little anxious.

'I'm curious to know which thing she chose to tell you.'

'Fiona told me that you're quite an accomplished cellist. So, we have music in common.' Stanley relaxed again.

'I wouldn't say accomplished, just competent. I learnt the instrument when I was young. Then work rather got in the way. When things weren't going well at work for a while, I turned to music to help me through. It was a lifesaver. Perhaps that's melodramatic, but that's the way it seemed at the time. After that, I took lessons again and kept up the playing"

'Do you make music with others, Stanley?'

'No, I don't. Do you know, it hasn't occurred to me to do so? Because of the circumstances that brought me back to the cello, I turn to it to ease my soul; to raise my spirits. Is that rather introverted of me?'

'Oh, I can relate to that. My piano has steadied me often. I wonder, though, would you be interested in playing together?'

'I would like that very much. I expect we'll find enough sonatas for piano and cello to keep us busy for quite a while. What a lovely idea!'

'Oh, here's the food,' said Julia, sitting back to let the waiter put the plate down. The conversation continued to flow around music. They discovered that both of them felt uncomfortable going alone to concerts in the City. So, they agreed to look through the Cambridge Concert Calendar for a few concerts they might attend together. After lunch, they fancied a short walk and went through the gate onto the meadows. In the third week of December, an icy blast from the Urals having discouraged most people from venturing out, they had the path to themselves.

Stanley offered his arm, which Julia took. Both of them were very fit and they walked at a brisk pace. They had to do so in order to keep warm. The sky had cleared, dropping the temperature, but with the advantage that the low winter sun cast a rather splendid mellow light across the shallow valley. The uphill walk back from Newnham went at a slower pace and they huddled together against the cold. This pleased both of them.

'Shall we choose Chopin's G minor sonata? I haven't played it yet, but I have the CD,' asked Stanley. Julia turned to him and smiled with pleasure.

'For me, he's the most romantic of the romantics. An inspired choice,' she said.

'How long do we need to get it up to speed separately, do you think, before getting together to practice?'

'Christmas will get in your way, I suppose.'

'Not in mine, actually. I'm not doing anything over the holiday.'

Julia brought the two of them to a halt. 'What do you mean by that? Are you alone on Christmas Day?'

'I'm used to it. The College shuts down until the New Year. There is a cousin to whom I go some Christmases, but he and his wife are away this year, seeking the warm sun.'

'Then join me on Christmas Day. Would you? Do say yes, Stanley. I shall be alone otherwise.'

'Now, I don't believe that.'

Julia laughed. 'Well, I would be alone were it not for the fact that Fiona and Matt insist I spend Christmas Day with them. I'm godmother to their youngest daughter. But Fiona was most insistent that I should get to know you. So, I think she would be impressed that I'm getting on with it. I can visit them on Boxing Day. Do say *yes*.'

'Yes! Thank you, Julia.'

Over the next few days, Julia ran about getting their Christmas together. She bought a small tree, and lights and tinsel to hang on it. She had received plenty of Christmas cards already; these were set out on the mantelpiece and on the tops of furniture. She found some pretty holly and mistletoe, which she braided together and fixed around the fireplace. Then, Julia concentrated on Christmas lunch: it would have to be a chicken, as it was just two of them, but she chose what she expected would be the tastiest. At any rate, she bought the most expensive one, assuming there would be a correlation.

Rather than mess about with cocktail sausages and bacon rashers, Julia bought a pack of oven-ready *pigs in blankets*, which would help upgrade the chicken to a Christmas dish. Sprouts, parsnips, potatoes and carrots would surely fill the two of them up. A small M&S luxury Christmas pudding and brandy butter settled the dessert question. Perhaps, she would serve baked camembert and salad with a freshly baked baguette as a starter. Stanley was bringing the wine, but she had some bottles in reserve. There, that would do. After all, it was up to them to make Christmas special.

Julia had to be pragmatic about the arrangements. She simply didn't have the time to come up with a home-made starter and pudding. Charity work and choir practice had not stopped. On Christmas morning, there was to be Sung Eucharist at St. Barnabas. So, she wouldn't be getting back to York Terrace before half past eleven. Rather sweetly, Stanley said he would like to hear the choir and asked if he could attend the service. She looked forward to having him with her for most of the day, and the two of them could get lunch ready together.

At the end of the Christmas service, Fiona left the group of choir members and went up to Stanley. She kissed his cheeks and said:

'Happy Christmas, Stanley, and congratulations. It's such a pleasure to see you again.'

'The pleasure is mine, Fiona. I got your letter, of course. Thank you for saying such nice things; and I'm also grateful to you for encouraging Julia to get to know me. She's lovely. Do you know, she's giving me Christmas lunch?'

'Yes, I have encouraged her, and I encourage you too. Oh, here she comes!' Turning to Julia, she said 'Now you two, do come to us for a drink in the evening, won't you? Meanwhile, have a lovely Christmas afternoon.' Fiona joined Matthew and the two of them went off to their family feast. Julia and Stanley followed them out. They had just stepped out of the church when a man came up. Julia didn't know him, though she had seen him at some Sunday services. He extended a hand to Stanley.

'How nice to see you at St. Barnabas, Sir Stanley. Merry Christmas.' He raised his hat to Julia, 'and to you, Ma'am,' and off he went. Julia turned to Stanley.

'Sir Stanley! So, I'm entertaining a Knight of the Realm. This *is* getting interesting.' She laughed and took his arm.

As Stanley followed Julia through the front door of York Terrace into the cheerfully decorated living room, he felt happy and deeply appreciative of Julia's thoughtfulness and kindness.

'This is fabulous, Julia; what a lovely tree! Just the right size. Thank you for being me to it........Now, that is a beautiful instrument!' He went over to the piano behind the tree and stroked the black glossed finish. 'If she sounds as good as she looks...'

Julia put on an apron and tossed another one at Stanley. 'I'll give you the chance to form an opinion later. Let's get things going so that we can relax.' Stanley reached for his rucksack, took out three bottles of wine and a corkscrew, with which he opened one of them. He filled the two glasses on the already laid table. Handing one to Julia, he said:

'We'll keep these near us as we cook. Merry Christmas!' They clinked glasses, drank a sip, and then moved into the kitchen. Julia took charge.

'I'll get the chicken and sausages ready. Could you scrape and slice the carrots and parsnips, please? Then, peel the potatoes and quarter them, would you? We'll roast them.'

'Sure thing. Just point me in the direction of the utensils drawer and the bin cupboard.' They worked quickly and everything was done in half an hour. Julia popped the chicken into the heated oven.

'That will take ninety minutes. I'll put the potatoes and parsnips in halfway through. The carrots and sprouts can be put to boil while you carve the bird. Don't worry about the starter. It'll just need ten minutes in the oven.'

'You're well organised!' said Stanley. Julia refilled her glass.

'Fill yours and come into the conservatory, Stanley. You must satisfy my curiosity. Tell me for what you've been honoured.' They sat in comfortable, cushioned armchairs, more opposite than next to one another. Each found the other attractive and it pleased both of them to be seated face to face.

'If you insist. Well, you know about my clinical practice diagnosing diseases of the brain. Really, though, I spent much more time researching the nature of a particular brain disease, which led me to a new scientific discovery. That's what the knighthood is for.'

'Please, give me detail. I'll tell you if you lose me entirely.'

'Well, I was interested in a very rare brain disease of man. Then, came bovine spongiform encephalopathy. I imagine you are familiar with the BSE epidemic.'

'BSE is the same as Mad Cow Disease, isn't it?'

'Yes, it is. Thank goodness, the epidemic is waning. It may be that we shall see the end of the disease in animals within the next five years.'

'Good news indeed for cows and for our meat and dairy industry, but a couple of years ago didn't the papers run a story about Mad Cow Disease passing to people who had eaten beef burgers and sausages?'

'Sadly, yes. That has happened. Some of us saw it coming. I'm sorry to say there will be several more cases in people before the illness peters out in humans too.'

'How did this horror come about?'

'I guess the easy way of putting it is like this. There was a mad sheep disease, called Scrapie, before there was a mad cow disease. The disease in sheep has been around for a couple of centuries and had never affected cattle before 1986. A few years before the start of the epidemic, farmers altered the conditions under which a protein supplement feed for cattle was produced. Farmers had been feeding cows with bonemeal from scrapie-infected sheep products.'

'What is in bonemeal?'

'Basically, cooked and ground leftovers of the slaughtering process, as well as from the carcasses of sick and injured animals such as cattle and sheep. The change to manufacturing conditions unknowingly prevented the Scrapie-causing agent from being destroyed. So, it passed to cattle through the feed supplement.'

'What role have you played, Stanley?' asked Julia.

'I worked out what the infective agent is; the cause of the disease.'

'Did it turn out to be something unexpected?'

'Yes, it was a new thing in all of biology. Everyone else thought the agent was a virus. Ironically, the main proponent of the virus theory, a chap called Gallagher, was awarded the Nobel prize some twenty years ago. I showed that the infectious agent consists solely of bits of misfolded protein that have the ability to spread round the brain by making other proteins misfold in turn.'

'Could you explain? Is the first misfolded protein different to the proteins that then come to be badly folded?'

'There's a particular protein that everyone – even people who aren't sick – have in their bodies. I discovered it and named it *prion protein*. The instructions that tell each cell in our brain how to make this protein are found in our DNA, on chromosome 20. In animals and people with the brain disease, a molecule of prion protein, which normally folds into several spirals, has its ends snipped off and the remnant changes from spiral form to zig-zag pleated sheets that fold over themselves. The curious thing is that, once one molecule is misfolded, the bad prion can induce a molecule of the normally folded prion to misfold. This proceeds inexorably until all the normal protein becomes wrongly folded. The misfolded protein disrupts a nerve cell's thread-like extensions that connect it to other nerve cells in a network. Once disconnected, glucose and other essential nutrients no longer pass from the bloodstream to the nerve cell. So, the nerve cell starves and withers. As more of them die, brain function deteriorates and the patient becomes progressively disabled.'

'If everyone has prion protein, then why do most people never get sick with the equivalent of the animal disease?'

'It's very rare for one molecule of the prion protein to misfold spontaneously, but it does happen. More unusually, an error can occur in the gene on chromosome 20, in which case all the prion protein made by the brain's nerve cells will be misfolded. As the error is in the gene, it is passed down the generations of that unfortunate family. In the case of mad cow disease in humans, the misfolded prion is eaten. Then, it travels from the gut to the brain, where it proceeds to misfold the normal prion in nerve cell after nerve cell.'

'Will your discovery lead to ways to stop the protein folding badly? Could a cure be found?'

'My work has been welcomed because it opens the door to a cure. There's a lot of scientists working on it now. They're excited because other brain diseases, which are much more common, have been shown to have a similar mechanism. Alzheimer's disease and Parkinson's disease are also caused by different proteins that can act in the same way as prion protein. They are cut at the ends, misfold into zig-zag pleats, and then get tangled up.'

'Is it this entangling of the badly folded proteins that does the damage?'

'Ah, the sixty-four-thousand-dollar question! For some proteins, yes. Generally, nerve cells may die either because some vital function is lost as the amount of normal protein reduces or a toxic effect occurs as the abnormal misfolded protein increases. The toxic effect could result from individual misfolded proteins or from the aggregates that form.'

'And the possible treatments?'

'Some scientists are trying to prevent the clipping of the end of the normal proteins. Others are trying to prevent the misfolded forms from sticking together into aggregates. Yet others are working on a vaccine that might encourage the body's own immune system to remove the aggregates of misfolded proteins after they form.'

'So, you've opened the way for doctors to make new kinds of parachutes for patients. That deserves more than a knighthood.' The oven-timer beeped. Julia got up to put the potatoes and parsnips into the oven. Stanley followed her into the kitchen and stood to the side.

'Julia,' he began, 'I did get more than the knighthood. Cambridge is a pretty small town and you'll hear about it sooner or later if we go out together, much as happened at Church this morning. I would rather get it out of the way, if I may.'

Julia went up to him. 'I would rather learn about you from your own lips. What is it?'

'I was given the Nobel prize for Medicine last year.' Julia put a hand on his arm.

'That's awesome!'

'Please don't make too much of it. Whether one's research works out as one hopes is as much a matter of luck as anything else... And, in my case, not a little kindness.'

'Modesty becomes you, but why not enjoy the plaudits?'

'Oh, I'll help the University and my College fundraise, especially when the money is intended for further research in my own field, but I don't want to miss out on other things that are important to me.' Julia still had her hand on Stanley's arm as she stood facing him. Now, he placed his free hand over hers. Julia smiled; then she kissed Stanley's cheek.

'Why have I been so pleasantly rewarded?'

'Because you've brought hope of a cure for so many... Hey, it's time to get our starter course ready.' Julia popped two small Camembert cheeses into the oven, dressed a salad and cut fresh bread. They sat down to a quite delicious late Christmas lunch and chatted away about anything and everything bar misfolded proteins until, at the end of the meal, Julia said:

'Something's occurred to me. You mentioned the other researcher... Gallagher...yes, that was his name. You said he was given the Nobel prize. What's happened to him since you showed he was mistaken about the cause being a virus?'

'Now there's a tragic tale. He's in prison in the United States for child molestation. He did his early work among the natives of Papua New Guinea. That's where the first epidemic of Mad Cow sort occurred in humans. Well, Gallagher took several native children who had been orphaned to his home in the US, over fifty of them I believe, mostly boys. He wanted to give them opportunities, an education, he said. It turns out he's a paedophile.' Julia was horrified and distressed, foremost because of Gallagher's betrayal of the trust placed in him, but also because the story reminded her that she too had been betrayed in part because of that insatiable male sexual urge. It had been a significant factor in the breakup of her own marriage. Trying not to show she was upset, she changed the subject.

'Now, I promised to play for you, didn't I?' she said. 'Let's clear away the dishes and go through to the piano.' Stanley realised it had been inappropriate of him to tell the story of Gallagher and he apologised.

'I'm sorry I mentioned that sordid story, Julia. And on Christmas Day. Clumsy of me!'

'Mozart will cheer me up.' She pointed to the sofa. 'The audience sits there,' she said. Julia sat at the piano and launched into the Allegro of Mozart's Sonata in C major. She didn't take her eyes off the keyboard for this fast and playful movement, but she did look up at Stanley with smiling eyes in the expressive Andante. Stanley thought: If I had my cello with me, I could answer her. He applauded when she finished the piece and complimented her both on the instrument and her playing.

'I'm looking forward to our Chopin,' he said. Julia came and sat next to him. He turned to her. 'May I ask you? What is the biggest and best thing that's happened to *you*?' She looked away and didn't speak for a moment. It seemed to him that he had got too close to the bone about something. But she looked up at him, took a deep breath as if to summon up courage, and said:

'*Biggest and best* don't always go together, not in my case anyway. In terms of something life-changing, it's cancer. I have had breast cancer.' Stanley kept his eyes on hers.

'I'm sorry that happened to you; though everything about you tells me you have come through, and strongly.'

'Strongly? Perhaps, but not without scars.' Self-pity raised its head but, recognising it, Julia swiftly suppressed it.

'Out of it came the best thing. I started a charity that provides support to people with cancer and their families. I love this work and, best of all, I can use my painting and music both to help people cope and to raise funds.'

'Then you're *the* Julia. I know of the Cancer Care Charity down at the hospital. Everyone calls it *Julia's*. Well done you. It's proving a tremendous support to so many.'

'It's a small contribution.'

'Modesty becomes you,' he returned with a smile. 'I heard this Julia runs marathons too.'

'Apart from the pleasure of being fit, marathons are one of the best ways of raising charitable donations.'

'Congratulations to you, Julia. You're the awesome one,' said Stanley.

17. MISFOLDINGS

Julia and Stanley spent more and more time together, regularly going to the theatre, concerts and art exhibitions in Cambridge and London. Whenever they were out, Stanley would offer his arm to Julia and she would take it. He did not reach for her hand; this would have presumed a desire for physical intimacy that might not be reciprocated yet. They had enjoyed working on the Chopin sonata and took great pleasure in playing it together once they had mastered it. This musical intercourse connected the two of them emotionally.

Naturally, they got to know more about one another during the practice sessions, which became regular weekly meetings as they extended their repertoire. The more Stanley heard about the Cambridge Cancer Caring Centre, the more impressed he was at Julia's achievement. Setting it up locally was one thing, but news of the Centre had spread to NHS Trusts and patient groups elsewhere in the Country. Julia was invited to speak in Newcastle upon Tyne, then Glasgow and Edinburgh. She was gone overnight on the first trip and for three days in Scotland.

Stanley missed her acutely when she was out of town. This emotion, this longing for another, was new to him. He had never married. Girlfriends had been great fun at times, but he had had no inclination to let things go further, deeper. His studies, then medical practice and especially research proved remarkably fulfilling and emotionally rewarding. Girlfriends didn't wait long enough to mount a serious challenge for Stanley's affection. Only now did Stanley question whether it need have been all or nothing. The really big question was whether any girl in his youth would have turned into a Julia. Impossible to rule this out, but his gut feeling was that

Julia was exceptional.

The *status quo*, pleasant as it was, seemed to be settling into just that until, in the early summer, Dorothy changed things. She announced her engagement to the young man she had been with for three years. They had been living together for some eighteen months. Dorothy joined Julia in the garden of York Terrace a couple of days after coming home with the news. These tête-à-têtes were frequent during Dorothy's childhood and teenage. Her parents had less time to attend to number three child. Dorothy would be listened to, but answers were rather matter of fact; kind of *that's what you should do, isn't it obvious?* In Julia, Dorothy had a confidante who made time for her; someone with whom she could explore whatever emotion was causing unease and work through the reasons why; from whom she could hear a gentle but clear presentation of options open to her and likely consequences; and from whom she would receive emotional and practical support.

Julia found her goddaughter radiantly happy. 'I do believe you're in love, Dottie darling,' she said. Dorothy's face lit up in a smile again; eyes widened, pupils enlarged, nose turned up and the corners of her mouth pulled in an upward curve towards flushed cheeks. She had one of those smiles that appeared in an instant, as if the Christmas lights in Regent Street had just been switched on. It was available to anyone, strangers as well as friends. By the time Dorothy reached the office, the newsagent, the bus driver, the *Big Issue* vendor and the *Café Costa* barista would have been on the receiving end, and all of them would feel better for it. In the office, Dorothy was known for her ability to connect with people and build teams; she was the genuine article when it came to people skills. She was always so happy when things went well for others; no surprise then that she seemed to glow at her own happiness and that everyone was happy to see it.

'I think I *am* in love. I felt so happy when Jeremy proposed. I thought he might be working round to it; my girlfriends told me so, but it came as a surprise nonetheless. You love him too, don't you?'

'Dottie, I shall love whomever you choose to love.'

'I wish Mum had put it like that. She asked me: does he love you?'

'What was your answer?'

'I said Yes, he must. He proposed marriage. Not many of my friends are married though they have partners. I think it's a rare statement of commitment. And between you and me, he wants to be with me all the time. He desires me too.'

'Darling, you're a beautiful woman. Any man will desire you.'

'Do you think that's all it is? Desire?'

'By no means; and if a man doesn't desire you, passionately, then lose him. The key question is: does he act in a way that suggests he wants your happiness and wellbeing above all; above his own, even?'

How can one be sure of that?'

'Ask yourself a few questions: Does he accept you fully as you are, without criticism? Can you talk about anything openly and honestly? Are you entirely yourself when you're with him? Does he show you respect, kindness and compassion? Does he think of *we* or *you*, instead of me?' Dorothy looked into Julia's eyes, seemingly with new understanding.

'It's just occurred to me that I can say *yes* to all these questions if they were asked about you.' She went to Julia and hugged her. 'Thank you for loving me.' Julia returned the embrace.

'Do you know, my darling, now you mention it, your mother loves me that way; as I do her... Now, back to Jeremy?'

'The answers to all are *Yes.*'

'Then you have as much as one can. The sixty-four-thousand-dollar question, as Stanley likes to put it, is whether, no matter what circumstance may befall you and through bad times as well as good, he will support you and care deeply for you; and vice versa. When this happens, you may say to yourself he loves me truly.'

The marriage ceremony was held at St. Barnabas. It was a musical treat with the choir in full and enthusiastic voice in support of one of their own. The reception was at the Gonville Hotel on Parker's Piece. They had considered having it at Matthew's College, but the College showed no enthusiasm for having a disc jockey and dancing after the meal. Dorothy simply would not compromise. She and her friends just had to dance. Her wedding dress had been designed to shed length à la *Bucks Fizz*, though from full length to mid-calf, rather than the original mid-calf to mini. The early dances were energetic, contemporary and utterly foreign to the ears of anyone over thirty. Then, late in the evening, the disc jockey (a misnomer, since there wasn't a disc in sight. Would *music lister* be acceptable?) switched to the slow-dance songs of yesteryear. Hey Jude, Bridge Over Troubled Waters, Yesterday, Massachusetts and other greats brought the older couples onto the dancefloor and into each other's arms.

Aware that Julia and Stanley were frequently together, Fiona and Matthew extended Julia's invitation to include a companion. Stanley was pleased to be drawn into the family celebration. He had always enjoyed contact with undergraduates and graduate students. So, the girls found him accessible, interesting, and interested in what they were up to. Julia was pleased to see him at ease with all the Jefferies. Of course, several guests were medical; close colleagues of Fiona. Fortunately, none present had been involved in the unpleasantness towards Stanley following the Marshall inquest.

Never mind the others though; the point is that for the first time Julia was in Stanley's arms, her hands placed lightly on his shoulders, his hands enjoying the latitude offered by the occasion to explore her back, with her fragrance finding a way to the sweet pleasure spot in his brain. His hands slipped down onto Julia's bum and drew her swaying lower body to him. Without breaking rhythm, Julia looked into his eyes. She saw affection. She embraced him, moved up against his chest, and brought her cheek against his. Stanley felt like an eighteen-year-old. Indeed, he reacted like an eighteen-year-old. Julia brought her head back and smiled.

'I'm flattered by your youthful reaction.' Stanley kissed her, rather passionately. At this, Julia drew away gently, took Stanley's hand, and walked him off the dancefloor. When they were out of the room and could hear one another again, she turned to him and said: 'Come into the garden, Stanley. I'd like to ask you something.' There was no-one else outside, so they walked over to a low wall, on which they sat side by side. She put her arm through his. 'Stanley, please tell me if I'm mistaken. That kiss seemed to me an invitation to take our relationship further, and in a new direction.'

'It is,' he assured her. She wanted the relationship to blossom, but she had not worked out a formula for just this moment. She had to speak plainly. What else could one do?'

'My breast cancer required mastectomy.' Before Julia had time to worry how this might have sounded, he said:

'I assumed that.'

'If you were to see my body and turn away, our relationship would end. Is it worth the risk?'

'Without surgery, you would not have been here for me to meet; my life would be empty still. You cannot know how much happiness I've found as we've shared more and more of life. That kiss wasn't only an invitation. It was a declaration. I love you, Julia.' Stanley leaned across, touched Julia's face, ran his fingers up into her hair and then kissed her lips gently, but lingeringly. Julia returned the kiss and embraced him. Encouraged by Julia's response, Stanley asked: 'Then, are you ready?'

'The possibility of intimate physical contact hasn't occurred to me. Frankly, I assumed you were content with a platonic relationship. So, you've taken me by surprise. Am I ready?' Julia thought about the question for a few seconds. Then, she said: 'Let's go back to the dance-floor and continue where we left off until Dorothy and Jeremy leave. Then come home with me, and love me,' she said.

'It's quite ridiculous that I should cry like this,' Fiona said as they embraced one another at the end of the evening, 'after all, she's been gone from home for a while; but she belongs to someone else now and I feel the loss.' Julia hugged her tightly.

'Dottie's focus is bound to shift, but isn't that as it should be. Their love will strengthen. Soon, she'll draw you into her life with Jeremy. She has a husband, as you do. Soon, she'll have a child, as you have had. This will change Dottie in a way that will bring her close to you again.'

'Thank you, that's helpful. I do look forward to having a son in Jeremy, and to love their children if they're blessed with any.'

'I'm the grateful one, Fi. We've had a wonderful day and it was such good fun to share the morning with you and the girls. The marriage service was beautiful, and this party has been just great.'

'Yes, and I noticed things seem to have heated up between you and Stanley. Is everything alright?'

'I'll know after tonight, Fi. Fingers crossed. Goodnight, darling,' Julia returned to Stanley in the bar. They took a taxi to Portugal Place, from where he collected a few necessities. Then they went on to York Terrace.

Julia led Stanley upstairs to her bedroom. 'I'll brush my teeth and make some room for your things by the basin. Then you can freshen up and I'll wait for you in the bedroom.' Stanley came out of the bathroom in a loose silk dressing gown. The lights were dimmed but Julia had lit several candles, at least one scented. She hoped the atmosphere was romantic, more for herself. She needed to be distracted from her nervousness.

When Stanley emerged, he found her seated on the end of the bed, apparently fully dressed except that she had removed her shoes and tights. He came up to her and she stood, kissed him, turned around. He unzipped her dress slowly and Julia slipped out of it without turning around. She was naked except for her bra. He unhooked the strap. Julia slipped it off, but still didn't turn around. Her heart was pounding. Stanley held her shoulders, kissed her neck, and then he turned her to face him.

'You are stunningly beautiful,' Stanley said, and meant it. The regular gym work and running had sculpted Julia's body over time. Her breast was round, full and pointed forward, unaffected as it was by pregnancy and breastfeeding. Well-defined pectorals and shoulder muscles minimised the asymmetry. Julia was statuesque: half Apollo Belvedere, half Venus de Milo. An Amazon, thought Stanley, as he took in her beauty. Needless to say, this was not the way Julia saw herself, but the attention he paid her body quickly dispelled any residual self-loathing and liberated her fully.

Whereas Julia had previously considered their relationship destined to be one of deep affection based on common interests and warm companionship, the new communication through caresses, embraces, and kisses drew them together physically and emotionally. Having been taken by surprise by Stanley's declaration of love at Dorothy's wedding, Julia had had little time in which to consider her answer to the question of whether she was in love too. However, every encounter validated her snap decision and it was not long before she decided to set up home with Stanley. He moved into York Terrace, partly because his property had a higher rental value; though the main reason was that Julia did not wish to leave the Mill Road neighbourhood.

The years that followed were the happiest for both Julia and Stanley. Their interests converged. They did almost everything together. Julia accompanied Stanley to College social events. He attended St. Barnabas with Julia and took up drawing; his determined and systematic approach leading to reasonable competence. They entertained regularly, mixing their friends and acquaintances, and people were happy to be with them as an air of contentment hung about them and their home.

Some seven years later, as content as they had ever been, Stanley and Julia were on a flight to Amman. Stanley had travelled all over the world, but never solely for leisure. Most of his time abroad had been spent in conference centres and lecture halls. Social and sightseeing events were attached to the scientific conferences and he received VIP treatment, but he was constantly interacting with other doctors and scientists or government officials. Traveling with Julia was altogether different. They took their time and stayed long enough in a place not to have to sightsee all day. Never having been outside Europe, Julia was excited by all that Stanley showed her in Japan, Southeast Asia and Latin America. The Middle East was put off because of the Arab Spring and subsequent clampdown by the army in some countries. When the situation there was relatively settled, Julia suggested they visit Jordan and Egypt.

They spent a couple of days in one of the Dead Sea resort hotels, then took in Jerash. Not having visited Pompeii or Herculaneum, Julia was astonished at the ruined Roman city.

'Wait till you see Petra,' said Stanley, 'it'll take your breath away.'

The drive to Petra had been long and monotonous, except for the visit to the stunning hilltop crusader fort at al-Karak. They were pleased with their hotel, which managed to create a calm and relaxing atmosphere despite the high turnover of guests, most of whom stayed only one or two nights. Having had a good night's sleep and eaten a delicious breakfast, Julia felt excited as she walked down the Siq on Stanley's arm towards the ancient Pink City. She marvelled at the carvings on its walls and the water gulley running along it, but her jaw dropped when she turned around the last bend and saw the Treasury in the crack of sunlight at the end of the Siq. Stanley watched with pleasure at Julia's wonder.

Then, they were out of the Siq and in the sunbathed open space before the Treasury, amidst the bustle of tourists, Bedouin with their camels, donkeys and carts, and hawkers of postcards, coloured stones and silver jewellery. The two of them moved to one side and Stanley began to read to Julia the section on The Treasury in their guidebook while she photographed it. Stanley's narrative stopped mid-sentence. A tourist who was being photographed with her back to the Treasury let out a scream and pointed behind Julia. She turned around and saw Stanley on the ground, bleeding and groaning in pain. Everyone rushed to help.

Stanley was conscious but battered and bruised, and badly cut on the back of his head. When he had worked out what had happened, a policeman ran back into the single-roomed police station and returned with a first aid kit. Someone, a tourist, said she was either a nurse or a doctor in heavily accented, broken English. She stemmed the bleeding with a pressure dressing, then cleaned the wound. For a while, Julia could do nothing more useful than comfort Stanley, hold his hand while others worked around his head, and attempt to understand what had just happened to him from the Babel of accounts around her. The eyewitness confirmed Stanley's own account that he dropped like a stone, without any warning. He had not felt ill or lightheaded. He had not lost consciousness; not even after his head had hit the ground. He had not slipped or tripped on anything. He felt himself fall, saw himself fall, and felt the severe pain of impact with the ground.

Once Stanley had been patched up, one of the Bedouins appeared beside Julia. In surprisingly excellent English, he said that his nephews would help get Stanley back to their hotel. Fortunately, the hotel was just opposite the entrance to the archaeological site. He called a couple of muleteers over and spoke to them. They collected a stretcher from the police station and arranged Stanley on it. Then, he put Julia on one of the horse-drawn carts that are used to carry tourists up and down the Siq and instructed the driver to get her to the hotel. He assured her that his people would carry Stanley to the hotel, but that they would do it on foot as the cart ride was far too bumpy. Julia was to alert the hotel doctor. She thanked them all and offered money, but they would take none.

'In our religion we are obliged to help anyone in need,' the headman said.

18. LOVE AND LET DIE (2014)

The Jordanian doctor who attended Stanley in Petra found nothing wrong with Stanley's heart and blood pressure; the electrocardiogram tracing showed a normal heart rhythm. He swung a torch from one of Stanley's pupils to the other, looked into the back of his eyes with an ophthalmoscope, and said that he could find nothing abnormal there. When he found no weakness in Stanley's limbs and they jerked appropriately when the tendons were tapped, the doctor seemed satisfied that nothing serious was amiss and suggested the problem may have been heat exhaustion. He sutured Stanley's head wound, left paracetamol tablets and said he would call again the next day. The next morning, he cleared Stanley for a flight back home.

When the plane was at cruising height and seatbelts had been released, Julia put her arm into Stanley's, drew him to her and asked: 'Now tell me what the problem is, darling. I could see you were skeptical when the doctor said you probably fainted.'

'I'm not sure what it is. It certainly wasn't a faint or heart exhaustion. It's just possible it could have been a form of epilepsy. Look, I don't want you to worry. As you see, I've come away with no more than a scalp wound. I'll see a neurologist colleague as soon as I can, I promise. I can't tell you how sorry I am that you're missing Egypt.'

'Don't be absurd. Nothing is more important than getting to the bottom of this so it doesn't happen again. Now promise me you'll tell me the results of the tests when they're done.'

'I promise.'

Chris Wilkinson agreed to see Stanley at the end of his out-patient clinic two days after Stanley made the telephone call to his secretary. 'Sir Stanley, it's a pleasure to see you,' said Wilkinson when the nurse showed him into the consulting room. 'I hope you're enjoying retirement.'

'I have been, Chris; thank you,' said Stanley as he shook Wilkinson's hand and sat down in the chair beside the consultant's desk. 'It's been spoilt by the episode that led me to call your secretary for a consultation.'

'Let's go through it, then. Tell me the symptoms. After that I'll examine you and take some blood for laboratory analysis. I have already asked for you to be sent appointments for an EEG and an MRI scan.'

'Thank you, that'll speed things up. Well, the fact of the matter is I just dropped to the ground. I had no warning at all. I didn't lose consciousness and I was completely aware whilst falling, even as I hit the ground. That was painful. However, I didn't lose consciousness as a result of the head injury and, if it hadn't been for the bleeding and the sore head, I may well have tried to get back onto my feet. I felt strong enough to do so, even if shaken by the event.'

'Was there nothing else that you experienced, no other symptoms, around this episode?'

'None at all.'

'Then, what about your general health?'

'Again, nothing; at least nothing I wouldn't have put down to early old age. I'm nearly seventy now.'

'Please, be specific. If I've grasped your turn of phrase correctly, you are concerned about something.'

'My vision blurs when I look up or down. It isn't a problem to read if I hold a book up. This has been troubling me for a couple of months. The other symptom is an odd feeling of stiffness in my left leg while swimming in a hotel pool a couple of weeks ago. It was disconcerting as I couldn't use the leg to stabilise my body when threading water. Looking back, there's also been stiffness in my neck, which may be related. I had put it down to arthritis and the problem of too soft pillows in hotel rooms when we travelled.'

'I see. You'll be wanting me to check your eye movements, then.'

'Yes, I'm rather fearful that you'll confirm my suspicion that I've got a gaze palsy. It's impossible to check one's own eye movements in the mirror, I've discovered.' Stanley sat up on the examination couch. Chris Wilkinson stood in front of him, held up the index finger of his right hand and, with his left hand, he steadied Stanley's head. Asking Stanley to focus on his index finger, Wilkinson moved it out to the right, then across to the left, then up and down. He watched Stanley's eye movements and saw that Stanley could turn his gaze fully to right and left, but not upwards. Stanley could get his eyes only midway up the normal vertical range. Next, Wilkinson held his index finger steady, asked Stanley to fix his gaze on it, and tilted Stanley's head downwards. This time, Stanley's eyes appeared to roll upwards fully.

'You're right,' said Wilkinson. 'You have restricted upward gaze and it corrects with the doll's head manoeuvre. Taking this together with your description of the fall and your other symptoms, it does look like PSP. Look, we'll get the MRI scan. It will serve as a useful baseline, against which we can compare future scans. Also, I think we might consider a trial of L-dopa at some point; just in case it's actually Parkinson's disease. Not just now though; let's review the situation in three months' time. Meanwhile, I'll send the test results to your GP with a copy to you.'

'Thank you for seeing me so quickly, Chris. I'll see your secretary about an appointment in three months' time. Should things deteriorate sharply before then, I'll get in touch sooner.' They shook hands and Stanley made his way to the car park. The irony was not lost on Stanley. PSP was another disease in which a protein inside nerve cells comes to be truncated and misfolded into tangles inside brain cells, killing them... killing him. He got into his car, placed his hands on the top of the steering wheel, leaned forward to rest his forehead on his hands, and closed his eyes. All my professional life I've been fearful of making a wrong diagnosis, he thought. This time, I hoped so much to be wrong. Is there anything worse than PSP? CJD, BSE are the nightmare scenarios, not that it's any consolation to have something a little less aggressive but equally incurable. How will I tell her? When will I tell her? I must think this through.

Stanley drove out to Grantchester, parked the car at the Rupert Brooke, and walked through the gate at the back of the carpark onto the path above the meadows. Mercifully, no one else was about. Stanley came to a bench. He sat on it and looked out across the meadows toward the City. He brought to mind his first walk there with Julia, wrapped up in their coats and scarves against the cold. He felt very emotional. Steady now old chap, he told himself, get things clear in your head...but things are clear enough, aren't they? I know about dying. What makes it all so painful is leaving Julia. I never thought I would know so much love from a woman and feel so much love for her. So much for thinking I had lived a full life. The greatest prize in medical science pales in comparison to the fulfillment her love has brought me.

When should he tell Julia? Should he wait until all the test results were in and the diagnosis was confirmed, to keep the terrible news from her as long as possible? Should he play down the terminal prognosis? The minute he considered their relationship he knew nothing could or should be hidden from her. Honesty and openness underpinned their relationship and their love. He got to his feet. Come on, he told himself, *force your heart and nerve and sinew to serve your turn*, and he set off along the path. But his pressing thought was the rest of the verse: To serve my turn *long after they are gone*. They will be gone, in five years, six. And I'll be trapped inside an immovable body. He found the thought terrifying and had to walk between Grantchester and Newnham several times before he felt able to face Julia without breaking down.

He returned home to find her at the piano. She was practising but stopped when he entered. She just smiled at him. He blew a kiss at her and went to the sofa across the room, facing her. When Julia saw that he had stayed, she placed the pencil with which she had been annotating the score on top of the piano, looked at Stanley as if to say *For You*, and started to play. Chopin, Opus 48 number 1, he said to himself, recognising the opening bars. He shut his eyes. It seemed to him she was speaking to him through the music: *Yes, I know you are sad and sorrowful, only let me in, take strength from me, and then I will lay you down and all will be well*. He looked at her through watery eyes. He thought: with these six minutes of music, she tells me she knows and that she's there for me.'

Julia crossed the room, sat beside him, took his hand, kissed it and held it in hers. 'You've been gone a long time,' she said softly. 'I have been worried. I telephoned the clinic to make sure nothing was amiss and was told you left; that was three hours ago.' She lifted Stanley's hand to her lips again and waited.

'The clinic didn't take long. Afterwards, I had to gather my thoughts.' Stanley pulled his hand free, but only to take hold of Julia's. 'I went out to the meadows in Grantchester.'

'Are you ready to tell me?'

'The characteristics of the fall in Petra were very unusual. Nothing about it pointed to a faint or a heart problem. There is an unusual form of epileptic seizure that could cause such a drop attack. For several reasons, not least my age, this too seemed unlikely.' Julia didn't interrupt. Stanley's rather circuitous opening was sufficient to alert her that the news was going to be bad. She rested her head against his shoulder. He read the body language. He kissed the top of her head, closed his eyes and let his lips and nose luxuriate in the softness and fragrance of her hair. 'I'm sorry, Julia. I should get to the point. When I put the fall in the context of some rather vague symptoms I've been experiencing, I began to suspect a disease called Progressive Supranuclear Palsy. We call it P-S-P for short. Chris agrees with the diagnosis. We'll be certain as and when I experience more symptoms. By then the MRI scan might show some shrinkage in certain parts of the brain that are typically affected in this disease.'

'Apart from the falls, what else happens?'

'It's similar to Parkinson's Disease. In the main, movement is affected; not so much paralysis as stiffness and a kind of freezing up.'

'Parkinson's can be treated, can't it?'

'Yes, Parkinson's can, but this is not Parkinson's, only *like* it as far as the problems that arise. There's no treatment for PSP.'

'You said the illness is called *progressive* something or other. You're saying it will get worse steadily, and more quickly than Parkinson's, aren't you?'

'It's a degenerative disease. Textbooks use the phrase *inexorably progressive* to describe the course, but the deterioration isn't necessarily steady. It can be stepwise, sometimes without warning.' Julia pulled her hands up to cover her face for a few moments. She was inwardly distraught and was trying hard to maintain a veneer of calm. Stanley waited.

'Stanley, tell me more about how this illness will affect you? How long do we have?' Stanley stood up and offered his hand to Julia.

'It's a depressing subject, darling; let's get outside, into the garden. The sunshine and your lovely flower beds will do their best to remind us that there's a lot of beauty left to us.' Julia took his hand and they walked out onto the patio and settled at the table there. The open air and sunshine helped check the downward spiral in her mood, as did the break in the discussion, but this respite was short-lived.

'You asked about the effects of the illness. PSP leads to a range of difficulties with balance, movement, vision, speech and swallowing. Sudden falls you know about already. Falls become more of a problem because of loss of balance, muscle stiffness, and decreasing mobility. Control of the eye muscles becomes more difficult. This results in blurred vision or double vision, which increase the risk of falls and making everyday tasks, such as reading and eating, more problematic.'

'Will *you* change, Stanley? Your personality? Your memory? Will I lose the man I love?' He hesitated, unsure about how much he should say, but Julia pressed him. 'Tell me,' she said.

'The personality may be affected. Irritability and mood swings occur. It's difficult to know how much of this is an understandable reaction to the frustration of increasing disability or to structural damage in the parts of the brain that determine behaviour. Usually, patients do not lose an awareness of who they are, but dementia can be yet another horror to bear.' Julia was stunned at this. Stanley squeezed her hand. 'Do you want me to stop?'

'I must hear it all. How will it end?'

'Over time, the initial symptoms of PSP become more severe. Walking becomes impossible and a wheelchair is needed. Sleep is disturbed for both patient and carer. For the patient, it's impossible to turn over in bed without help. New symptoms can also develop because of increasing difficulty controlling the muscles of the mouth, throat and tongue. Speech may become increasingly slow and slurred, making it harder to be understood. The loss of control of the throat muscles can lead to severe swallowing problems. This leads to the insertion of a feeding tube to prevent choking or chest infections caused by fluid or small food particles passing into the lungs. Constipation and difficulty passing urine are common. Most lose control over their bladder or bowel movements. The end is inhuman. It comes in five to seven years.'

Julia could bear it no longer. She bit her lip to stifle the sobs that were welling up inside. She put a hand on Stanley's shoulder to keep him seated, stood up, hugged his head and whispered into his ear that she would be back. Have I been too blunt? Stanley asked himself as he listened to Julia crying upstairs. It was more than a half-hour before Julia returned, red-eyed. She kissed Stanley and sat down next to him.

'Don't worry about me,' she said to him. 'I'm strong enough. I love you. You won't be alone. I'll see you through this.' Stanley touched her face and looked into her eyes.

'I don't want to go through it. I don't want to put you through it. I would be trapped in a painful coffin of a body that has ceased to function. I would end up unable to communicate, being tube-fed, catheterised, and painfully constipated or incontinent. Julia, I still have some three years that are worth living, and I shall live as fully as the disease allows, but thereafter I shall be dying. I don't doubt that you have the strength to care for me. I don't doubt the constancy of your love, but you will be loving a man long gone. The man you will be nursing will not be me. A changed personality, severe depression, emotional swings, odd behaviour, paranoia, and possibly dementia will leave nothing of me for you to love. I don't want to do this to you, Julia.'

'No! I won't think of you like that; never! I love you. I'm not afraid.'

'I'm the one who is afraid. I know too much about what's in store for me. I don't want to go through that pointless suffering. I need to stay in control and to decide when enough is enough.' Julia knew what Stanley was getting at from her long experience with her Cancer Care charity and links to palliative care. 'Do you mean to take your own life, then? Please, don't think that way.'

'But, Julia...'

'Stanley, no! Please stop! It's too upsetting. We need time to think, to get a second opinion, to investigate proper care facilities. Then, you'll feel differently, I'm sure.' Stanley's heart sank. I've spelt it out, yet she doesn't see; she can't appreciate the torments in store for me. Will I have to endure a lingering death by starvation? Even that will be better than being kept alive by tube-feeds. He checked himself. I mustn't be brutal.

'Darling, I'm so sorry to have brought you such horrible news. I couldn't think of an easy way to do it. You're right, though. This isn't the time to work out what to do.' The two of them stood up. Stanley opened his arms and Julia went in to hug him tightly, her head against his chest. They held one another for a while. Then, there was nothing else to do but continue living their lives again, albeit with heavy hearts.

Over time, it became clear to Julia that Stanley was deteriorating. He couldn't learn new pieces of music because of difficulty reading musical scores. Julia became even more concerned when his left hand stiffened up to the point that he couldn't play the cello. His appearance was changing too; as if he were ageing rapidly. He became stooped and shuffled as he walked. His face lost its ability to communicate the affection and love that previously Julia could so easily read into it. He looked blank, expressionless. What with the shuffling and difficulty focusing his eyes, Stanley would catch his foot on irregular paving, on a carpet edge or a step, and trip up. After a couple of these falls, he took to using a Zimmer frame.

Then came a frightening turn for the worse. Over the course of a few days, Stanley began to have difficulty swallowing solid food. When some meat stuck fast in his throat, Julia had to rush him to the Emergency Department at the hospital. It took an injection of a muscle relaxant and a strong sedative before the bolus of food passed down his gullet. A neurologist was asked to review Stanley. After his examination, Julia followed him out of the room and asked how he had found Stanley.

'Sir Stanley's condition is entering the phase when the stiffness and spasms you've already seen in his hands and legs begin to affect his throat muscles. He will develop difficulty with his speech: a weakness in the voice with some slurring. The swallowing is also likely to get worse. I recommend that you cut all solid food into very small pieces.'

A couple of weeks after this episode, Stanley was sitting on a chair in the conservatory. He was listening to the Goldberg Variations arranged for a string trio. Julia came to sit beside him. He reached for her hand, slowly, stiffly. She took his hand as it wavered in the air and held it while the music played. When the piece finished and the CD turned off, she knelt at his feet, looked up at him and said:

'I see now what you will have to endure. Tell me what you want.'

Stanley had not broached the subject of suicide since the day when he told Julia about the PSP diagnosis. He knew the decision was not his alone to make; that he must have her support. As the illness began to take hold of him, Stanley hoped that Julia would find, in her love for him, the strength and courage to let him go. Time was running out. There would be a lot of paperwork to put together, which would take time, and he had to retain sufficient movement to bring the barbiturate medication up to his mouth and to swallow it. Crucially, he had to demonstrate that his judgement was sound. Stanley was all too aware that his intellect could deteriorate unexpectedly at any time. So, Julia's words brought him relief.

'Let me go to Zurich. It may be too late in just a few weeks. I have to get there by myself.'

'I shall take you. That way we can enjoy a little more of our life together. If you aren't mobile, I'll get you there in a wheelchair.'

'Darling, it's not simply about mobility. I have to be of sound mind. It will take several weeks to compile the medical reports and for *Dignitas* to consider my application. While I'm able to indicate my wish for assisted dying now, I don't know how long that position will hold. And there is another issue. I can't let you come with me because the authorities in this country could prosecute you. The penalty for assisting anyone to take his or her own life is something like seven years imprisonment.'

'Never! I am coming with you. You are not going to die alone.'

'It's too risky, Julia.'

'I don't think the Director of Public Prosecutions will think it in the public interest to prosecute me. If a prosecution were to be brought, I think my cancer charity work would speak in mitigation. If it comes to it, though, I'm prepared to bear even imprisonment.'

'Are you serious?'

'Never more than now.' Stanley thought for a moment; then he looked into Julia's eyes and said:

'Marry me.'

'What on earth for, Stanley?' she said. 'I am yours, completely.'

'Because I adore you and want you to be my wife, and for you to be known as such. Also, the DPP is likely to be less inclined to prosecute Lady Posner than someone who isn't legally my next-of-kin.'

Julia kissed Stanley. 'I accept,' she said, 'because it would be a joyful thing to do and because I'd love a honeymoon with you. There is another reason,' she added, 'I expect *Dignitas* will consider your case more favourably if they know you have the full support of your wife and that she will accompany you.' Stanley saw that there were tears in Julia's eyes.

'Thank you,' he said to her gently.

'For what do you thank me?'

'For your compassion.'

'You don't need compassion. These tears are mine; for me. I weep selfishly; for the loss I shall endure.'

'Thank you, then' he said, 'for your enduring love.' Julia grabbed his head in both hands and leaned in till her lips touched his. Her kiss grew intense, then furious. Startlingly, Julia got to her feet, pushed him backwards on the chair's back legs and spun him round, away from the table. Then, she sat astride his lap and with her mouth and tongue wildly explored his own. She delighted in the surge of pleasure and emotion of this embrace. She whispered into his ear.

'I have loved you since our first shared Christmas. I will love you always. It's the reason I shall endure my tomorrows without you.' She drew her head back to look at Stanley directly. 'I know that you love me; that you were prepared to suffer if I asked you to stay with me. I owe you so much. You made me feel that I was beautiful to a man again. Much more than that, we have had a beautiful life together in our music, in our art, in the love of our many friends, in our work for others, and in each other's arms. When the time comes, I shall give you up. I do not want to see my beautiful man destroyed by this horrible disease.' She took his hand, helped him to the bedroom, and loved him.

EPILOGUE

I n the old days, he really could rub people up the wrong way. The kindness of Charles Marshall's son and daughter saved him, changed him. He repaid their generosity with the significance of his science and with his own gift of the Nobel prize money to the Charles Marshall Access Fund. They were the templates that refolded him into the kind and magnanimous spirits of which they themselves were made. And Julia reshaped him further with her love.

He is dying in her arms, in the comfort of her embrace. At the last, she gifts him compassion so that he can be merciful to himself. What was that story of his? He had heard Carleton Gallagher tell it: a native chieftain euthanises his wife by snakebite to spare her the horrible terminal stages of Kuru. An act of love.

He is dying in her arms. He asked for Janet Baker's recording of Mahler's Rückert-Lieder to be played while she held him. He meets his end with *Ich bin die Welt abhanden gekommen;* soon to be *dead to the world, resting in a quiet realm, alone in heaven, in his love, in his song.*

She has painted him. He hangs above the piano to greet her when she enters the house and to be next to her while she plays. He sits at an open window and the warm evening light of summer falls on his face and hands. His blue eyes smile at her with gentleness and love. His right hand reaches out to her, as it did the night he first touched her chest and made her whole.

She'll be surprised to see me here. How could I not have come? She'll be exhausted, heartbroken. I'll take her into my arms and hold her tightly though I yearn to caress her sweetly, and stroke her head consolingly when I would rather finger those soft curls teasingly, and kiss her cheek when I want those lips, and dry those eyes that do not see the nature of my love... There she is!

> *Be still my beating heart*
> *It would be better to be cool...*
> *Be still my beating heart*
> *Or I'll be taken for a fool.*

Julia stood on the steps of the clinic, dazed, almost overcome by a sense of loss. A woman hurried towards her, arms out-stretched.

'Fi? Fiona! Thank God!'

AUTHOR'S NOTE

The novel draws inspiration from the scientific achievements of Stanley Prusiner, Carleton Gajdusek and Vincent Zigas, and from the altruism of Maggie Keswick Jencks and her husband, Charles Jencks, founders of Maggie's Centres (The Maggie Keswick Jencks Cancer Caring Centres Trust).

The author has quoted or paraphrased from the following sources:

Roy Blatchford – *Excellence as a standard: what makes a great school leader. The Daily Telegraph Friday 8 March 2019*

Maggie Keswick Jencks – *A View from the Front Line (including the Forward by Marcia Blakenham)*

Michael Lerner – *Choices in Healing*

If I were you – *System failure*

Simani – *Music and friends*

Rudyard Kipling – *If*

Sting – *Be still my beating heart*

And from various short blogs on the internet.